UNLAWFUL JUSTICE

VISH DHAMIJA is the bestselling author of five works of crime fiction. He has gained a reputation as the master of legal crime and courtroom drama in India. In August 2015, at the release of his third novel, *Déjà Karma*, *Glimpse* magazine called him 'India's John Grisham' for stimulating the genre of legal fiction in India, which was almost non-existent before his arrival on the scene. *Unlawful Justice*, a legal thriller, is his sixth novel.

Vish lives in London with his wife Nidhi.

UNLAWFUL JUSTICE

VISH DHAMIJA

HARPER
BLACK

First published in India in 2017 by Harper Black
An imprint of HarperCollins *Publishers* India

Building 10, Tower A, 4th Floor, DLF Cyber City, Phase II,
Gurugram Haryana – 122002, India
www.harpercollins.co.in

P-ISBN: 978-93-5264-416-2
E-ISBN: 978-93-5264-417-9

2 4 6 8 10 9 7 5 3 1

Typeset in 11/14.6 Adobe Garamond at
Manipal Digital Systems, Manipal

Printed and bound at
MicroPrints India, New Delhi

To all my friends who have never read any of my books…

'Justice? You get justice in the next world. In this one you have the law.'

— William Gaddis

Part One

6 June

'A worthless person, a wicked man, is the one who walks with a perverse mouth, who winks with his eyes, who signals with his feet, who points with his fingers;
Who with perversity in his heart continually devises evil...'

—Proverbs 6:12:15

ONE

He shouldn't have been there.

Maheep Singh shouldn't have been where he was that fateful afternoon. But he was. He was eighteen, spoilt rotten by his parents, particularly his doting mother, Jaya. Not that his father, Maninder Singh, ever really, truly endeavoured to stop his wife from indulging the male heir, born after three daughters. Daughters were supposed to be reined in, their freedoms curtailed, but a son should be exempt from any and all discipline, Maninder Singh believed. The immunity from his parents coupled with the unaccounted wealth, accumulated from equally unmentionable sources by his father, though envied by his friends, made him like the allegedly impermeable Titanic racing towards the iceberg.

He tried smoking at thirteen. He smoked sporadically for the next few years. However, he became a regular smoker at sixteen, occasionally with cannabis when his friends could stealthily procure it from insalubrious sources.

He started drinking spirits at sixteen. His dad had occasionally allowed him a sip or two from his own drink at parties earlier, but that was enough for him to start liking it.

He spent the night of his seventeenth birthday with a prostitute. His money fetched him friends who loved his money more than they loved him. These supposed friends had hired a hooker as his birthday gift.

Anyone with a little sense and experience who had been watching him all along could predict that Maheep would disgrace himself and his family if he continued along the same path. He could only escape till his luck held out. Anyone with a reasonable IQ could foretell that his luck was about to run out on him like it ran out on Napoleon at the Battle of Waterloo. Just as Napoleon should not have been anywhere near Waterloo in Belgium when he was, Maheep Singh should not have been anywhere near Defence Colony in New Delhi when he was. Maybe it was not the same quantum of bad luck. But it was similar. Simply put, sometimes people are in the wrong place at the wrong time. That is pure kismet. Even if they have no sinful intent when they start from wherever, they get reckless or greedy or fail to control themselves when something is too tempting to resist. Sometimes, the brain is too fazed to compute the consequences, at other times it is too confident to fret. And if someone is intoxicated, it makes the whole slippery slope a whole lot more lubricious. Sadly, for people like Maheep, the end is never elegant.

Maheep Singh was tall and bulky for his age and looked considerably older than eighteen. The usual suspects—drinking, smoking, drugs, fast food and virtually no physical exercise—had dutifully colluded to do their bits. He would look far better if he shaved his jowls and lost the excess weight, but he couldn't care less. He had just finished school that summer, on his eighteenth birthday in April, a little over a month before it all happened. His Board results were expected by the middle of June, which would decide which college, or colleges, he got admission into. Although his father was influential enough to pull strings or bust bollocks to get him admission into a few colleges, Maheep still had to obtain a respectable score. Maheep wasn't too concerned about which subjects or course he would pursue; he had made up his mind, long ago, to follow in his father's enormous footsteps—sail the heretofore-charted waters—and make money, a lot more of it than his father had acquired. The means, however dubious, didn't disturb him.

His father, Maninder Singh, tall and bulky like his prodigal son, was essentially a bagman behind the façade of a proclaimed businessman. He worked for corrupt politicians and criminals, collecting and distributing their money, illicitly earned through bribes and criminal enterprises—hafta, hookers, hawala, hooch; nothing more than a pimp laundering dirty money. The commissions were a small per cent, but the turnover was high—someone had once run some complicated algorithm in the eighties and surmised that 25 per cent of all money printed by the Reserve Bank of India went missing from circulation almost immediately; it exchanged hands in a parallel economy. And tax on such a stained income was as little as Maninder Singh fancied declaring in a particular year. To front it all, he ran a large dairy farm that supposedly generated tax-free income and washed clean the unaccounted black money. To his credit, he had never been caught out or even had a finger pointed at him, which wasn't unusual when you were under the wings of political apparatchiks and notorious criminals. With not much to do, on most days Maninder Singh was at Delhi Gymkhana Club, whiling away the hours playing billiards or cards or drinking with someone important in the seedy world he operated in, at one of the three bars in the club. Easy money, spent without a thought.

Maheep's mother, Jaya, was a mousy looking woman with hundred per cent hennaed hair and lifeless eyes that echoed her listless personality—she might have been good looking in her twenties, maybe even fit for a miniskirt, but time had been uncharitable to her. At forty-seven, she looked sixty. She had little ambition and even littler achievements. She had been brought up rich and like her mother, she was a socialite: too much money and time on hand and not enough ways to spend either. There had always been servants at home to mollycoddle the kids when they were growing up, to cook, to clean and to attend to the everyday needs of the household. She was forever away during the day, playing cards and sipping gin and tonics with ladies of similar ilk or hosting a gathering at her own residence.

On the day her unchecked son brought down the house—which had always been doomed for subsidence—she was away at a party at a friend's place in Vasant Vihar.

Maheep Singh didn't love his parents, but he didn't despise them either. They provided all the money and gave him enough leeway to carry on with his life. Two of his older sisters were married. The eldest was Ritu, now twenty-five; she had married early and already had a son of three. She was the misfortunate who had fallen in love with a middle-class boy in her college. Maninder was dead against the relationship. How could his princess live a bourgeois life in a small town? But Ritu, being her father's daughter, was equally determined. She eloped with her boyfriend Raj, got married, and the two moved to his hometown of Mussoorie, a quaint little town in the foothills of the Garhwal Himalayan ranges in the state of Uttarkhand. Under strict orders from Maninder, no one in the family was permitted to have any contact with her; she was an outcast, a disgrace to the family.

The middle sister, Reena, a year younger than Ritu, had married only a couple of years ago and had moved to Los Angeles with her husband, whose education in the United States was funded completely by his father-in-law. She visited once a year, but aware of how her father had amassed his wealth, she had no plans to ever return to New Delhi and live and socialize in the same circles.

The third sister, Ragini, was in her final year at Lady Shri Ram College. Even though the college was in Delhi, she had insisted she wanted a taste of hostel life. Truth be told, she was dating a not-so-rich guy, and she spent more nights at his pad than in the hostel. No one knew her secret except Maheep, but knowing his dad, and his nasty temperament, he didn't rat her out. To avoid a repeat of his eldest daughter's flight, Maninder Singh would definitely use his ruthless connections to kill or maim the boyfriend.

Maheep was alone on the day, 6 June, and as such, he had nothing much to do except squander time, which he was proficient at doing. When he had got out of bed, his parents had already left for their daily activities. He had rudely ordered breakfast in bed and swore at the old lady—older than his mother—who had served him, merely because the eggs weren't runny enough and the coffee was weaker than he preferred. Aarti bai had been in the household for twenty-eight years now; she had come with Jaya at the time of her wedding as her caretaker and despite having literally brought up the four kids, Maheep treated her like a worthless maidservant. He often misbehaved with her. Correction. Maheep misbehaved with everyone. Anyone lower in financial status than his dad, people who worked for his dad or their children were not people; they were his property.

After breakfast, he raided his father's liquor cabinet in the face of Aarti requesting and begging him not to. To avoid Aarti's urgings to stop, he shouted: 'Stop it, bitch!' and carried a bottle of Bells whisky to his bedroom, which had a small refrigerator for everything else he required—water, soda, ice, Coca Cola. He took one straight shot from the bottle and opened the bathroom window to light up.

Two drinks later, the liquid made his mind wander. He put on a Coldplay CD, but got bored after a couple of tracks. His mind was somewhere else. He thought about calling Vamini, whom he thought was his girlfriend, but who was just a friendly, good-natured, well-mannered pretty girl.

Vamini was the only child of Priti and Vansh Diwan, both advocates.

Priti Diwan was in her early forties. She was five-four in socks, petite, olive-skinned, with a well-maintained body and dark auburn lustrous locks that ended at her shoulders. She had been the heartthrob of many a guy in college, but she fell in love only once: with Vansh. She had taken an eight-year break from her career when Vamini was born, and had returned to work for a large multinational consumer product company. She was very good at what she did—corporate law—and quickly making up for her time away, she scaled the corporate ladder faster than others and was now the chief of the company's legal department. With the number of mergers and acquisitions happening across corporate India, her hands were full, but her daughter was always her first priority. If she had to decide between work and Vamini, she would choose Vamini every single time, no doubt about that. Priti had a caretaker to look after Vamini, twenty-four/seven. Gayatri was from Bihar, a widow, almost the same age as Priti, but the years hadn't been generous to her. She had a daughter called Baby, who was sixteen. Baby's early education in a village school in Bihar had disallowed her attending the same school as Vamini, but Priti Diwan had seen to it that Baby continued her studies in another school.

Vansh Diwan was a pedigreed criminal advocate. His father and grandfather had been criminal advocates too. A six-foot-tall, trim, salt-and-pepper haired, clean-shaven, sophisticated man who, with Priti, formed a made-for-each-other couple since law college, Vansh had continued the family's legal practice and was the sole proprietor of Diwan-e-Khaas, which was started in the 1950s. The office was now on Barakhamba Road, an entire floor in one of the towers. Vansh had added other functions of arbitration, banking and finance, competition/antitrust law, dispute resolution, employment law, intellectual property and insurance to the business and had opened affiliate offices in Mumbai and Bengaluru. Business was good. Vansh was a decent man, but being a criminal advocate, mixing with unsavoury characters was unavoidable, which was something Priti found disconcerting. One such character was Vansh Diwan's largest client in terms of annual billings: Maninder Singh.

Priti found it extremely difficult to spend time with Jaya and Maninder Singh whenever they socialized. Unpleasant, pathetic but unavoidable, exactly like shit, was how she described them. However, they had to meet occasionally since their son was Vamini's classmate. Vamini, too, had taken the same Board examinations as Maheep and was awaiting her results. However, the difference between the two children was stark—chalk and cheese, cardboard and cream, take your pick—Vamini was expecting to be in the top ninety-eight percentile to pursue a career in law, just like her parents.

Maheep had eyes for Vamini. He wasn't the only boy in school who did, but he had a perfectly legitimate reason to meet her outside school, as the Diwans were family friends. His access to the Diwan household wasn't restricted, but it wasn't as regular as he would have liked it to be. Vamini was gene-blessed—taking the best of both her parents. Taller than her mother—five-five, but petite, she was pretty with the same lustrous, straight shoulder-length hair. The plus side was her positive and happy disposition, which gave Maheep the idea that she was interested in him as her boyfriend. He completely ignored the fact that she was polite and personable to everyone.

As Maheep got drunk in his bedroom, he switched on his computer and started surfing insalubrious websites, gradually moving on to the hard-core variety. He imagined the women on the screen with Vamini's face on them and the idea of hooking up with Vamini danced its way to the forefront. His father had bought him a Honda Civic for his eighteenth birthday and the drive from his farmhouse in Chhatarpur to Defence Colony, a distance of thirteen kilometres, suddenly shrank in his inebriated mind. He thought, once again, about calling Vamini, but dropped the idea: what if she made an excuse, what if she didn't want to see him for some reason; but if he simply showed up at her place, she would obviously welcome him. He was her classmate, their families were friends, and his father was, after all, her father's client. Mega-bucks client. Wasn't she obliged to entertain him?

He was determined to see Vamini now. To declare his desire for her; he so wanted her to accept him as her boyfriend and to let everything follow from there.

He was tipsy, not smashed drunk, but nevertheless certainly over the alcohol limit permitted in any part of the world. Including Columbia if they enforced any limits on alcohol and drug consumption when at the wheel. He picked up some extra cash just in case some random policeman stopped him, although he was conscious that it was rare that the police stopped cars to check at eleven-thirty in the morning—that was more a late-night drill. However, if he had an accident on the way, however insignificant, the police wouldn't require a breath analyser to detect he was under the influence. He would later reflect that had he had a slight brush and, for any reason, been detained by the police till daddy dearest got him released, it might have been a cloaked blessing. At least the alcohol level in his body and his over-heightened libido would have declined. But life isn't a happy song that you can rewind at will.

He shouldn't have been there.

As he drove through traffic, left hand on the horn, cigarette in his right, all he could think about was how his encounter with Vamini would be. Would she let him kiss her? Would she undress a bit? Would she allow him to go all the way? He could see her smiling at him from the huge billboards, he could see her in the car in the next lane. She was everywhere. He knew she wanted him too. Which girl in her right mind wouldn't want Maheep Singh? Dashing, loaded and someone who could promise her a secure future. Vamini would live like a princess, attend socialite parties, and not have to work in some office like her mother.

He was delusional without being aware of it. His brain wasn't working because the blood was rushing to somewhere between his legs. Part of his brain acknowledged he wasn't exactly going to Vamini's house to light a candle. He had questionable intentions when he left home.

Nevertheless, he hadn't gone there to do what he eventually ended up doing.

Regrettably, the future wasn't for him to see or anyone to judge. Wasn't that something The Zombies had wanted to express: *how do I know and why should I care?*

Defence Colony, or Def Col, as it had come to be known, was built in the sixties for retirees from the defence services. Given the south Delhi location, it became a posh address for anyone with money, and restaurants, cafés and top-end shops opened up; retired defence officers could hardly afford to buy property there now.

Maheep didn't go directly to Vamini's place. He still had enough sense to know he needed to make a stop before he got there. For condoms. What if she agreed? Wasn't that what he had driven out to Def Col for? It would be such a bungle if they had to stop at the last minute for lack of them. How ridiculous would that be? Palling with Vamini was specifically for carnal motives at the moment, so why not be prepared? Be one step ahead.

He drove to the main Def Col market and stopped his car behind a parked car. The attendant rushed up to him to stop him from leaving his vehicle blocking another, but Maheep took out a hundred-rupee note and handed it to the attendant. 'I'll only be gone a minute,' he winked and opened the door and jetted out.

'Thank you, sir, please leave the car in neutral.'

Standard parking rules in Delhi. If you blocked an already parked car, and the owner of the car came along while you were away, the attendant would call in a few buddies and push your car out of the way. An ingenuous remedy for crowded parking spaces in a megalopolis that housed an overabundant population.

Maheep had never bought condoms before; his friends had always got them for him. Garnering all the confidence he could, he briskly walked past all the shops and people without looking up and rushed straight to the pharmacy around the corner. Still a little unsteady on his feet, a cigarette in his hand, a desperate attempt to disguise the high testosterone, he asked the old man at the counter for condoms, handed him a five-hundred-rupee note and without waiting for the change, sprinted to his car, backed it out of the parking lot as if he were Michael Schumacher's first cousin and sped away. Turning right at Diana Dairies, he passed the Defence Colony Service Apartments and entered 'A' Block, where the Diwans lived. The house was quite large, but it was not even two-tenths the size of Maninder Singh's sprawling property.

Maheep left his car outside the gate and walked in. His mind was playing tricks, but he could still walk straight. He opened his mouth and sprayed breath freshener, then brought his palm in front of his mouth and exhaled to see if he still reeked of alcohol. Just in case Vamini agreed to kiss. There was still a faint odour so he sprayed again and rechecked. Better. Then he rang the bell. And waited. No response. Was she in the shower? Scrubbing and cleaning herself for him? For a wink, he thought no one was home and almost returned to his car. But he changed his mind and decided to give it one more try. He rang the bell again.

He could—and should—have walked away, but he didn't.

Inside the Diwan residence, Baby was alone and feeling miserable. Vamini Jiji and she were supposed to have gone grocery shopping in the morning. Priti had given them the money and explained to the two teenagers that it was good experience for the two girls to go with the driver and buy provisions for the household. It was a good way of utilizing the girls' vacation, a way for the girls to learn about running a home. But her mother had had to go instead. Only because

Baby had lazily overslept and wasn't ready. She had been alone for a while and contemplated if she should have a shower now or after Vamini Jiji and Ma returned. She had just taken off her clothes when the doorbell changed her decision. Were Jiji and Ma already back? But why would they need to ring the bell, surely they had the keys?

Baby was a short, sinewy girl. Sixteen, but slightly underweight, skin tone a tad dark, which was predominant in the region where she came from; she looked like the typical girl next door. She had long hair, which she normally kept in a braid, but at the moment she had unbridled it to shampoo. She slipped back into the nightdress she had just taken off and rushed to the door. She saw Maheep through the peephole in the large double front door. She had met him before, he had visited them with his parents, and he was also Jiji's friend from school.

'Hello, Maheep bhaiya,' she said with a guileless smile.

'Hello, is Vamini home?'

'No, she's gone out with Ma.'

'When will she be back?'

'I don't know … maybe an hour.'

'Hmmm … '

'You can wait here or if it's urgent, you can call on her mobile. You have the number?'

'Yes. Okay.' Maheep turned to go. She heard him tread away from the door and then, through the peephole, saw him walk to the gate.

Maheep felt disappointed, as if he had been left stranded. In fact, he felt cheated. He had risked driving in an intoxicated state only to find out that Vamini wasn't even home. He closed his eyes and, instead of Vamini, Baby flashed. Young and blithe. And she was a servant in his dad's client's house. A domestic help's daughter. She wasn't bad looking; he recalled the face and body he had just seen. How bad could she be for a one-time fuck? He'd pay her, if need be, and get rid of some of the weight he had started feeling in his tautness.

Maheep Singh should not have been there. He had been given an opportunity to walk away.

He spun around, walked back to the bungalow and pressed the bell once more.

'Hello again, changed your mind? You want to wait?' Baby asked innocently.

'Could I have a glass of cold water?' The word 'please', for obvious reasons, did not exist in his dictionary.

'Of course, come in.'

Maheep closed the door and walked behind her. Her white floral cotton nightdress was thin and crumpled. It wasn't short; it ended only an inch above her knees. He watched her small derrière move as he lecherously followed her through the large living and dining room into the kitchen, and by the time they got there he had figured that no one else was home and that made up his mind.

He saw her stretch up on her toes and pick up a glass from the kitchen unit on top of the counter; her dress lifted a little more as she reached up. As she turned around with the glass in her hand, he moved closer, and was barely a finger's breadth away.

'Oh!' Baby exclaimed finding him so close.

'Take your clothes off,' he said without warning.

'What? No. Please move away.'

'I'll give you five thousand rupees.'

'No, I don't want your money, please go.'

In that moment, he grabbed her hair and dragged her to the floor. Her dress rose higher as she struggled to escape. He held her loose hair with his left hand, brought down his right hand and tore her thin nightdress in one swift, violent motion. Baby started shrieking, tears in her eyes. He knew that she wasn't that naïve to not know what his intentions were. And, despite the mouth freshener, even he could smell the alcohol on himself now.

'Please spare me, I promise I won't tell anyone this ever happened. Please … '

'Shut up or it will be painful.'

'No … ' she screamed again when she felt his big hand on her panties.

He released them, slapped her harshly across the cheek and then punched her in the face. Her lower lip got cut in the corner and blood gushed out. However, it had the opposite effect to what Maheep had anticipated. Baby didn't stop howling out of fear of being hit; she did not give up the fight. Instead, she hollered even louder, her hands were now on his forearms, her nails digging into his flesh. She folded her knees and put her entire body weight behind them to push Maheep off her. However, it was a losing fight. She was forty kilos, he was sixty-three. He was on top and she was pushing him against gravity. In his frantic effort to stop the girl's high-pitched voice being heard by the neighbours, and to overpower the girl, Maheep raised himself a bit, placed a knee on either side of her slight flank to stop her from escaping. Then with both his hands he grabbed her hair, raised her head and banged it with all the force he could summon, against the stone floor. A yelp escaped Baby's lips and then her eyes rolled backwards, her body shuddered once violently before she let out a groan. The blood started running from the wound caused by the heavy hit against the cold stone floor. Semi-conscious, she surrendered to her attacker. Maheep unzipped, pulled out one of the condoms he had purchased, rolled it on himself and pierced Baby. By the time he finished, Baby had passed out.

Maheep left Baby on the floor, dashed out of the house shutting the door behind him, made his way through the main gate and zoomed away in his car.

Maheep Singh shouldn't have been there. Split second, wrong turn. Disastrous consequence.

TWO

Vamini tried calling home from the car as Gayatri and she were stuck in traffic and were getting delayed on their way back home.

'Why isn't Baby picking up the phone?'

'Must have got up late and gone to shower. I'll have a word with her when we get back,' Gayatri's tone was a bit sheepish, as though she was embarrassed by her daughter's lassitude.

'Gayatri bai, there's no need to reproach her. It's vacation time, so what if she lazes around a little longer one day?'

'Still, it is nearing one o'clock now. Wasn't she supposed to go shopping with you today?'

Vamini shrugged. It was futile debating with Gayatri bai. Instead, she tried calling Baby a couple more times, then gave up. They'd be home in the next five or ten minutes. Why bother if Baby was in the shower?

They got out of the car and walked to the main door. Shiv Kumar, the driver, would carry the provisions and bring them into the house. Realizing that neither of them had taken the house keys, Vamini rang the bell. No response.

They waited a minute and buzzed again.

'Did she say she had to go somewhere?' Vamini asked.

'No.'

Gayatri stepped forward, put her finger on the bell and kept it pressed for a long time.

Still no response.

'I need to teach this girl a lesson.'

'Gayatri bai, stop fretting. It's okay. Sometimes you can't hear the bell in the shower if the bathroom door is shut.'

'Baby,' Gayatri shouted, as if her voice would carry farther than the electric doorbell.

A few minutes rolled by.

'Shiv Kumar, please go around to the back of the house and see if you can call Baby and ask her to open the door.'

Gayatri and Baby's room was on the first floor at the back of the house. Shiv Kumar left the bags on the ground and rushed around the right side of the house to approach the rear. He returned after a few minutes and told them that no one had responded to his calls.

'Where has this naughty one gone?' Gayatri's face was red, the heat and humiliation both taking their toll.

'Let me call Mom, she'll send the spare key.'

As Vamini called and asked Priti to send the spare key to the house with her office boy, Gayatri strolled to the rear of the house, with Vamini following her. The house was eerily quiet. They couldn't hear the shower or water moving through the pipes and drains.

Vamini walked to the kitchen window and peeped through it. It was difficult to see much while one stood in afternoon sunlight in June and tried to see what was inside an unlit kitchen. From that angle, she could see something on the floor. Slowly, as her eyes adjusted to the dimness, she realized it was Baby's head on the floor, lying still in a pool of some dark liquid. Maybe she had slipped and fallen and got hurt.

'Shit,' Vamini yelled.

'What happened?'

'Baby is on the floor, it looks like she's hurt herself.'

'How?' Gayatri was glued to the window now. She wasn't any taller than Vamini and given the angle of the window, and the kitchen counters in between, they could only see Baby's head. Their eyes now adjusted to the darkness, both Vamini and Gayatri concurrently comprehended that Baby was lying in a pool of blood.

More screaming.

'Baby, Baby, BABY … '

The distance between Nehru Place and Def Col is roughly four kilometres. The office boy, on his 100cc motorcycle, cutting through traffic, jumping a couple of lights, could still take twenty to twenty-five minutes, Vamini reckoned.

'Shiv Kumar, can you break down the door?' she pointed towards the kitchen door that opened out to the rear of the house.

'Sahib will not be happy,' he uttered.

'Just break it if you can, I'll talk to Dad.'

Still seeing Shiv Kumar flinch, Vamini picked up a stone, the size of a hen's egg, and aimed it at the window.

'That won't help. Even if you break the glass, there's still the safety grill. We won't be able to get in anyway, Vamini,' Gayatri called.

'Wait a minute. I'll run and get the jack rod from the car.' Shiv Kumar ran back to the car while Vamini and Gayatri kept calling out to Baby in the hope that she might wake up. Gayatri was in tears, her breath rising and falling with the fear of the unknown that had happened to her only daughter.

'How could she have slipped?' Vamini asked, well aware that Gayatri had no answer, but the question was more to distract the mother.

'She must have been clumsy.'

Vamini dialled her mom again.

'He's left,' Priti answered the call.

'Mom, Mom … it seems like Baby is badly … injured.'

'Injured how? Take a deep breath, Vamini, and tell me what's going on.'

'We don't know.' Vamini succinctly narrated the scene.

They had no idea of the how or the severity of the injury, but it didn't appear good if Baby had fainted. And all that blood …

'Good God, I am coming there right now. And don't you worry; I'll call the ambulance from the car. If you guys can break open the door, go ahead. Give me a call and let me know as soon as you get in, okay?'

'Should I call Dad?'

'No, the ambulance should get there first, and I'm on my way too. Dad's office is too far off and it will not be of any help. I'll call him after I call the ambulance.'

Shiv Kumar returned with the jack rod and hit the doorjamb hard where it met the lock. Then another strike. Nothing gave till the sixth strike. A slight clicking sound indicated that the lock was coming loose on the inside. Good.

'Hit it hard, Shiv.'

Shiv Kumar dropped the jack rod, took a step back, then with his right leg kicked at the lock with the flat of his big, size-ten foot. The wood splintered and the lock gave way. The force sent the door slamming into the wall behind.

He was the first to rush in but stopped.

Gayatri and Vamini followed and were horror-struck too.

Baby, as they had partially witnessed from the window, was out for the count and lay with her head in a pool of blood, which was now a shade deeper than what Vamini had seen in her biology lab. Baby's eyes were closed. Her nightdress was completely torn off, her panties ripped off and lying next to her torso. There was blood on her lip and chin, which had congealed and stopped running. Her legs were open wide and there was some blood smeared near her groin.

Gayatri went berserk, screaming, hitting her forehead with her palms. Vamini, too, understood that Baby hadn't slipped. She had been beaten and raped. Shiv Kumar had slipped out rather than look at the naked body of the young teen.

Vamini bent down and checked for Baby's pulse. She was alive, but with the amount of blood loss, the fact didn't provide much solace. 'Baby, wake up,' she said softly, as if Baby had been sleeping.

No movement. Nothing.

Behind her, Vamini heard a thump. Gayatri had slumped to the floor.

Shiv Kumar returned with a bed sheet that had been hanging on the clothesline to cover Baby with, but Vamini declined.

She had read somewhere that a crime scene should never be contaminated.

In the near distance, before Vamini broke down, she heard the faint siren of an ambulance.

On his way back, Maheep drove like a maniac on steroids. He didn't quite accept that what he had done was terrible; the bitch had asked for it. Her fault. She was the daughter of a domestic help, her education and livelihood was financed by the Diwans who, in turn, earned money off his dad. Didn't he have a right to ask her to do something simple for him? And he had requested her. What would it have cost her? But he was terrified. Not because he had forced himself upon the unfortunate girl, but because he had left her in a state of shock, passed out with blood all around. And that might be graver than the little sexcapade. Well, if it was any consolation, he had offered money to her, but the slut hadn't budged.

He parked his car in the driveway and hurried in. He saw Aarti rushing to him as he lumbered through the entrance lobby and almost stumbled.

'Where did you go, Maheep baba?'

In that instant, his clouded brain told him that she could be his only saviour.

'Just outside. I was outside in my car listening to music.'

She didn't question or challenge. He knew she would have known he hadn't been outside. The bloody car hadn't been there either. Knowing her, she would have covertly peeked out of the window first, and then stepped out to see if Maheep baba had driven off the property. Stupid illiterate.

'I didn't go anywhere.' His words sounded to him like they were uttered to convince himself more than Aarti. He felt comforted that she didn't contradict him. 'Aarti bai, if anyone asks you should say I didn't go anywhere, you understand?'

'Is everything okay, baba?'

'Yes … yes. Nothing to worry, just a little … '

'Did you have an accident?'

'No … oh yes, just a little scratch.'

He saw her eyeing his forearm. It was the forearm where that little urchin had scratched him with her fingernails. She had managed to peel off some skin and the scratches were beginning to redden. Thin streaks, like little tributaries of a river when seen from thirty thousand feet above the ground. Not bleeding, but still red as the flesh was torn.

'What happened?'

'Nothing. Just a little streetside skirmish.'

'Come, let me put some Dettol and clean you up.'

'Don't tell Mom and Dad.'

'No, I won't.'

After the antiseptic cleansing, Maheep went into his room and changed into a long-sleeved T-shirt. The wretched marks now concealed, he took another large swig of whisky and dozed off.

Priti arrived before the paramedics who, on their arrival, instantly comprehended that it was a crime scene. They called the local police station without wasting precious time and started the process of reviving Baby. Her breathing was shallow, but her airways were open and her heartbeat was a little slower, too. The police arrived at the scene soon after and took photographs, after which the paramedics lifted Baby without disturbing anything around her, put her on a stretcher and wheeled her away.

Assistant superintendent of police, Arvind Kapoor—an IPS probationer in the second year of his service—looked like a sharp and polite man with oodles of patience. Well groomed, he gave the impression of someone plugged in. He nodded to show he understood what had happened within minutes of his arrival. Rape of a minor. He went around the house twice, checking all the doors and windows and expressed to Priti that the perpetrator was known to the victim or, at least, someone in the household, to have been let into the house without a break-in. Then he apologized and left saying he had something more critical to attend to before questioning everyone. He promised Priti that he'd be back in the evening after he had been to see Baby at the hospital. Priti called Vansh and told him of the tragedy at home, and he said he would head to the hospital. He advised her that it was better if she stayed with Gayatri and Vamini, as it wasn't prudent to crowd the patient.

Safdarjung was the ruler of the State of Awadh. His legacy is the number of public places named after him: an airport, a road, a bus terminal, a colony and one of the largest government hospitals in India, and it was to this hospital that Baby was transported by the ambulance. ASP Kapoor travelled the less than four-kilometre distance in his jeep while Vansh Diwan was driven in his 5 Series from Barakhamba Road.

Baby was still unconscious when Vansh arrived at the hospital and met with ASP Kapoor outside the intensive care unit.

'How is she?' Vansh asked after the introductions.

'She's stable now, Mr Diwan. Still unconscious, as she's lost a lot of blood due to the head injury, but her breathing, heartbeat and even blood pressure are normal now.'

'Any prognosis so far?'

ASP Kapoor candidly narrated to Vansh Diwan what he had been told by the doctors: that Baby had been beaten and raped, and then left in a badly injured condition. The major damage had been due to loss of blood. The doctors were attending to her, and would only take her out of intensive care once she was conscious. The IV was in; they had been waiting for someone to arrive to sign off on a blood transfusion, and ASP Kapoor, in his official capacity, had approved the same, considering the criticality of the situation. They couldn't wait for Baby's kin to arrive, as it might have been detrimental to recovery.

'What do the doctors say, when will she regain consciousness?'

'They're attending to her, no further info … '

'Any leads?'

'None yet, but we'll catch him, whoever he is.'

'Is there evidence in the body? Semen?'

'They are checking. The immediate need was to ensure her survival. What do you do, Mr Diwan?'

'I'm a criminal advocate.'

An informal introduction followed and the duo realized that albeit in separate capacities, both men had similar professional backgrounds: dealing with criminals. ASP Kapoor found it easier to explain to Vansh that nothing had been broken to gain entry into the house, which surprised Vansh. He couldn't think of anyone known to them or Gayatri or Baby who would brutally rape a minor girl.

'That will make it more difficult to find the bastard … till Baby wakes up,' he finally said.

'Why do you say so?' The ASP looked surprised.

'Simple, because if it is someone known to us then this would be his first crime, which means you cannot match the semen recovered from Baby's body to any registered criminal. What chance do you have of catching a first-time criminal till Baby wakes up?' Vansh thought and spoke like an advocate.

'There will be other clues. A first-timer couldn't have been meticulous. He'd have left enough clues to lead us to him in no time. Even before Baby wakes up.'

Vansh Diwan shook his head. *How?*

Vansh recollected Edmond Locard from his law college days: *A perpetrator always brought something to the crime and took something away from it. That provided the forensic evidence.* While that was reassuring to a point, Vansh also knew of numerous cold cases that police around the world hadn't solved. He had seen police and investigators falter, miss the clues and evidence. Mistakes were expected, they came with any criminal investigation's territory. But he remained reticent; it wasn't something he wished to convey to the ASP.

Later, when the sun was packing up for the day, a young resident doctor in the usual white coat with a stethoscope roped around his thin neck delivered the bad and good news to Vansh Diwan and ASP Kapoor. Baby was still unconscious.

The injury to the back of the head had caused severe trauma and, though she was now out of any imminent danger, she was still diagnosed as being in a coma, Glasgow Scale three, he explained. Her eyes were responding to voice stimuli, but her speech was incoherent—just random, incongruous words—and there was abnormal flexion to painful stimuli. The doctors had performed an X-ray Computed Tomography—aka CT scan—and were continuously monitoring her brain waves. The good news was that if statistics were any indicator, then there was an over 95 per cent chance of a full recovery in the next four to six months, though allowing for the age of the patient, recovery could be a lot faster—maybe even weeks.

Vansh let out a cold sigh.

'I'm sorry if you find it inappropriate at this time, but when will we be able to speak to the patient?' ASP Kapoor asked. He was talking to the doctor, but he looked at Vansh for corroboration.

Vansh wasn't affronted at all as he, being a criminal advocate, had been in similar precarious situations himself. He understood that the more time you lost after a crime, the more chances it gave the perpetrator to get away.

To Vansh, even the doctor didn't appear shocked by the ASP's question. 'I cannot tell you just yet. Let us get the test results and, maybe, I can give you a time frame tomorrow morning. But I'm sorry I cannot make any predictions at this moment.'

'Is it positive that she was raped?' questioned the ASP. A medical confirmation was required.

'Yes. There are tears in the genitals that are evidence that she was forcefully penetrated.'

'Semen collected from her?'

'No. We found traces of the chemical lubrication found in condoms. The rapist was cautious.'

'What?' Vansh asked. 'A planned rape?' He couldn't wrap his head around it.

'Any other trace evidence found?'

'The girl was brave, I can tell you that. She fought hard. We found skin residue of whoever it was under her fingernails, and given the amount of skin she tore, the scratches on the malefactor won't heal for a few days, maybe an entire week.'

'Thank you, doctor. The girl's mother and my wife and daughter would certainly like to see Baby as soon as possible. Will that be all right with you?'

'I wouldn't recommend tonight, honestly. Ideally, I wouldn't like the patient to be disturbed, because if you bring her mother here, she will likely talk or cry and I would rather we speak to Baby, so that we can clinically gauge her responses. However, if you must, I insist that they merely peek in at the patient from the other side of the glass. No communication or any physical contact whatsoever with the patient, please.'

'I appreciate that,' Vansh conceded. The doctor was only making sure his patient was top priority.

'ASP Kapoor—the forensic report will be ready latest by tonight. You can ask someone from your department to collect it from us.'

'Thanks, doc.'

The crime scene had been combed and cleaned, all evidence collected and sent to forensic labs, when Vansh and ASP Kapoor arrived at Def Col. Priti told both men that she had given Gayatri a sedative and made her go to sleep in Vamini's room, as she was hyperventilating. Vamini was with her in case she got up.

Vansh updated Priti on Baby's condition.

'What a bastard,' Priti blurted.

'Do you suspect anyone?'

'No idea, ASP Kapoor. I can't believe we know a brute who could have raped the poor girl,' Priti responded.

'But someone did, Mrs Diwan. Someone got access to your house, someone Baby herself let in, which tells us that the perpetrator was known to the girl.'

'Unimaginable.'

'It might come as a shock to you, but in a large majority of rape cases, Mrs Diwan, the victim is known to the offender.'

'ASP Kapoor is correct,' Vansh validated.

Priti looked at her husband. After all, he was a criminal advocate.

'But how could that someone have known that Baby was alone at home at the time?'

'I don't know that yet. Maybe he did, maybe he didn't; maybe he came around for some other purpose and found that she was alone and vulnerable, and he took the opportunity—'

'And he carried a condom in his pocket?' Priti looked angry.

'Again, it's too early and we have awfully little information to establish if the person came here with an evil intention, or having found Baby alone, overpowered her. The condom could well have been in his wallet for some other encounter, perhaps … '

'But he had enough presence of mind to roll one up before the rape, which surprises me,' Vansh added.

'I find that surprising too,' ASP agreed.

'When can we see her? I know Gayatri will ask to see her daughter as soon as she wakes up.'

'Unfortunately, we'll only know that tomorrow.'

'Would you like to have a drink, ASP Kapoor?' Vansh segued from the ugliness of the day.

The ASP looked at his watch. It was around seven. 'One drink only, thanks.'

Maninder had called to say he wouldn't be home until late, which was hardly unusual, and which was good, Maheep thought. Dad had a habit of asking too many questions: *What did you do today? Did you meet anyone? Call anyone?*

If his mother noticed anything strange about him, she didn't show or mention it. All in all, a good sign. He maintained his usual demeanour—he was reticent on some days, chatty on others—so why should his mother question it if he was quiet today and wanted to keep to himself? If that useless Aarti hadn't told his mother anything yet, why would she tell her anything later? The fright he had earlier in the day, though, hadn't subsided. He didn't know what had happened at the Diwan residence after he left, but maybe that servant girl had ultimately realized that it was her fault for not accepting the money for a fuck. He decided to give it a few days before he went there again, and maybe passed on some money for her silence. Maybe he could arrange to see her again sometime soon. It was just a little scuffle. She'd be fine, he convinced himself.

Neither Vamini nor Gayatri came down for dinner. Priti, too, was in no mood to dine and she retired early. Vansh had a few more drinks after ASP Kapoor left and then scrambled a couple of eggs and noshed them with bread and whisky before joining Priti in the bedroom.

'Poor girl. She must have suffered.' Priti was still awake.

'Priti, please don't say all these things in Gayatri's presence, as she will become even more fretful than she is currently… Yes, I understand her daughter's been through an ordeal, but what's done is done; there's not much we can do now except let the police find the guy and make the arrest. '

'How can you say that?'

'What? What else do you want me to say? Or do?'

'It could have been your daughter, Vansh, our daughter.'

'What do you mean?'

'What do you think would have happened if Gayatri and Baby had gone shopping and Vamini were alone at home?'

'Vamini isn't as naïve as to have opened the door and invited some crook into the house.'

'Baby isn't a fool either. She only opened the door because her attacker was known to one of us. I'm shocked that we know people who can actually come to our house and rape. Who could it be?'

'Damned if I know.' Vansh was getting peeved by the conversation and what, he guessed, Priti was alluding to. In his mind, Baby—yes, she must have suffered both physically and mentally—would be okay by the morning and she'd tell the police who it was. From there on, it was an open and shut case of apprehending the guilty party. What he didn't know then was that Baby wasn't waking up any time soon.

Priti was a bundle of nerves, and her uneasy tossing and turning kept Vansh from having a restful night.

THREE

Everyone in the Diwan household was up well before the morning broke. Unlike other mornings, there was no knock on their door with Gayatri bringing them tea. The house was unnervingly quiet. Vansh couldn't hear anything other than the humming of the air-conditioner. He could sense that Priti still wanted him to deliberate over the question she had posed the night before, but he didn't want to be taken down that alley once again; the thought of the victim being Vamini, and not Baby, was not something his brain was capable of imagining or processing. He was an advocate, and advocates weren't trained to dwell on the what-ifs; advocates focused on the realities on the ground. The actual crime, the hard evidence and not *what could have happened.* Priti too, being an advocate, should be reflecting on the facts, and not extrapolating them or substituting the victim to make the case more personal than it already was. Wasn't she unnecessarily trying to emotionalize the whole thing?

Gayatri was a sight in the morning. Her eyes were red and puffy, the result of crying and an after-effect of whatever strong sedative Priti had given her, which, too, worried him. Administering sedatives or any prescription medicines without medical intervention wasn't a practice he condoned. He decided to tell Priti that later when they were alone. If Gayatri needed help, Priti should take her to a doctor who could prescribe tranquillizers, should they be required, as Gayatri was inconsolable even now. Vamini was running around, making tea for everyone and preparing breakfast.

'We need to employ a security guard,' Priti said when Vamini and Gayatri were out of earshot.

Vansh nodded. If that would calm his wife and her fears, so be it. It wasn't going to bankrupt him. He would ask the company that provided security at his office to add another guard or two in the contract and place them at their residence round the clock. 'What's your plan for the day?'

'I've taken a few days off.'

'Fair enough. I'll head to work and speak to ASP Kapoor to check if the police have some clues or if they suspect somebody. Could you check with the hospital before you take Gayatri there, please?'

'Gayatri and Vamini. She wants to see Baby too. You know they're close, and at any rate, I'm not comfortable leaving Vamini alone at home till you get the security sorted.'

'Your call.' He didn't want to tell her that she was being paranoid. Whoever attacked Baby the day before wouldn't come around to attack someone else in the same house, but he let it go.

As Priti had expected, Gayatri went mental when she saw her little girl intubated and sedated. The doctor hadn't allowed any of them near the patient, and as such, they only looked at Baby through the Plexiglas window.

The entire back of Baby's head was in a cushioned cast to prevent any damage to the sutures they had put over the injury that had been inflicted by the rapist. The left side of her lower lip had stopped bleeding, but it was a shade of purple and swollen to twice its original size. Gayatri put her hands on her mouth and screamed. Shock. Horror. Anxiety. The human brain is several times more complex than the most advanced ultra-chip Intel will come up with any time in the foreseeable future. It can run the entire gamut of emotions without a stop-start. Outrage. Disbelief. Fright. Priti could imagine Gayatri asking herself: *What if Baby never wakes up? What could she do to facilitate her daughter's revival? Why her daughter?*

Vamini was at Gayatri's side, holding her hand. 'It's all my fault, Gayatri bai, I should have gone shopping alone,' she uttered, her eyes brimming too.

After a few emotional moments, the nurse came around to tell them that the doctor treating Baby would like to see them and answer any questions that they might have. Priti, cognizant that doctors typically didn't like to sugar-coat the truth, decided it was best to let Vamini wait with Gayatri while she visited the doctor unaccompanied.

Dr Shah's office was at the end of the corridor on the floor above, Priti was told. Dr Shah was a senior paediatric neurosurgeon. He had been assigned Baby's case after the doctors and forensic experts had completed the initial formalities, and they were convinced she was out of any imminent danger. He was sitting at his desk when Priti knocked and entered his office. He was a balding man wearing rimless glasses, in his mid-to-late fifties with a few silver strands. He stood up courteously and walked out from behind his desk to greet her.

'Thanks for seeing me, Dr Shah.'

'I can't say it's a pleasure to see you, which is what makes my profession a bit intense.' He managed to summon a mirthless smile.

'It's okay.'

'Sit, please.' Dr Shah pulled out a visitor's chair and gestured to Priti to sit, then walked around and took his seat.

'How is she?'

'She's out of danger, which I'm sure the doctors at the ICU would have already told you.'

Priti nodded, said nothing. Partly because there wasn't anything to say, but also because she was conscious of the lump in her throat, and she had no intention of breaking down.

'She's in a coma caused by what we medically call epidural haematoma, which in plain English is blood between the outer membrane of the central nervous system and the skull.'

'When will she be a hundred per cent okay, doctor?'

'Is she your daughter?'

'No, she's the daughter of my household help.'

'Do you have her permission to discuss her medical condition, Mrs Diwan?'

'Baby is like my daughter.' Priti bit the inside of her cheek to stop the waterworks starting, but her eyes eventually welled up.

'I'm sorry, Mrs Diwan. I know you're an advocate. You should know better.'

Doctors, by law, aren't permitted to speak of any medical condition of their patients to anyone except the patient or their guardians. The Access to Medical Reports Act, 1988, in India categorically states that the insurer or employer cannot be shown a medical report until the patient or their parent or guardian has seen, commented and consented to its disclosure. However close Priti Diwan was to Baby or Gayatri, she was still the employer of the patient's mother.

'Is Gayatri Devi not around?'

'She is. She's with my daughter on the floor below us.'

'Apologies for being pedantic, but I strongly advise you to take this form—' he bent forward and pulled out a two-page form from one of the drawers in his desk and handed it to Priti— 'and get it signed by her. This relieves me of the burden that none of the information on Baby that I provide to you today can affect the employment of Gayatri Devi.'

This wasn't the first time such a thing had happened and it wouldn't be the last, Priti knew. Legalities are put in place so that malicious people don't take advantage of the sickly and the old. So even if your intentions are clear as sky, it is the paperwork that attests it. All argument would be a waste of time. She excused herself for a few minutes and left Dr Shah's office.

She was back in eight minutes.

Dr Shah looked at the signed form and kept it to one side. 'I'll ask someone to send you a copy later.'

'Thanks.' Priti sat down.

'Do you know exactly what a coma is, Mrs Diwan?' Dr Shah commenced.

'In broad layman's terms, yes.'

'It's a protracted state of unconsciousness, caused by bleeding in Baby's case. By the reports I've read, she had also lost a considerable amount of blood before the emergency services got into action. She is unresponsive to her environment, apart from her eyes reacting to speech. However, although she responds to the stimulus, she doesn't comprehend what is being said. And she hasn't spoken a coherent sentence, just mutterings. However, these two factors are good points, actually, since they indicate that it's not permanent.' Dr Shah stopped. Maybe he realized he had gone far too much into the medical description, which wasn't required. 'Also, age is a major plus for Baby, as younger bodies are known to recover faster.'

'When will she wake up?' Priti had a lone question.

'I was coming to that. Unlike deep sleep, a person in a coma cannot be awakened by doctors with any sort of stimulation, including tickling or pain.'

'So, there's no medicine to facilitate that?'

'Sadly, no.'

'So, we have no idea if she will even—'

'No. Like I said, it's temporary, but it could be a fairly long temporary.'

'What is your honest opinion, doctor, you must have some past references to have some idea?' Priti almost beseeched.

'I don't. In America, apparently, there was a case where a man woke up after nineteen years. The best research says that the patient should be visited often to keep their mind going. She needs to be spoken to, reminded of happy times spent with family and friends. Everything helps in recovery, including prayers. So, we'll ask you to visit her regularly after we complete all tests to ensure she's out of any kind of danger, so to speak.'

'Will she have disabilities?'

'Unlike my colleagues, who believed Baby was on Glasgow Scale three or four yesterday, I'd say Baby is fourteen on the scale, so there is an above 85 per cent chance of a full recovery. And, as I said before, children always have a higher rate of recovery. However, I'd advise you not to raise too many hopes when you explain this to the patient's mother, since statistics only tell us past results. It isn't an exact science.'

Dr Shah advised that he'd ideally want the family to visit Baby only after a couple of days. A full forty-eight hours.

Vansh Diwan sat in his office. Having been through files, memos, routine office tasks, returning calls and two coffees, Priti's words still resonated in his brain despite his best efforts to impede them: *what if Vamini had been alone at home?*

He called ASP Arvind Kapoor for an update.

ASP Kapoor explained that the forensics team had recovered the skin from under Baby's fingernails and had found it to be from a male; no surprises there, since she had been raped. Skin residue of the same individual had also been recovered from scouring the kitchen floor. Two body hairs were also recovered from the scene and the lab was presently comparing them to the skin to establish if both samples were from the same guy. Further tests might reveal the skin elasticity, which could provide the age group of the offender. Besides that, there was only a tiny portion of a paper box recovered from under the kitchen units, the type that one found on strips of medicines, which, too, was being analysed, although the investigators weren't pinning a lot of hope on that. It could have been there for a while and gone unnoticed. And in any event, on first appearances, it looked too ordinary to lead anywhere.

Given the nature of his profession, Vansh understood ASP Kapoor easily; he had used similar forensic evidence in several criminal cases. Evidence based on science was the only evidence that never lied. He remembered it all so clearly: it wasn't a case he had been involved in, but he had read about it in detail. Manu Sharma had shot Jessica Lal in the head at the Tamarind Court restaurant for refusing to serve him a drink. A lot of people had witnessed it. Over thirty witnesses had turned hostile. They had lied before they were coerced to tell the truth, eventually, and not take the secret to their graves. In his long and illustrious legal career, Vansh Diwan had seen scientific evidence win more cases than human testimony.

The ASP wanted all male members, occupants and recent visitors to the Diwan household, including Vansh Diwan, to provide a sample for DNA fingerprinting should they fall into the age group determined by the forensic team: standard operating procedure to check if the hair was one of theirs.

'Anything else?' asked Vansh.

'The lubrication from the vaginal walls has given us the brand of condom, but we haven't got any further on that, since it's one of the three largest brands sold in India.'

'So we have no pointers ... ' Vansh felt deflated. Twenty-four hours since the crime and not a single pointer. He had just received a call from Priti on his mobile, telling him there was little chance that Baby would be waking up in the next couple of days to narrate her sordid story and point a finger.

'I'm sorry, but you're correct. We have nothing else to go on at this moment. I have asked my team to scour the entire area, go door-to-door, ask around the neighbourhood stores. Someone will have surely seen something. Some person, some vehicle, some anomaly, some disruption of routine. Give me a little more time, I'm equally concerned, Diwan sahib.'

'Thank you. Anything we can do to help?'

'Yes, Mr Diwan. I need statements from all of you. When could we come over or do you want to come to the Andrews Ganj police station?'

'I don't mind. I've been to, literally, every police station in Delhi by now. But, I would really appreciate it if you could send someone over, as none of the women in my household are in the best of form, as you can well imagine.'

'No problem. I'll personally come over with a senior inspector this evening, say after six?

'Fine by me. I'll see you later.'

Maheep was uneasy throughout the day. He didn't go out, he didn't drink. His head was still numb from all the alcohol he had consumed the previous day, but memories were coming back as if dropping out from the folds of time. He stayed in his room, toyed with the notion of calling Vamini, just casually, to chat, to ferret out if anything was amiss but eventually let the idea pass. His brain, now clearer than it was yesterday under the influence of alcohol, was beginning to twig the gross blunder he had committed. No, it was not regret, it was the fright that bothered him, playing tricks on his mind. The only comfort was that if the girl had divulged the details about the escapade, wouldn't the police have come to his home already? Aarti had certainly not squealed, which was good. Otherwise, his mother would have been all over him to see and nurse the little scratches. He was still wearing a long-sleeved T-shirt to conceal them. The wounds had started healing, but the marks were still visible.

If the police came for him, he would say that Baby had invited him in for sex, and even insisted that he put on a condom. That reminded him: two out of the same pack of three still remained in his wallet. He got up and flushed them down the toilet. He could say she gave him one to put on, how could the police verify where the damn packet came from?

And if the servant girl did not complain, it meant she'd be willing to do it again, wouldn't she? Maybe it would be a bit more unhurried, more gratifying the next time around?

At the time, he didn't know that there would be no second time.

ASP Kapoor was at the Diwan residence as agreed. Senior inspector Anupam Verma was present as Priti and Vansh gave their statements for the record. Their versions were either hearsay or they narrated the post-event situation, since both of them were not present when the others in the household had discovered the victim.

'I will kill him,' yelped Gayatri when she was asked about the incident. She was under a lot of stress, which both the policemen, fortunately, realized. First the rape of her minor daughter and then the looming uncertainty if Baby would ever wake up, and if she did, what were the odds that she would be totally fine and not left damaged physically? From experience, ASP Kapoor knew that there would always be psychological scars of the torment she had gone through. He had seen a lot of victims. Gayatri narrated that one of her friends in her village in Bihar had been raped and she never recovered. She was always scared of the dark, of strangers, of new places. What would happen to her Baby? With polite nudges and references, the trained policemen somehow managed to segue to her daughter's case. Between intermittent crying and howling, she narrated how Vamini had, at first, seen the motionless head of Baby from the kitchen window, and how the driver Shiv Kumar had broken down the door before the three of them rushed in. 'If I come to know who did that to my Baby, I'll kill him sahib, I will … '

Vamini's and Shiv Kumar's versions of the event were ditto. They had all returned together and figured something was wrong. There were no fractures in the story.

'Any new developments?' Priti asked after Gayatri and Vamini left the living room, and SI Verma left with the recorded statements.

'We're expecting some laboratory results tomorrow, so that should give us an indication of the brute's age group. My team has been canvassing the area, but nothing has come up yet. Maybe no one was around or no one saw any incongruity.'

ASP Kapoor could see that this surprised Vansh Diwan. In fact, it surprised him every single time too. Someone should have seen the intruder walk through the gate. Or seen someone drive up to and park outside the Diwan residence. When the person left, what were the odds that he would have leisurely strolled out: between minus one to zero? He would have jetted out. Maybe reversed the car rashly? Maybe his running out or driving recklessly would have turned a head or two. Maybe someone had shouted expletives at the person if he had driven irresponsibly. And if the offender had come by car, someone should have seen a car parked outside the residence for, what, twenty minutes, at the very least? Maybe it was parked haphazardly; maybe it had blocked part of the road. How could no one have noticed anything?

'Something will turn up, Diwan sahib,' ASP Kapoor said, more to reassure himself than Vansh.

Four

Tales travel. The episode at Vamini's house—no, not the full scope, extent and the calamity it had triggered—commenced its journey from Vamini to another friend from the same class, same school, when her friend, Aditi, called to ask Vamini out for a film. Vamini, desperate to talk to someone her age, confided that there had been a misadventure at her place, which the police had been called to investigate. Aditi, albeit promising to keep it to herself, had to narrate the story to another friend who, when asked if she was coming for the film, enquired if Vamini was joining them. It didn't take long for the tale to travel to the boys from the same class and from there it found its way to Maheep's ears, eager and waiting to pick up any noise regarding the same.

Should he tell his parents now that the police were involved, he pondered. He was aware that his dad was moneyed, notoriously powerful and indeed, had some hold on the Diwans. Plus, he had police connections, but this was nastier than any mischief he had committed in the past; maybe this wouldn't even be considered mischief, this was proper, dirty transgression. Getting into someone else's house and having sex with the maidservant's daughter. With a couple of quiet days in between, the confidence that had started to return was flattened when he heard about the police involvement. What he found strange was why the girl hadn't reported him yet. And if she had named him, why hadn't the police come looking for him? He wanted to call Vamini, but once again could not bring himself to. He wondered if he could ask one of his close friends to check with Vamini but in the end, discarded that notion too. He shouldn't pay much attention to an incident that he shouldn't even have any knowledge of or people might start to question his unnecessary interest. His only regret was that in his haste to be with Vamini, he had brought upon himself the curse of not being able to see her. It would have to wait. Turning up for a social call at Vamini's house could be asking for trouble to find him.

He replayed the incident with Baby in his mind several times. There were parts he realized he had enjoyed immensely: the touch, the sense, the smell, the taste, the actual act, the time when that bitch had squirmed while she was snared under him. If only she hadn't been so stubborn. She had asked for it. She was to be blamed. She could have avoided the nasty situation by complying with his need. He hadn't even driven there to have sex with that girl, had he? No. The purpose of his drive to Def Col on that fateful day had been to see Vamini, to express his love for her. That scraggy girl in the little nightdress should not have opened the door. What was she thinking?

She had lured him in. And now, that one moment of weakness could decide the balance of his life. What could be the consequences? How dire? How imminent? Was it only a matter of multiple moments before it all became too unbearable for him?

He wouldn't let that happen.

ASP Arvind Kapoor, having assigned to his team the task of looking out for any anomalies on the day of Baby's attack, couldn't do anything but wait. Investigation is known to be a game of patience. You can't let disappointments drill holes in your confidence. The team checked with local cycle-rickshaw pullers. Auto-rickshaws travelled from one locality to another, but a human being pedalling a rickshaw could only wander so much. For instance, you could not hire a cycle-rickshaw in Def Col to carry you to Connaught Place; the sheer physical effort required was a constraint. As such, most guys tended a neighbourhood, taking commuters from their residences for local shopping trips or ferrying them to taxi stands or bus stops. Unfortunately, there was no cycle-rickshaw stand near the Diwan residence. The neighbours, of course, hadn't seen anything irregular on the day. However, ASP Kapoor wanted results and insisted that the team canvass more, widening their circle.

Persistence, sometimes, does bring results. Finally, a police constable came across a rickshaw-wallah who had crossed the Diwan residence that day, at the time of the incident, and remembered having seen a white car parked carelessly, it's rear portion taking up a third of the space on the blacktop of the road, obstructing traffic. Any diversion the person pedalling it has to take—cycle-rickshaws being slow-moving and human powered—even a few extra pedals to go around a small hindrance, counted. On further questioning, the rickshaw puller told the police that he even remembered that the lady customer and the small kid, whom he had been carting, had said something about the negligence of the driver of that white car. The poor guy, however, failed to provide any details about the make and registration of the car. A white car in Delhi with no other details was like the proverbial needle in an automobile haystack. Nevertheless, that information on the car helped further investigations yield several leads—hawkers, other rickshaw-wallahs and a tea shop owner came forward to acknowledge that a white car had driven rashly past them in the area a couple of days back, overtaken them, crossed them from the opposite side, swayed a bit on the right, wavered a bit on the left. All those probed admitted it was being driven fast, but no one remembered the driver or any other details.

ASP Kapoor looked at the data coming in. Most people who had provided a statement were working-class. Recognition of makes and models of cars wasn't expected. A car was a car was a car, and the best identification was colour, which they had all agreed on. Then it struck him. It was possible that the lady and the kid, who were in the rickshaw when it crossed the Diwan residence that morning, might be able to give some further information about the car—make, model, registration number. The same rickshaw-wallah was contacted again. He had picked up the lady and her son from Def Col main market and dropped them in the same lane as the Diwans, to a kothi only eight doors from them. The police finally got the make of the car from the mother—Honda, a hatchback—but the six-year-old boy was more observant than his mother, and ASP Kapoor learnt that the car that had been haphazardly parked outside the Diwan residence at the time of the crime was a white Honda Civic. The registration number was still missing from the files.

Pictures from Honda Civic brochures were cut out and circulated. There was instant recognition from all those who had claimed to have seen the white car.

ASP Kapoor called Vansh Diwan to check about the white car.

'Were you expecting any of your friends that day, Diwan sahib?'

'No, most people know I'm at work so why would anyone come to see me at my residence?'

'Do you know anyone who has a white Honda Civic?'

'I honestly can't think of anyone, but then I wouldn't know of all the cars owned by the people I know personally.'

'Was Mrs Diwan or Vamini expecting anyone?'

'Priti is also in office during the day, so I doubt anyone would visit her at home. I'll check with Vamini and get back.'

True to his word, Vansh called back after having checked with Vamini and her response was also in the negative.

The investigation seemed to have hit a wall yet again.

Nevertheless, something else gave.

The little piece from the paper box recovered under the kitchen unit was enough to tell the experts it wasn't from a medicine box; it was from a box of condoms.

ASP Kapoor asked if the same could reveal anything else. Buried in the corner of the box was the batch code. The last two or three characters, alpha/numeric, had been torn off. However, the first part was enough to reiterate that it was the same brand identified by the lubrication earlier.

Telephone wires started buzzing.

The condom manufacturer's PR office was called. ASP Kapoor succinctly told them why the police were enquiring about the said batch number. It was something that wasn't in any way detrimental to the brand or the company, and any association of the crime to the company and its product would only be used to identify where the particular batch of contraceptives had been bought. Once assured, the international pharmaceutical company gave the names of two carrying and forwarding (C&F) agents in Delhi, one in south Delhi, the other in west Delhi. The south Delhi C&F, even with the last three digits of the batch code missing, was able to determine which store this particular stock had been supplied to: Angel Pharmacy in Def Col main market. That put ASP Kapoor in a dilemma. It was, of course, possible that the perpetrator had purchased the box of condoms from Angel Pharmacy in Def Col, but given its vicinity, it was equally possible that Vansh Diwan had procured the same. It could well have travelled down from the bedroom to the kitchen as a little piece from the waste-paper basket. ASP Kapoor didn't have the heart to ask Vansh Diwan if he had ever had sex with anyone on the kitchen floor. He decided to go down to the pharmacy and talk directly with the owner or manager or whoever manned the shop.

The pharmacist called for tea when ASP Kapoor told him he had come for a chat and a routine query.

'How can I help?' Krishna Chand, shop owner, despite the ASP being polite, was visibly perturbed by the police snooping around his store. ASP Kapoor was aware that there were a lot of cash transactions and unaccounted merchandise from small C&F agents. Krishna Chand didn't want unnecessary headaches.

'Don't worry, Mr Krishna, it is a small thing. We are looking for someone who bought something from you in the last few days … '

'For cash?' Krishna Chand interposed.

'Maybe. Most likely, yes. We believe he bought a pack of condoms from you.'

'That has to be cash if the person bought only condoms. It is such a small amount, sir.'

'I know.'

'The guy drove a white car.' ASP Kapoor realized when the words left his tongue that there was no way Krishna Chand could know that. Whoever bought the condoms must have left the car in the parking lot. How had he missed that?

'Uh-huh!'

ASP Kapoor changed course immediately and explained that they were looking for someone who had bought condoms from this store on a certain date between certain times. Anyone who didn't look local? Or anyone who looked to be in a rush? Or anyone who stood out in Krishna Chand's memory?

'Yes. A young man, eighteen or nineteen. Unkempt beard, big build, reeked of alcohol—these young guys these days, SP sahib, they have no shame left,' Krishna Chand went off on a tangent; the diatribe covered society, new films, the sleazy content on television and item numbers. ASP Kapoor had a feeling that he could have carried on for the next two hours so he stopped him.

'Mr Krishna, is there anything more you can tell me about this young man?'

'Which young man?'

'The one who bought the condoms from you that day … '

'Oh, him? Yes, he was big built, thick eyebrows, teen beard, unruly hair …'

'Wait a minute.' The ASP turned to the constable. 'Call the office and tell them we need someone to make a sketch for us from the description Mr Krishna Chand is giving. Also, get the person responsible for the car park for this complex. I need to speak to whomever is in charge.

The car park attendant also described a boy who was in such a hurry that he was virtually running. Yes, the car was a white Honda Civic. Yes, it had been parked without a ticket and hence, the registration number hadn't been recorded. Cash business.

Vansh received a call in the late afternoon from ASP Kapoor to say that the E-FIT of the boy driving the wanted Honda Civic, who had also purchased the condoms, the partial batch-code of which had been found under their kitchen unit, was ready. Two of them, in fact, both worked upon separately by two artists using the descriptions given by the two eyewitnesses—the pharmacist and the car park attendant. ASP Kapoor finished the call and drove straight to Vansh's office on Barakhamba Road.

Vansh cancelled all meetings for the rest of the day. He didn't want anyone to know why he was meeting the police. It was better if everyone believed he was working on a client's case and not his own.

'I can't lie that, under the circumstances, it's nice to see you,' Vansh quipped when ASP Kapoor came in.

'I know. I get a similar reception everywhere else too. No one seems to be happy to see the police.'

'Tea or coffee?'

'Something cold would be nice, if that's not a problem.'

'Not at all.' Vansh swivelled around in his leather chair. His office had polished rosewood bookcases, filled with legal books and journals, from floor to ceiling on both sides of his desk. Behind him, below a big glass window, was a credenza that housed a little refrigerator, from which he pulled out cans of cola and orange soda and showed them to his guest.

'I'll have a Coke.'

'Orange for me, then.'

Without any preamble, ASP Kapoor opened a file and extracted the two E-FITs and said, 'There's a striking resemblance between both E-FITs, Mr Diwan, and they were both drawn using independent descriptions, so we suspect this is our young man.' He passed both of them to Vansh. 'Also, the forensic experts have come back with the results of tests done on the skin and hair left behind at the crime scene, which confirm that the offender was a young man, maybe a teen to about twenty-two or twenty-three.'

'Let me have a look.'

Vansh's mind went into overdrive the moment he glanced at the sketches. The resemblance wasn't merely between the two E-FITs; he was shocked to see sketches of Maheep Singh's face in his hands.

'You know him, Mr Diwan?'

Vansh was silent for a while, gazing at the sketches, attempting a poker face till he thought his anxiety had subsided enough to speak. 'Looks familiar, but I can't place him right away,' he lied.

'Don't worry, we'll find him. Could I come over this evening to show these sketches to your family members for possible identification?'

'It's best that I do that, if that is okay with you. Is it possible for you to leave copies with me, please? I'll show these sketches to all at home, including Gayatri and Shiv Kumar ... Maybe they will remember seeing him.'

'Of course.'

'Anything else you have so far?' Vansh asked. He wanted the meeting to conclude without another word exchanged and the ASP gone as soon as possible. Being an advocate, he recognized the imprudence of lying to the police, the penalties of obstructing or misdirecting the police in an ongoing criminal investigation ... He was all too familiar with the possible consequences.

He also realized that he had to speak to Maninder at the earliest.

'No, but I'll keep you posted.' The ASP took the last sip from his Coke can, got up, shook hands, turned around and walked out of his office.

And Vansh Diwan called Maninder Singh.

Five

After Vansh Diwan's phone call disclosing that the ASP had left the E-FITs with the advocate, Maninder Singh went home, pulled up Maheep, gave him a verbal thrashing and a few slaps and handed over the keys to the Honda Civic to one of his unscrupulous men, instructing him to drive it out of Delhi and destroy it beyond possible recognition. *Char it*, he said. Using his police connections, he lodged a police report—backdated two days before the sordid incident in Def Col—at a south Delhi police station. However, that was merely one part of the problem taken care of. Maheep's sketch still remained, and it was obviously a close enough likeness if Vansh had called him. Vansh had, of course, declined to send a fax or a photograph of the same but had been sure that the sketches were sufficient to make the identification. But Maninder was a criminal, and like all criminals, he knew how the law worked, how it could be circumvented and he had adequate resources and connections to rely upon. He had called Vansh to ask him to stay in his office so he could visit him after seeing Maheep.

It was one of the rare times Maninder Singh went to Vansh's office; the vile Mr Singh had visited his office maybe only once or twice before. They either met at the club or Vansh would go to his client's office. But this was an altogether different occasion. Maninder needed to curry favour with him. A rotund, tall, balding man, he was huge. A thick neck, wide shoulders and a large stomach on a six-foot two-inch frame. He looked callous, which given his line of work, worked to his advantage. And he didn't do anything to fight people's impression of him either. The trick in his business was to be meaner and harder than the guys who worked for him. It wouldn't have worked any other way. If the politicians and other criminals whom he fronted thought he looked weak, he'd lose business right away. And he was a textbook example of the nouveau riche. Gold bracelet, a thick gold chain around his neck, dressed in a short-sleeved shirt to display the gold Rolex on his wrist. Even his prescription glasses had diamonds studded on the frame, a level above your average vulgar guy. He was loud-mouthed, impatient and had serious halitosis, which no amount of Colgate could remedy. A manqué who would prefer to mix with the right sort of who's who, but the dichotomy was that his riches were earned courtesy of the cruder section of society.

It was late, and consequently a lot of staff had left Diwan-e-Khaas for the day. The office was quiet, except for the humming of the air conditioning and the random clacking of a few keyboards somewhere in the distance. No chance of someone eavesdropping outside Vansh's personal office. This wasn't a meeting to discuss just another case, this was personal for Maninder and he had come alone and not with any of his associates, which was atypical for him, since his cronies forever surrounded him like he was some crown prince.

'Sorry to have to drop in at such short notice,' Maninder said, shaking hands and attempting to give the impression that it was simply a routine call, which Vansh knew it wasn't. Maninder was visibly perturbed.

'It's fine. What are friends for?'

'Thanks.'

'Drink?' Vansh asked.

'Do you have anything here?'

'Of course,' Vansh opened one of the lower drawers in his desk and pulled out a bottle of Balvenie. Then he turned around to reach into the credenza, which housed the crystal and the refrigerator. He poured the whisky, added ice and club soda and offered one of the glasses to his client. 'Cheers.'

'Show me the sketches.' Maninder made clear what he was there for. The sooner they approached the topic, the better.

Vansh passed both the sketches to him.

'There is indeed a resemblance,' he said within seconds.

'Did you speak to Maheep?'

'Yes.'

He wanted Maninder to confirm if Maheep had actually violated Baby. 'Did he go to Def Col that day?' asked Vansh when Maninder stopped after the mere *yes*.

'Unfortunately, yes.'

'That doesn't sound good,' Vansh said as he took his first sip.

'Has the girl or anyone in your home seen these sketches?'

'I didn't give you all the details on the phone. The girl, Baby, has been in a coma ever since.'

'What?'

'Yes. She's been in a coma as she sustained injuries to the back of her head that resulted in a lot of blood loss. She hasn't spoken at all.'

'God.'

For a moment, Vansh thought that his client-friend was actually empathizing with the little girl. Then:

'Don't get me wrong, Vansh. I'm as sorry about Maheep's little misdemeanour as you or anyone else, but Maheep was a bit drunk. And you and I both know about testosterone. We, too, were young once and went through the same urges and we know how strong those itches can get.'

'I know, Maninder, but raping a girl violently ... ?'

'Look, Maheep told me that she was teasing him by lifting her frock or whatever she was wearing. She invited him in when he requested her to bring the water out. He didn't even want to go in.'

Either Maheep had convinced Maninder or he was making up a story that it was entirely Baby's doing. Vansh knew the evidence vehemently suggested otherwise. The cut lip, the head injury, the blood loss, the resulting coma ...

'Then how do you explain the violence?'

'That's water under the bridge, over the dam or whatever else you may want to call it, Vansh. Whatever's happened has happened and we can't change that now, can we?'

'The police have enough to identify Maheep and his car, they will get to him whether I tell them anything or not. I can pretend for a while that I cannot recollect anyone who looks like these sketches, but I still have to show them to Priti, Vamini and Gayatri. There is no way Vamini won't identify Maheep from these.' He pointed at the two sheets that lay between them on his desk. 'And if I don't show them, there is no reason why ASP Kapoor won't show these to them himself. He's not just going to walk away because I cannot—'

'You can always tell the ASP that you've shown them to people at home and no one recognized the person in these sketches.'

'They will find out that I lied, sooner or later, what then?'

'Then we need to find another way out.'

We? *We?* Vansh closed his eyes.

'Priti and you have done a lot for Gayatri and the girl. She's a little educated now. Honestly, had she been in her native village, some old man would have fornicated with her right after puberty. Or maybe before. You know how it is in those villages.'

Vansh didn't say anything. He looked blankly at Maninder while taking civilized sips from his glass.

'What I'm saying is, she's proletarian. Servant class. We don't know who her dad is or was.'

'How does that help Maheep?'

'May I have another drink?' Maninder upended his glass and stretched his hand forward. 'I'll tell you in a minute.'

'Of course.' Vansh turned to make another drink.

'Don't bother with the soda. Just give me the whisky.'

'Tell me how not knowing who Baby's father was, or is, helps Maheep?'

'Pay the mother off. You have to convince the mother to drop the charges. Everything will be okay. It's entirely feasible at this moment, if you act fast, believe me, it'll go away.'

Vansh finished his drink and poured himself another. He had, in the past, defended criminals; sometimes they were innocent, but most times they were not. Maheep wasn't innocent, but that wasn't what bothered him; the affected party was in *his* home and that was the worry. It wasn't his conscience he was trying to rein in. It would be an almost impossible conversation to have back home. If Baby's mother withdrew the police complaint, ASP Kapoor could be dealt with. But getting Gayatri to roll over meant going through Priti, and he had always reassured Priti that even though he was a defence advocate, he had some ethics and principles.

'You have to somehow convince the mother to drop the charges.' Maninder took a generous sip. 'However much money she wants … I'll pay for all the medical expenses of the girl, pay them to move back to their village or whichever other town they wish, buy them a house, give her lifelong employment, lump sum money, just tell her to name a figure.'

Vansh waited for Maninder to continue.

'I'll ensure the girl has a future, I'll send her to college, higher education … ' Maninder appeared smug now, a hackneyed confidence anyone with his kind of cash and clout carried as their entitlement.

'I'm not sure how to approach it with Priti and Gayatri.' Vansh sighed.

'I've taken care of the car.'

'What do you mean?'

'Reported stolen on June fourth. First Information Report, all above board. And now the car has been destroyed beyond recognition.'

'What about Maheep?'

'I've told him to prepare to move out of India soon. He can stay for a few weeks with his sister and depending on his results in the Boards, I'll send him to whichever university accepts him in the United States for undergrad. He'll be away for a few years and everything will be forgotten.'

'How soon can he go?'

'I can send him to the States within a week. Actually, now as I talk to you, I think I should send him straightaway, maybe in a day or two. He doesn't need to hang around in Delhi for anything.'

Something in Vansh's countenance might have communicated to Maninder that his advocate wasn't a hundred per cent convinced because his next attack was on an emotional level. 'What would you do if it was your own child's future at stake, Vansh?'

Vansh understood a father's pitch. He could equally appreciate how Gayatri would feel if he approached the topic, but he nodded. 'I need to think,' he uttered.

'Do the right thing. Do it for a friend. I know you'll do the right thing.' Without asking for permission, Maninder got up and picking up the bottle of Scotch from Vansh's desk, poured himself a generous portion.

Then, for no apparent reason, Maninder dived into a protracted panegyric on the brilliance of Vansh's firm, his commitment to loyalty and friendship, all the years he had worked as a star advocate for him and indirectly for others who had been behind the scenes and wished to remain anonymous. The eulogy was filled with hints of more work, more money, more prestige for Vansh and his firm. And should anything ever bother or trouble Vansh, how easily it could be eliminated. The monologue also implied that this was just another assignment that Vansh, the criminal advocate, was being asked to carry out for a fee. He just stopped short of mentioning the proverbial *the sky was the limit* to Vansh.

'How much are you willing to spend?'

Maninder's eyes shone at his question. Perhaps he saw a glimmer of hope: if Vansh was talking about price, then maybe the sale was made. 'No cap on that. It's my son's life, you know I won't hold back.'

Money; Vansh knew he could extract as much as he wanted for making this case go away from Maheep's life, no question about that. He had Maninder's precious gonads in a bottle here.

Maninder had another drink and rose to go. 'It's best that I leave now. It's only eight o'clock so you can still go home and have this conversation tonight itself.' He smiled innocuously.

Vansh's mind was in a turmoil long after Maninder left. He poured himself another drink, his third, and pondered. He recognized he needed to have a conversation with Priti. There was no way around it. He couldn't just go to Gayatri and have this discussion alone. He needed to convince Priti that paying Gayatri off and letting her move to another town or city of her choice was the best way forward. It would be the least embarrassing exit plan for Maninder, Maheep and also the Diwans. If Maheep were arrested and convicted, wouldn't their neighbours in Def Col look at them weirdly—a family friend's son being convicted of raping a girl in their area? It was a lose-lose situation.

By eight-thirty, he had convinced himself that the only way out of the problem was the way Maninder had prescribed. He got up, picked up his bag, switched the lights off, took the elevator down and sat in the car as his driver took him home.

With the office rush hour long over, the drive took less than twenty-five minutes.

Just as he had anticipated, the vibe at home was still sombre. Baby still hadn't come out of the coma, though Dr Shah, who was treating her, felt very positive after the new series of tests. He had seen certain responses—which were obviously imperceptible to Gayatri, Priti and Vamini—that suggested that Baby was better today than she had been yesterday. However, that hadn't lightened the mood. Even if Baby regained consciousness tomorrow morning, and no physical damage was diagnosed, it would still be a long road to psychological recovery. She was, after all, a rape victim.

Vansh patiently listened to Priti but didn't mention anything about the E-FITs or Maninder's discreet visit while the three of them had dinner. He waited until Vamini and Gayatri retired and the couple was alone in the living room.

'Do ASP Kapoor and his team have a suspect?'

'Yes.'

'Yes, and you didn't call me? When did you come to know about it?'

'It's complicated.'

'What's complicated about it? Who is it?'

Notwithstanding his resolve to speak to Priti the moment they were alone, the words dried up in Vansh's mouth.

'What's wrong, Vansh?'

Vansh poured himself his fourth drink of the evening and spewed the discovery in one long discourse: the car, the

E-FITs, the meeting with Maninder and the father's lament and proposal.

'He's got some cheek to ask Gayatri to forget about her daughter who is fighting for her life ... I warned you from the very beginning that Maninder was an outlaw, and his son, that little animal is only eighteen at the moment ... the apple didn't fall very far from the tree.'

'You're overreacting to the situation, Priti, he isn't totally wrong—'

'What?'

'Listen to me, Priti,' he implored.

'Disgusting. How can you be in cahoots with that criminal? God, listen to what you're saying, Vansh.'

'Maheep is their only son.'

'And Baby is Gayatri's only daughter.'

'But—'

'But what, Vansh?'

'It's different—'

'It's different because she's a maidservant's child, she's less of a person than Maheep?' Priti was interjecting at every sentence now. Rage seemed to have taken over.

'Would you please listen to me because—'

'Because?'

'Because I wasn't saying that.'

'Then say it, because as far as I am concerned, that's precisely what you want to say.'

'Not at all.' Vansh stalled. He had known arguing it out with Priti would be tough, but this tough?

'What are you saying? God, Vansh, how could you even think I would let this outrageous idea pass? I didn't really expect you, at least not you, to propose such an idea, like some third-rate criminal!'

'What do you want me to do? Go against my firm's biggest client?'

'Either that or go against me and my daughter.'

'You're unnecessarily making it personal, Priti.'

'It is already personal. You know I only went back to work after Gayatri came into our lives. She has always treated Vamini like her own daughter, at times even dearer than her own daughter. Vamini tells me that Gayatri sometimes ignores Baby to attend to Vamini first … '

'That's because you pay her bills.'

'How ungrateful of you! You think money can buy that kind of love? Vamini thinks of Gayatri as a surrogate mother and Baby as the sibling she never had. Do you even know that Vamini hasn't eaten or slept properly ever since Baby went into a coma? She's been beating herself up over taking Gayatri shopping with her, leaving Baby behind. Does any of this mean anything to you?'

Vansh grappled for words to dampen his wife's wrath, but failed. He could tell that this debate was going nowhere. Strike that. This debate was going only one way: Priti's way. He couldn't think of any argument except the financial impact, at the moment. He had anticipated resistance, but not to this degree.

'I don't see any point in discussing this further tonight. I suggest you think it over and we'll have a frank chat tomorrow morning. It's late, why don't you go to sleep? I'll join you after my drink,' he concluded.

'Don't be optimistic,' Priti said before she left the room angrily. 'Just think what you'd do if it was your own daughter, and not Baby, who had been raped.'

Melodrama, he said, under his breath.

He sat thinking, sipping his drink. He could see himself getting crushed between mortar and pestle. Priti Diwan's ideology versus Maninder Singh's muscle; his wife against his biggest client; his home or his legal practice. There was certainly merit in accepting Maninder's offer, he still reckoned. What would be the benefit of sending Maheep to a cell besides revenge? Of course, the boy had done something reprehensible, but how would destroying the rest of his life make any difference to what had already happened? Okay, so Priti and Gayatri don't budge, he extrapolated, as he had nothing better to do other than argue with himself to come up with a decent comeback for Priti. If Maheep Singh was sent to prison, how would that benefit Baby or Gayatri? Wouldn't it be better if Maninder took on the financial responsibility of medical care? And education? A kind of penance—a father asking forgiveness for his son's actions? In time, when Maheep grew up, he'd repent too. Priti was pointlessly being maudlin, maybe even overzealous. Perhaps the despicable incident had been too recent; but he recognized that they didn't have a lot of time, he had to get back to Maninder with an answer. And now that he had spoken to Priti, if she wasn't persuaded soon, nothing stopped her from calling ASP Kapoor. Should he speak to Gayatri directly?

Six

Vansh woke up when Priti came down to the living room in the morning. Still tired and dazed, his head hurt with a hangover to be reckoned with. He managed to open his eyes fully after several minutes of blinking them as if he had been dragged into direct, scorching sunlight, straight from the dark. Priti was beside him with a mug of coffee in her hand, which she placed next to him. She looked equally tired, as if she hadn't slept well.

'You slept here?' she asked. He had crashed in the living room, a little whisky still left in the tumbler on the coffee table near him, emitting fumes that didn't seem as enticing as they had the night before.

'Yeah,' he said rubbing his eyes. 'Do you have some pills to make this headache go away?'

'I knew you'd need them so I brought them along.' She gave him two white tablets, which he washed down with the hot coffee.

'Thank you. Did you sleep well?'

'No.'

Which was not what he wanted to hear. Neither did her disposition show any sign that she had calmed down since the night before.

'What have you thought, Priti?'

'No.'

'No, what?'

'No to whatever you asked for last night, Vansh. I cannot let this happen on my watch.'

'Then take some time off, go see your dad in Dehradun and I'll speak to Gayatri. Take Vamini with you, her results won't be out for another week, and when they are, she can apply for admissions remotely too. In any event—'

'That's not what I meant, Vansh.'

'Oh?' He looked at her questioningly, as he took another sip of his coffee. 'What did you mean then?'

'I'm not going anywhere and we're not paying Gayatri to withdraw her complaint.'

'It's not us, it's Maninder—'

'It doesn't matter who's footing the bill here.'

'You know that is going to be a big problem, don't you?' Vansh was almost pleading now.

'Yes, you might lose the account of a bona fide criminal, we might lose a family friend that I always despised, Vamini will surely cry at the loss of a classmate and a friend who was never worthy of being her friend in the first place. Anything I've missed?'

'Yes, the fact that Maninder Singh is a bona fide criminal, as you just said; he won't just walk away from us. He can make life difficult for us, all of us.'

'What can he do? He'll send hoodlums, like that wretched son of his, to our place?'

'I don't know what he'll do, I'm only assuming it.'

'So what if he threatens us, what are the police for?'

'Aren't you blowing all this way out of proportion, Priti? Isn't it all just a storm in a teacup? I mean, I am not saying that what happened is in any way insignificant or pardonable, but think about it. You're a mother too, and aren't mothers known for forgiveness? Where has all that love gone? Maheep is mentally a kid, after all. I know he's physically an adult, but his brain is not fully developed. And to top that, he was drunk—'

'Oh, so now being drunk is an excuse?'

'I am not making excuses for him. I want you to think. Let's not take any decision in haste only to repent later. Please think again. We don't have to speak to Gayatri today, I'll ask Maninder for a day for us to decide, but please … ' Before he could complete his sentence, he heard footsteps coming down the stairs. Either Vamini or Gayatri. In either case, it was best to discontinue the debate.

'Good morning, Vamini,' Priti said, turning to see their daughter walk into the living room. Her eyes were red, the skin under them swollen, as if she, too, hadn't had a full night's sleep.

Some good news finally found its way to the Diwan residence.

Priti's phone rang around half past eight when she, Vamini and Vansh sat for breakfast laid by Gayatri. Sandwiches with tomatoes and homemade green coriander chutney. Nothing elaborate or fancy. Whereas Gayatri cooked and served meals to the family before she sat down to eat on her own, in the kitchen, Baby always sat with the Diwan family at the dining table and ate with them. And her absence from the table was a conspicuous reminder of the tragedy that had struck their household.

Priti glanced at the phone's screen and announced: 'Dr Shah.'

'Yes doctor, really?' Her voice was suddenly jubilant, but then it sounded despondent. Vansh wondered why and as they looked at her mutely, he saw the waterworks begin. Tears rolled down Priti's cheeks as she carried on a hushed conversation with the doctor. Something was wrong. Or right.

'I want both of you to come upstairs with me,' Priti said as she finished the call.

Father and daughter looked at each other and then followed Priti.

Vamini entered her parents' bedroom, followed by her father. Priti sat on her bed, sobbing, rubbing away tears. Vamini knelt on the floor in front of her mother, with Vansh standing close by.

'What happened, Mom?'

'Baby is conscious,' Priti uttered and broke down again.

'So why are you crying? That's good news, isn't it?' Vansh asked.

'The doctors want to observe her for the next twenty-four hours to check if she is a hundred per cent okay. Dr Shah has strictly told me not to tell Gayatri yet or let her go to the hospital, as he doesn't want Baby to go through any kind of anxiety. He thinks that as her memory rolls back and she relives the nightmare she's recently been through, her anxiety levels will be very steep. There can be serious repercussions if that isn't controlled. They have put her on sedatives for now because she woke up screaming. They will keep her under observation and let her wake up for a few hours a day until they think she's stable enough.'

Vansh and Vamini gaped at Priti as she paused and broke down again.

'Anything else?' Vansh asked.

'He said there is a serious possibility of her attempting to commit suicide—'

'Why?' asked Vamini.

'Vamini, she was violated recently, and this will be the first time she'll comprehend that. For her, it's not been days since the rape, it will be her first waking moment after the brutal attack. She's a kid. Who knows how her mind will work? Dr Shah told me that some girls—especially the younger ones, who see their entire lives looming ahead—end up convincing themselves it was their fault and now that they've been debased, they might as well kill themselves rather than live a life of shame.'

'But Baby didn't do anything wrong. She's not at fault here, why should she feel any shame?'

'Come close,' Priti pulled her daughter to her and hugged her. 'This world is cruel, Vamini.' Still keeping her daughter close to her bosom, Priti looked up and glowered at Vansh. He gathered that the words *world* and *cruel* were cited for him. He had been the one proposing that they request Gayatri to forget the entire thing.

'I'm sure Baby will tell us who the offender was, who knocked her out, right, Mom?'

Vansh simply wagged his head in frustration and walked out of the room.

Priti and Vamini joined Vansh ten minutes later as he noshed on the sandwiches and sipped coffee. There was a strange silence for a few minutes. No one spoke. He reckoned the decision to break or not to break the news to Gayatri had already been taken upstairs, in his absence, and he didn't mind that. He had been married twenty years, and he knew Priti was more level-headed than he was. She would do exactly as Dr Shah had suggested, she would give the news to Gayatri in small doses and ensure that she did not rush to see Baby at the hospital till Dr Shah gave them a clean chit. He finished his breakfast and got up to go for a shower when, as if on cue, his iPhone rang. Maninder Singh. Without announcing it, like Priti had earlier when Dr Shah had called, he walked from the dining table to the living room section and slumped on the sofa.

'Good morning, Maninder,' he almost whispered. 'How are you this morning?'

'I'm fine. Did you manage to convince that maidservant to drop the case against Maheep?' Maninder sounded part growling, part frightened.

'No … I mean yes, we had a little chat but …'

'But?'

'Maninder, you have to understand that she's a mother, she isn't going to agree to something in the first attempt.' Vansh omitted the fact that Gayatri had not even been part of the first round of the discussion and that he had miserably failed in convincing his own wife. He didn't see the need to furnish all the details.

'So how long do I need to wait for Her Royal Highness to come around?'

'I don't know, what can I say?'

'Is someone around that you can't talk?'

'Yes.'

'Okay, give me a call later.'

'Ah, Maninder, before you go, I wanted to tell you that Baby, the little girl who was attacked at our place recently, has woken up.' Vansh was constrained in what he said. He couldn't say any more as both Priti and Vamini were now gaping at him.

'How does that change anything?'

'She will be able to identify her attacker.'

'What the fuck! Call me the moment you leave your home, and please do that as quickly as possible.' He ended the call.

Priti glared at him when he returned to the dining table.

'What have I done now?' Vansh asked meekly.

'Why did you tell Maninder about Baby when we're not even disclosing that info to her own mother?' Priti asked softly.

So despite his whispering, a part of his conversation had still been overheard.

'Because it's good news. And he isn't going to rush to the hospital to see her,' he whispered back. 'Anyway, I'm going for a shower and then I'll leave for office. I'll call you from the car.'

'You didn't call me?' Maninder rudely asked when Vansh took his call in the office.

'There was nothing to update you on.'

'What do you mean there is no update, what happened to the offer I made last night?'

'Well, I can't say it was well received at my place.'

'Does that stupid female want more money?'

'No—'

'Then what? My son had sex with that dirty piece of tail because she teased him and I'm still prepared to pay her and her mother more money than they could ever dream of to forget about it. What does that woman want—that Maheep should marry her daughter, damn it?

'Maninder, relax. They'll come around.'

'Who's *they*?'

'I spoke to Priti and she thinks it's too early to speak to the aggrieved mother—'

'You mean you haven't even spoken to the maidservant?'

'Not yet, but—'

'And what does Priti mean by *too early to speak*? The little floozy has already woken up in the hospital, you told me. I want this to go away before she starts talking to someone in the hospital or to the police.'

'Nothing like that will happen, Maninder. Baby is under medical observation, sedated most of the time, so she won't be giving any statement to any doctor or the police, so please stop fretting.'

'If only it was your son, you would have felt the pain.'

'I can understand your pain, believe me.' Vansh shook his head in disgust. Maninder was as hyper as he had expected.

'Do you want me to talk to Priti?'

'No, leave that to me. I don't think your talking to her will help.' The last thing Vansh wanted was for Priti to go on an offensive and take a stab at Maninder. That would be the end of their relationship and give Maninder an opportunity to, maybe, take his business elsewhere or get belligerent and contemplate carrying out something untoward against them. It was only a question of time.

'How soon can you get back to me?'

'Give me another day.'

'I'm happy to come over to talk to Gayatri personally.'

'Oh no, that won't be required, it might aggravate the issue.' In his mind, Vansh could picture Priti, Gayatri and Vamini pelting shoes and stones at Maninder if he proposed paying Gayatri to retract the police complaint against his son. It was best if Gayatri didn't know who the culprit was.

'I'll call you tonight.'

'Better if I call you, Maninder.'

'Okay.' Maninder slammed the receiver down so hard that Vansh had to rub his ear after he put his own phone down.

Vansh heard his iPhone buzz: ASP Kapoor. It seemed like one nightmare running into the next, a never-ending horror tale. He did not answer the call. What could he say? That he had recognized the guy in the two E-FITs and had therefore decided not to share them with his family? That the guy in the E-FITs was the son of one of his biggest clients, and the client was a dangerous criminal in a rakish, albeit ill-fitting suit? That the guy in the E-FITs was also a classmate of his own daughter? His training advised him that avoidance at this juncture was the only prudent course of action.

Seven

'I think you should go to your room while I have a chat with Gayatri,' Priti requested Vamini. She didn't think another discussion on rape and assault was something the teenager needed to hear. As it was, she had witnessed too much spectacle in the last few days.

'No, I want to be with Gayatri bai when you give her the good news.'

'I'm not giving her any good news, I'm only setting the stage. Remember what I told you Dr Shah had said?'

'I promise to keep my mouth shut while you two talk.' Vamini put her finger on her lips, as if that would add weight to her words. Her eyes had turned moist, too.

'It's not only what you say, sweetie, but if you break down and start crying, it will have a negative impact on Gayatri and she's not in a good state of mind, either, and you know that.'

'Please, Ma ... '

'Okay,' Priti relented. 'But remember your promise. Not a word, and no crying.'

'Yes.'

They left the living room and walked towards the kitchen. As Gayatri spent a lot of time there, it was as if they were entering her domain, which, Priti believed, would be a little more comforting for her as Priti initiated a chat and segued into Dr Shah's evaluation of Baby's recovery, rather than calling Gayatri out and delivering it as a piece of news.

Gayatri must have seen something in Priti or Vamini's expression because she looked expectant when they walked in purposefully. 'What happened to Baby?'

'Gayatri, be patient, believe in God. Everything will be all right.'

'The same God who let a monster attack and rape my little Baby?' The scathing words came rushing out of Gayatri's mouth.

'Yes, the same God will restore everything, we cannot lose our faith in Him.'

'Nothing will ever be the same, madam.'

'It will be. He will also punish the criminal.'

'He will suffer in hell.'

The silence hung in the kitchen like steam released from a pressure cooker after the whistle.

'When can we go to see Baby?'

'I spoke to Dr Shah, and he told me that Baby is recuperating quicker than he had anticipated.'

'What does that mean?'

'Sit down first.' Priti pointed to the folding stepladder that everyone in the household at some point unfolded and used as a stool. 'Baby has regained consciousness.' Priti saw Gayatri's eyes bulge as she took a deep breath like a long-suffering asthma patient; her body shuddered. 'Vamini, fetch Gayatri bai a glass of water.'

It took a while for Priti to explain what Dr Shah had summarized, in part due to the caution that Dr Shah had warned Priti to exercise, and in part because Gayatri needed sips of water intermittently and to take deep, agonizing breaths; at times it felt like she could hardly breathe.

When Priti finished, Gayatri let out a shrill yelp, a cry of bittersweet, albeit shrouded, joy, then got up from the makeshift stool, staggered towards Priti and embraced her, and then hugged Vamini. The three stood in an embrace, tears flowing.

'Promise me one thing, madam,' Gayatri eventually broke the silence. 'Whatever happens, you will be with me to punish whoever did this to my Baby.'

'Yes, of course.' Priti didn't have the heart to tell Gayatri or Vamini that she already knew who the perpetrator was. However, she wasn't worried: if all else failed, Baby would certainly identify her attacker. The primal instinct of any mother is to seek and destroy anyone who harms her child. Gayatri wasn't overreacting. If put in her shoes, Priti knew she'd do exactly the same. This was one crime no one could become inured to, especially not a mother who herself had a teenage daughter. Nevertheless, if Vansh, for some flimsy reason, did not, she knew whom she could ask to fight Baby's case in court. Maninder Singh could go and start digging his son's grave.

A few hours later, Priti lay on her bed, deliberating her next step. She knew Vansh would try to convince her otherwise, and she, being an independent, strong-willed woman, did not want to let Vansh dictate what actions she took. She wasn't normally difficult, but there were times when one had to take a stand. She had never seen Vansh being weak, bending over backwards to oblige that sleazeball, Maninder. She came up with the best course of action, one from which recanting wasn't possible: she called ASP Kapoor and asked him to visit her at home, later in the day. Then she called up Vansh to inform him.

'What have you told him?' Vansh went mental.

'Nothing yet, but he said he'll come by this evening.'

'Why are you trying to take the lead on something I'm already handling? We can let events take their own course ... '

'I'm not taking any lead. I want you to be here when ASP Kapoor comes around after seven.'

'What?'

'You're still not convinced he should be convicted, are you?'

'I don't know.'

'You seriously think Gayatri should retract the police complaint?' asked Priti.

'It's not what I want. It's being pragmatic. We cannot fight Maninder.'

'We're not fighting your client, Vansh.'

'Who else are we going against then? Who else is in the fight?'

'We're only helping the law by telling the police what we know. We didn't come up with the name of the offender, but we cannot lie that we don't know who it is in the sketches the police have got. The police will eventually get Maheep, and we'll become accessories to the crime, trying to protect a rich and powerful friend. You, of all people, should know that.'

'And what good would telling the police be to any of us, including Gayatri and Baby? I was only trying to keep it under wraps for Baby—she'll be the one who will have to deal with police interviews, not once but several times, and then be dragged into court to narrate the nightmare in public. She'll have to go over the terrible episode again and again. You seriously think that'll help her forget the ordeal or expedite her recovery? And don't underestimate how irresistible this story will be for the media ... Irrespective of who's wrong or right and who wins or loses, Baby will eventually lose and consequently, both she and Gayatri will be forced to run back to their village to seek shelter. At the moment, they have an offer on the table, an opportunity to get more money than the two of them could ever make, and return to their village as if nothing happened. You're not only stymying that opportunity, but by hauling Baby into the courtroom, you'll ensure that the poor girl will be subjected to pointless humiliations that will only stigmatize her as a rape victim for the rest of her life. What's the point, Priti?'

'So by that axiom, every girl who gets raped should just keep shtum? Or maybe accept money for being sexually violated?'

'Why don't you understand, Priti, Maninder is not a man to be crossed.'

'Too bad, he should get used to his path being crossed.'

'Listen to me, Priti—'

'No, you listen to me, Vansh. If you stop me from talking to ASP Kapoor today, Vamini and I do not want you to come back home. We do not want someone who thinks we can be raped and offered money in lieu of justice, to be in our lives. I'm sorry. If it had been Vamini instead of Baby, I bet your response wouldn't have been the same.'

'Please, rethink, don't act in haste—'

Priti didn't want to listen to any more excuses and justifications; she hung up.

Vansh left the office almost immediately. He wanted to be home before ASP Kapoor came by, but he ended up being caught in the tail end of the rush hour, and the car moved an inch every few minutes. He tried calling Priti to check what time the ASP was coming, but Priti did not answer her phone. He saw little point in calling the landline or Vamini's phone. He eventually reached Def Col at eight, and ASP Kapoor was already sitting with Priti in the living room, looking grave.

'Mrs Diwan was about to identify the young man from the E-FITs,' were ASP Kapoor's first words when Vansh entered the room.

'Look, I can explain … '

'You don't need to. I understand you are a defence advocate and you wouldn't have told me till you were a hundred per cent convinced who it was. But, thanks for seeking help from your wife.'

Vansh glanced at Priti and grasped that she hadn't thrown him under the bus. ASP Kapoor's words made it clear that Priti had given him some hogwash about Vansh consulting Priti to confirm who they thought the guy in the sketches resembled. He wanted to thank her, but not in the presence of the police. He just gave her a timid smile.

'Thank you for understanding my position.'

'Maheep Singh,' Priti commenced. 'He studied in the same class as our daughter, Vamini.'

ASP Kapoor had taken out a notepad and was scribbling in it. 'And is he a frequent visitor to your place?'

God, this is embarrassing, Vansh thought.

'No, he doesn't come here often and not alone, anyway,' Priti responded.

'You mean, he comes when Vamini's other friends come over, like for a party or something?'

'No, he's visited our place with his parents a few times.'

'So they are … family friends … ?'

'I wouldn't go that far. It's merely a social connection. Maninder Singh—Maheep's father—is a client of Vansh's firm.'

'Interesting … ' ASP Kapoor looked at him now.

Vansh was certain his face was red with humiliation. If the ASP had any inkling why he had failed to recognize Maheep the evening before, he did not let it show.

'As I told you when we met the first time, ASP Kapoor, I am a criminal advocate and hence, I have a lot of clients. Only a small fraction of them are actually criminals, not all.'

'So … he's just another client who also happens to have common interests, which is why you socialize with him?' ASP Kapoor fervently scribbled in his pad.

'Yes, we're all members of the Gymkhana Club.'

'Oh, I see.' Again, it was impossible for Vansh to detect if ASP Kapoor was being sarcastic or just making conversation. 'So, an occasional client, but more of a club association, then?'

'More a client than a social contact.' Priti was not having any more of this Maninder being a social friend rather than a client.

'What sort of business is Mr Maninder Singh in?'

'Unfortunately, as an advocate, I cannot divulge anything about my client or his business, which I'm sure you'll appreciate.'

Vansh hid behind the advocate-client relationship. Unless the police believed and had strong enough evidence that an advocate was withholding information about a client that had a direct bearing on an investigation, the police couldn't coerce the advocate to disclose any information about the client. That is the law. Of course, it could all be overruled by a signed court order if the police could convince a magistrate or a judge that the said material was pertinent to an ongoing investigation.

'Of course.' ASP Kapoor seemed to accept the response discontentedly.

'Maninder Singh is a businessman, but all his fingers aren't in sanitized pies, that is all I can tell you.' Priti, for whatever reason, thought it was prudent to mention.

ASP Kapoor looked puzzled. He had certainly not heard of Maninder Singh or his extracurricular activities, which was hardly surprising. Those close to Maninder, like Vansh, knew he stayed behind the scenes, protecting and being protected by the ones he worked for.

'Okay. What can you tell me about Maheep?'

'Nothing much, actually. He seemed like just another teen, a bit spoilt by his parents, but we didn't think he was capable of attacking Baby.'

'Hmm … ' ASP Kapoor noted that too. Then he changed course: 'By the way, has Dr Shah spoken to you?' He spoke to both, but he was looking at Priti when he asked this question.

'Yes, and I have communicated what he told me to Gayatri. I've also explained to her that we must let the doctor decide when we can visit her.'

'I was told the same, but I'll be going to the hospital tomorrow morning to check if I can get the victim's statement.'

'Could I ask you for a favour, ASP Kapoor?'

'That depends on what you ask for, Mrs Diwan.'

'Would it be possible to provide some security for Baby?'

'Why?' ASP Kapoor looked at Priti, then at Vansh.

'Because Maninder Singh isn't the most sincere guy in the world.'

ASP Kapoor looked puzzled. 'You're not thinking that he'll attempt to thwart Baby's statement in any way, are you?'

'He's quite capable of doing something as crazy as that, especially now that his son's life and freedom are at stake.'

'I'm sorry, but I think you're overreacting, Mrs Diwan. And unless we find some factual reason to believe what you just said, I cannot deploy resources. You are, of course, free to hire private security, if that's what you want.'

'We shall.' Priti looked at Vansh for support.

'I think I have enough for now to go and see Maheep Singh. Of course, we have the DNA fingerprint of the perpetrator from the skin under Baby's nails and the hair we collected from the crime scene. We can wait to speak to the victim until the doctor advises. However, I might need to speak to Vamini and Gayatri in time, if that's okay.'

'Sure.' Priti seemed more than happy to get Maheep arrested, convicted and hanged.

'ASP Kapoor ... is there any way you can conceal how and who identified Maheep as a suspect?' Vansh was simply trying his luck. Or buying time? He was aware that unless ASP Kapoor provided some evidence or testimony that identified Maheep as a suspect, there was no way under the blazing sun that Maninder Singh would allow a sample collection from Maheep Singh for DNA fingerprinting. Even with the E-FITs indicating that it was Maheep, Maninder would not permit his son's DNA fingerprinting voluntarily; he would raise objections and make the police go through the long and convoluted process of procuring a court order, which was the only option available, if the suspect refused to cooperate. The police could not just walk in and collect DNA samples from any suspect against their will.

'You know I cannot promise that, Mr Diwan.'

Vansh pursed his lips and nodded.

EIGHT

'Where is Vamini?' Vansh asked after seeing ASP Kapoor off.

'I sent her out to Def Col market with Gayatri since I didn't think it was wise for either of them to partake in this conversation or eavesdrop.'

Vansh poured himself a drink and returned to slump on the sofa facing Priti, gazing at a lovely painting of big sunflowers behind her. For some reason, he felt drained. He exhaled noisily, but didn't say anything. What was there to say? The cat he had packed in the proverbial bag and wished to throw away had already been let out by Priti. It was now just a matter of hours before things turned ugly.

'What are you thinking, Vansh?' It felt like Priti was reading his thoughts. They had been married for a long time, and had known each other even longer. They had met when they were both law students in Delhi University. Priti was still a gorgeous woman, her dark auburn hair, coiffed in a loose French twist, reflecting light from the recessed halogens in the ceiling. She was wearing jeans and a T-shirt. She was an attractive woman, a loving wife, a doting mother and a great corporate lawyer. She had always been a brighter student than Vansh, though she chose to take the corporate route and not the courtroom, which she was completely capable of. She had had the option of joining Vansh's family firm, but she had declined, because she wanted to be independent. Vansh was a handsome man too, but he had aged more than her—both were in their early forties—and looked older because of the grey hair he didn't colour, or perhaps the stress of dealing with clients like Maninder had gently crept in over the years and showed.

'Where this is headed is what I'm thinking.'

'We did the right thing.'

'What is right for one person may not be right for another, Priti.'

'You mean we should have kept quiet about something as severe as this?'

'This might be right for Baby, but where does this take us? We could have waited and let it pan out on its own. We didn't have to be the torchbearers.'

'You amaze me, Vansh. I never expected you to fall so low—'

'Stop attacking me with your holier-than-thou speech. I've done nothing wrong. All I'm worried about is the safety of my family and myself. I have a teenage daughter, damn it.' Vansh lost it. He took a sip from his glass to calm down. 'I don't want anything untoward happening to the people I love and care about. Is that so difficult for you to comprehend? The police are paid to do their job, we didn't have to call them home and tell them about Maheep, is all I'm saying.'

'What if everyone thought like you? No one would ever identify any criminal.'

Vansh just shook his head. His anger stemmed from being in the middle of it all. Priti took his silence as a sign to carry on.

'You're the father of a teenage daughter. Let me ask you how you would feel if it had been Vamini at the receiving end and all the people who could identify the culprit left it for someone else to do that? Why should anyone get involved—is that your logic? And in this instance, the crime occurred in your house … in the very place where the people you claim to love and care for live. Have a heart.'

'Have a heart for what? Have a heart to not only sacrifice my biggest client but also to openly go against him and declare war? Do you have any idea how dangerous Maninder can be?'

'So we all zip our lips and let his son go around raping girls. Why don't you call him and tell him to take Vamini out on a date?'

'Please, spare me the histrionics.'

Priti, who rarely drank, got up and fixed herself a whisky and took a generous sip.

'What, pray, are you going to do now?' Vansh asked.

'You seem to know how everything should be handled, why don't you tell me?'

'I could have, had you left it to me. Now what do you want me to do … file a court case against Maheep?'

'You don't need to do anything. It looks like a simple, unambiguous case for any public prosecutor. However, I will be talking to Akash for advice, and should something go wrong, I will hire him to appeal and I'm telling you that now.'

If there was one criminal advocate that Vansh Diwan acknowledged was better than him and his firm, it was Akash Hingorani, a batchmate of Priti and Vansh from law school. Vansh could see how Priti's mind worked: her engaging Akash Hingorani scored many points against Maninder in a single throw of dice. First of all, Akash, with his tremendous experience, would definitely help whoever the public prosecutor was, albeit as a consultant. Secondly, the best advocate in New Delhi would no longer be accessible to defend Maheep Singh and ergo, Maninder would either have to settle for some marginally successful advocate or go shopping for someone in Mumbai. Because, considering the circumstances—with Priti backing Baby's case—it was highly unlikely that Maninder would even entertain the idea of hiring the second best, which was Vansh Diwan. And there wasn't a chance in heaven or hell that anyone could buy Akash Hingorani once he was engaged by a client, least of all if he had been approached and hired by Priti or Vansh. It was game, set and batchmate against Maninder Singh. However, as Vansh pondered, he got more infuriated.

'Priti, don't you think you're overreaching to go against Maninder? I mean, you've already delivered a near-fatal blow ...' Vansh didn't want to dwell on the retaliation by his biggest client.

'Vansh, this is the last time we're talking about this. I am going ahead. I don't see this as a trivial disagreement between us, this is a breakdown in our relationship—I cannot live with someone who thinks so radically different on a matter as serious as this.' Priti's eyes had welled up, her face was red. There was no indication on her countenance that she didn't mean everything she had just voiced.

'Priti—' Vansh got up to sit closer to his wife.

'No, Vansh, this is not acceptable. This is not what I want my daughter to grow up seeing ... that her parents pussyfooted around such a serious issue and let down someone who depended on them, that her parents were nothing more than rapacious socialites who, for money or connections or both, disregarded simple ethics and sacrificed justice for a young girl because she wasn't a daughter of someone important, even though the girl was her close friend, a surrogate sister.'

Vansh realized that Priti wasn't in any mood to listen. She had already set the ball rolling on events that he had desperately wanted to stall. And now she didn't want him to be a blasé spectator; she had decided that he had to bat for her too. 'No.'

'No to what?'

'I'm not getting into this mud fight.'

'Then we have a big problem.'

'What do you mean?'

'Vamini and I don't want you in our lives.'

'What shit are you talking? For your information, Vamini is eighteen, you cannot decide for her, she can choose what she wants.'

'You want to have this discussion when she's back?'

'Of course, and I'll also have a chat with Gayatri.'

'You're making a huge mistake, Vansh.'

'From my perspective, you've already made a huge mistake.'

As he sat there, Priti got up, poured herself another drink and stomped up the stairs to the first floor. Then he heard the door of their bedroom slam and he got up to make a drink for himself.

Nine

Vansh decided to go out. He took his bottle of Chivas—he needed a few drinks to unwind and he didn't want to leave it behind for Priti—and asked the driver to take him back to the office. He didn't want to be home when Vamini and Gayatri returned. He had no desire or patience or energy to participate in a discussion and defend himself against three women concurrently, as group dynamics would block out anything he said, however pragmatic. It was best to let the fire wane and then talk to them individually. There was little he could do now that ASP Kapoor had taken Priti's statement. Maninder would soon be calling him, shouting expletives, when the police descended upon his home to inform him of their discovery or maybe even arrest his son. Even if it took a few days to get a court order to collect samples from Maheep for DNA testing, ASP Kapoor, once he saw Maheep, would instantly recognize him from the E-FITs. There was no doubt about that, none whatsoever. The fact that Maheep had been in the Def Col area at the time and day when the rape and attack had happened was enough for the police to, at least, question him as a suspect. Everything else would follow.

As he sat in the car, which was moving faster than it had on the drive home only a few hours ago, he couldn't help but think about the options left if he were asked to defend Maheep. What would be the best way to convince Maninder Singh that he, Vansh Diwan, was still beside him? The simplest way would be to retract the police complaint. If Gayatri and Baby were willing to say that it wasn't Maheep who had raped Baby, a defence wouldn't need to be constructed. The case would just go away. But by the look of it, that wasn't happening.

By the time Vansh arrived at his office, he had consumed half the bottle of whisky, worked out the entire defence strategy for Maheep Singh and also concocted a believable enough shaggy-dog story to tell Maninder Singh that could possibly impede him from declaring full-scale war on the Diwans.

If serial killers like Harvey Louis Carignan could escape capital punishment on a rape and murder charge in 1950s America due to what his defence pointed to as tainted evidence in an appeal to a prior ruling, Maheep's defence was actually quite straightforward. Harvey Louis Carignan raped yet again and the subsequent rape charge was dropped because of lack of evidence. It is laughable how many loopholes lawmakers around the world have left in the law. If Carignan had been convicted, he would have gone to prison for life, thereby saving the countless innocent lives that he snuffed till he was finally convicted in 1974. Through the years, Vansh Diwan had crafted strategies and argued some exceedingly astute defence cases, sometimes even—as in the case of Maheep—when he was absolutely certain that his clients were guilty of the ghastly crimes they had been accused of, but he had still put up an impenetrable defence. He, of all people, knew that it didn't matter that they were guilty as the Devil's hell; if the accused couldn't be proven guilty, then they were not guilty. Unless there was incontrovertible evidence of the client's guilt, he could vouch that an accused would walk free. In the initial days of his career, Vansh had wondered how some defence lawyers slept at night. Experience had taught him that money and morals weren't exactly siblings.

He dwelled further upon what could transpire since the whole thing hinged on one factor: Baby had to state that Maheep hadn't attacked her. And with Priti so vehemently disagreeing to that, he couldn't envisage how he could get to Gayatri and persuade her to convince Baby. A second tier tactic, a fallback plan was, therefore, essential if Baby and/or Gayatri didn't relent.

Vansh started making notes on his yellow pad the moment he sat down. Even in his inebriated state, it was quite simple.

In Maheep Singh's case, any abecedarian defence advocate could prove him not guilty, as defending someone was a lot easier than prosecuting someone. That is a universal fact. Prosecuting someone required untainted evidence. Defending someone meant tenaciously squashing anything that the prosecution presented. The cogs in Vansh's brain had commenced moving; he could envisage what he would do next, and how he would build a defence for that nasty little Maheep Singh.

The car park attendant's claim that he had seen the white Honda Civic in Def Col market could be refuted. One: it was solely the car park attendant's testimony. Two: Maheep Singh could not have been driving that car, as it had already been reported stolen two days prior to when the attendant claimed to have seen it. Hence, either the car park attendant was being deliberately deceitful or he had seen Maheep and the white Honda Civic on the same day but as two separate events and had managed to somehow mix the two up when he pulled them out of his memory. Certainly possible, considering the number of customers he had during each working day. His testimony would prove that Maheep was in Def Col at the time, but so were ten lakh other people. What did that prove? Nothing.

The pharmacist's testimony would also prove that Maheep was in his shop in Def Col on the same day, but that would only corroborate the parking attendant's evidence. And Vansh wasn't even questioning Maheep's presence in Def Col and thus, it couldn't work against Maheep. He couldn't have been the only customer Krishna Chand, the pharmacist, had attended to on that day. Maheep was there, of course, but how did that prove he had attacked and raped Baby? Yes, Maheep had bought condoms from Angels Pharmacy. But what could that prove? The partial code on the fragment of cardboard found under the kitchen unit could only identify the batch of which the box was a part; it couldn't identify the exact box. There was no way to prove that the box Maheep had bought was the same one that had found its way to the Diwan's kitchen. Could Mr Krishna Chand line up all the guys who had bought condoms from the same batch that were sold from Angels Pharmacy and prove that any of them had raped Baby? No. Could the police issue a circular to ask all those who had bought that particular brand of condoms from Krishna Chand's store in the two or three weeks preceding the incident to come forward and identify themselves? No way.

Maheep's car couldn't have been spotted outside the Diwan residence either, since it had been stolen and ergo, it was someone else with a white Honda Civic who had come to the Diwan residence on the same day. Could the police round up all the white Honda Civic owners in Delhi and NCR? And if they did, could every white Honda Civic owner provide an alibi to prove that their car wasn't parked in Def Col on 6 June? No. How, then, could they prove it was Maheep's stolen Honda Civic?

Maheep's skin under Baby's nails was a sheer accident. When Baby served water to Maheep, she slipped, and in an attempt to stop herself from tumbling, she had grabbed Maheep by the arm, and hence, his skin got under her nails. How was that a crime?

It seemed obvious that the attacker had come to the Diwan residence shortly after Maheep had left the property. But why did Baby open the door if she didn't know the attacker? Probably an innocent mistake. The two events—Maheep leaving the premises and the attacker knocking on the door—had occurred minutes apart and maybe she thought Maheep had returned for some reason. Hence, she didn't bother to check who it was through the peephole and had carelessly opened the door. Everyone made such minor mistakes in life. It wasn't something that had never happened in history.

Would the prosecution have any more questions, mused Vansh? Oh yes, they might want to know how, if the white Honda Civic had been stolen from Maninder Singh's residence two day prior to the attack, Maheep had gotten to Def Col?

That would be a silly question. As a matter of fact, it would only help his defence. Apparently, after his son's car had been filched, Maninder Singh had instructed his driver to drive his son around so he wouldn't have to stay at home all day and get bored. The driver took Maheep around in Maninder's car. The fact that no one saw Maninder's silver Audi in Def Col did not, in any manner, prove that the car hadn't been there. And in any case, Maninder would pay his driver enough for him to be happy to turn up in the witness box and narrate the events to a T.

Vansh poured himself another drink. It was close to midnight, but he didn't want to interrupt his line of thought.

Nothing stopped him from raising the question: who was lying? Baby had no witnesses. The story that she had slipped when serving water to Maheep and had grasped his arm to avoid falling could still stand, especially if the driver, who had accompanied Maheep, had witnessed it and was willing to validate it. Two witnesses against one would indeed carry added weight and impress any judge more; it may not convince the judge that the two guys were speaking the truth, but it would certainly place enough doubt in any judge's mind. And that, in most cases, was enough to get a not guilty verdict. Why was Baby being mendacious? A few theories could be floated: a greedy indigent girl from a village, who might have been coached by her mother to use the incident as a ticket to a good life by attempting to malign a vulnerable, rich boy and coerce his family to cough up cash. It wasn't an outlandish explanation. Another story that could work was that Baby, having suffered a spell of weakness—she had prevented the fall that could have injured her seriously by clutching Maheep—was still dazed or unsteady or maybe semiconscious and had imagined that the guy who attacked her was Maheep, as he was the last person she saw before she became comatose. Vansh knew he could get as many specialists as he wanted to take the stand to talk about hallucinations; they would cite adequate examples of people who had been through some kind of trauma, however insignificant, and had been diagnosed as delusional soon after, and had got mixed up between two incidents that took place one after another. Hence, Baby unfortunately took Maheep, who, in point of fact, had been her saviour only minutes before the attack, to be her attacker.

The testimonies from the car park attendant and Krishna Chand didn't require any tweaks. Neither one of them proved Maheep's guilt.

Of course, Vansh recognized that both tactics were fraught with risk. But what wasn't in a courtroom trial? Even if you had the best possible evidence in the bag, a million other last-minute things could take the case away from you in a moment. Everything was a risk till the judge or the bench gave their verdict.

Vansh wasn't one of the best criminal defence advocates in the country for nothing. However, there was one monumental thorn in the way. All the defence tactics that he had considered and jotted down would already have been thought of by someone like Akash Hingorani. Chess would have been an extremely simple game if you merely had to know how each of the five other pieces moved on the board to defend the king. But it isn't. Some mathematically astute person had once calculated that there were approximately 5,900 possible moves, provided people adhered to the fifty-move rule in a chess game. So, even if you had the chess God on your side, it would be impossible for him to run permutations and combinations of all the moves that the opponent might make. And the opponent here was Akash Hingorani and the board, a courtroom. If and when he was engaged for the case, Akash would work out these scenarios, and many more, as well as counter tactics to shred and slice all that Maheep's defence presented to bits. Those advocates who had had the misfortune of facing Akash Hingorani in court often admitted that his greatest skill was his speed in reacting. The guy veritably thought on his toes. Quick as lightning. Everyone agreed that like a genius chess player, he could work out the opposition's game by their first few moves, and react instantaneously. And once he discovered tiny chinks in his opponent's game plan, he proactively led the opponent till he defeated them by crushing all their arguments within a matter of minutes. Add his charm and histrionics to his brilliance, and you were looking at a pretty unassailable opponent.

Vansh thought of calling Akash but couldn't muster the courage. If Priti had mentioned Akash's name in their conversation earlier, he was certain that she had already spoken to him. If he called, he would appear to be a defector and would have to wash dirty linen in Akash's presence. Why was he doing something if Priti abhorred it? Besides being a brilliant advocate, Akash was also a long-time, loyal friend. Whichever way he looked, Vansh knew he was royally screwed; he couldn't remove Akash from the game. Unsettled by the thought, he poured himself another drink and decided to call it a day. There was a huge sofa in his office that doubled as a day bed when he needed forty winks during long days. He decided to sleep on it tonight. Tomorrow he'd return home to talk to Priti. He called his driver to tell him to leave and return the following morning, but keep his mobile on, just in case.

The incessant, irritating vibration of his iPhone woke him up; the phone, kept on the side table, seemed to thrash about like a fish out of water. He didn't have to look at the screen to know who it was. But the first thing that caught his eye was the time: 07:42. He pressed the side button on his iPhone that stopped the vibration and went back to sleep. Maninder Singh would have to wait.

TEN

To say that Maninder Singh was angry when he was told that the police wanted to talk to his son was an understatement—it was like calling a kettle of boiling water lukewarm. He seethed. Maninder's farmhouse was in a remote, vast acreage with fencing and barbed wires for protection, abutting an uninhabited rural area, in the rear of the property and a high concrete wall and large electronically operated gates in the front. The gates were remote controlled and were generally locked at night. All visitors had to announce their arrival through an intercom before they were let in. The drive from the front gate to the main building where the Singhs lived was almost three-quarters of a kilometre. On average, after the conversation with the visitor at the gates, opening the gates, driving the vehicle to the main portico and allowing time for the visitor to get out of the vehicle, it took about seven minutes before the visitor pressed the bell at the main door. That was all the time Maninder needed to gather everyone in thc house—his wife Jaya, Maheep and Aarti—and ask Maheep to exit from the rear kitchen door and disappear into the wilderness of the farm, carrying his mobile but on silent, and not return till he heard from his mother, and not take any calls except from his mother—not even calls from him. Jaya and Aarti were directed to speak as little as possible to the ASP, who had called from the main gate. Maninder would say that Maheep was out with some friends for a couple of days and if the policeman insisted that Maninder call Maheep, Maheep was not to take any calls from his dad; the policeman wouldn't tell his mother to call as well. Maninder would use the two days to hide Maheep somewhere even Sherlock Holmes couldn't find.

10:17 pm. The doorbell rang precisely eight minutes after the intercom had buzzed. Maninder had, in the meantime, served himself a cognac, lit a cigar and gone into his study, which was accessible through the generous living room, and was sitting there nonchalantly, as though he wasn't concerned about why the police wanted to speak to Maheep. He had sent Jaya up and told her to come down only if called. There wasn't any point in exposing more people to the police. They hadn't had much time to prepare the lie and the last thing he desired was for them to contradict one another's statements and give the police any clues.

Aarti opened the door and led the two policemen into the study. Then, as ordered, she returned to the kitchen. There was a fridge in the study, and if the visitors asked for water, it would be served by Maninder himself.

'Mr Maninder Singh?' ASP Kapoor courteously asked when he was shown in.

'Yes,' Maninder looked up, then got up from the recliner and walked towards the policemen from behind his desk. 'Hello, inspector,' he said patronizingly, knowing full well that it was an ASP he was addressing, accompanied by a senior inspector.

'ASP Kapoor, and this is Senior Inspector Anupam Verma.'

'I apologize, ASP Kapoor, please sit.' He shook hands with them both and gestured to the chairs across from the recliner he had been sitting on. 'Drink for either of you?'

'No, we're on duty.'

'How may I help?'

'We're looking for Maheep Singh.'

'Why?'

'Just an enquiry at this stage ... '

'Enquiry into what, ASP Kapoor? What has my son done?'

'We have a sketch of a suspect that resembles Maheep. We're only here to look at him and hopefully eliminate him from our enquiry.' ASP Kapoor looked at his colleague who passed the two police sketches to Maninder.

Maninder looked at them as if it was the first time he had laid eyes upon them. 'I have to admit there's some resemblance, but could I know what crime you are investigating, where someone who has a good enough likeness to my son has popped up as a possible suspect?'

'It's a violent attack and rape of a minor girl.'

'Oh my God!' Maninder hadn't thought he could fake such surprise, but he outdid himself. If either of the police officers suspected it was feigned, their countenances did not reveal it.

'Sad world we live in, Mr Singh.'

'I guess so,' Maninder uttered, taking a sip of his cognac. He wasn't going to volunteer any information about Maheep. But he didn't have to wait long.

'Could we meet Maheep, then?'

'He's not at home at the moment.'

'Where can we find him?'

'He's gone out of town with some friends, he'll return the day after tomorrow.'

'I see.'

'Is it urgent?'

'Even you acknowledged that this sketch resembles your son, Maheep, so the earliest we can see him to rule him out, the better, isn't it?

'That is true, ASP Kapoor, but it could well have been an error on the part of the person who described the individual they saw or some misunderstanding on the part of the artist who drew this ... '

'That's not possible, Mr Singh.'

'Why not?'

'Because two separate individuals saw this person and described him independently of each other to two different artists, who then drew these sketches. It is highly improbable for any of the four people to make a mistake and still get to the same result.'

'Maybe there's a lookalike then?'

'That's precisely why we'd like to meet Maheep—so we can eliminate him from the enquiry.'

'I couldn't agree more. You sure you don't want anything to drink ... water, cola, anything else?' Maninder craftily changed course.

'We're fine, but thanks. Can we not reach Maheep where he is to expedite this?'

'I can try.' Maninder pulled out his mobile, dialled Maheep and put the phone on speaker, praying that Maheep wouldn't answer the call. They heard it ringing thrice before it went to voicemail. 'I told you he's away. He must be somewhere where there's no signal. I'll try after a while.'

'Okay.'

'Could I ask one more question ...?'

ASP Kapoor nodded.

'How, from millions of people, did you zoom in on a few people in Delhi who could resemble these sketches your artists have made?'

'He was identified as a probable by someone who saw the sketch.'

'And it would be safe to assume that whoever that person is, knows Maheep well enough to recognize the resemblance, is that correct?'

'Correct, Mr Singh.'

'So someone known to Maheep or us could be framing my son?'

'It could well be, and hence the resemblance notwithstanding, there are other ways to eliminate Maheep from the suspect pool—'

'Hold on a minute, ASP Kapoor,' Maninder interjected, his voice raised an octave. 'Are you saying my son is actually a suspect in some sexual crime against a minor girl?'

'Mr Singh, you might be aware that everyone's a suspect till a police enquiry closes. And if we have a sketch that resembles someone, then that person is added to the suspect pool; that's routine.'

'It may be routine for you and your investigations, ASP Kapoor. It is certainly not routine for us. It's not like we interact with the police on an everyday basis or get paid a visit in the middle of the night often. We are a law abiding, tax paying, respectable family. I'm sorry, but when you arrived at my gate, you said you just wanted to ask my son a few questions, and I took it to be about some school fight Maheep had got into, which he hadn't told me or his mother about ...'

'I can explain, Mr Singh.'

'I'm sorry.' Maninder got up. 'I request the two of you to leave my property this instant.'

ASP Kapoor and SI Verma got up. 'But this issue isn't going to go away till we meet Maheep.'

'Do you have a warrant for my son?'

'No.'

'So you think you can just enter my property and do whatever you want?'

'We didn't break in or enter using any force, we were let into the property by you.'

'I invited you in because you lied.' Maninder's patience was running out. He wanted this meeting to end. He needed the policemen to leave so he could plan the next course of action. 'Please leave. Now,' he gestured towards the door.

ASP Kapoor and SI Verma, realizing that their friendly visit was over, got up to leave.

'And do not come anywhere near my property till you have a search warrant or an arrest warrant for my son. And I'm going to call my advocate; you need to speak to him before you come anywhere near my son. I want my advocate and me to be present when you visit Maheep. Good night.'

Left with little choice, ASP Kapoor left with SI Verma in tow.

Maninder Singh regretted that he had flared up a wee bit earlier than he probably should have. If he had carried on with the conversation, it was possible that the policeman would have revealed what other clues they had to link Maheep to the crime. Well, there was always Vansh Diwan to check that before the bloody cops returned.

He called out to Jaya to tell her to call Maheep and ask him to return.

'I'll get you another phone tomorrow,' he told Maheep when the boy was back inside. 'One that no one else will have the number for but me. Totally untraceable ... for times like these, okay? Now, go to your room and we'll decide how to handle this mess tomorrow.'

ASP Kapoor was fuming. He realized that he shouldn't have gone to the farmhouse without the appropriate papers. What had he thought? That Maninder would allow his son to come forward and agree to give a sample of his blood for DNA fingerprinting? He should have arranged for a search warrant, at least. Stupid, impetuous decision. He was also annoyed because there was something about Maninder that he didn't like. Well, everything actually. Maninder had come across as a real moneyed prick to him.

'He's lying,' SI Verma said as he drove ASP Kapoor out of the gates of Maninder's farmhouse.

'About what?'

'That Maheep Singh has gone away for two days.'

'Why do you say that?' ASP Kapoor asked, even though Maninder's demeanour had screamed that he was prevaricating, changing lanes.

'Just a hunch, sir.'

'We'll need a search warrant to return for a look around. He won't allow us to come anywhere near his farmhouse without one.'

'I'll get on the task first thing tomorrow morning.'

'Thanks. I don't think any magistrate will shy away from issuing a search warrant, based on the identification of the sketches made by the Diwans. Hopefully, I should be able to speak to the victim tomorrow, and that will settle whatever dust Maninder Singh is trying to blow into our eyes.'

They drove in silence towards Def Col. Then: 'I want someone to look into Maninder Singh. We need some insight into this guy. He seemed quite a character to me, sipping Cognac and acting undaunted when he came to know that his son was being accused of rape. I want to know all we can about his businesses, his activities, his connections, whatever we can dig up.'

'Okay, sir.'

'Thanks. You can drop me at any taxi stand, I'll head home now.'

Eleven

Priti was already up when her phone buzzed. She had been in and out of sleep practically the entire night. The tension in the household had only moved north since the previous evening, with Vansh and she not subscribing to the same point of view. She couldn't get her head around how Vansh could have a different opinion on an issue such as this. How could he have gone down the road they had promised each other never to travel, back in their college days? She knew he was a criminal advocate, she understood losing Maninder as a client meant the loss of considerable income, she also recognized crossing Maninder could entail consequences, but still … there had to be a limit to how low one could fall for greed or out of fear. Vansh was no longer the guy she had married, and she needed to make him see that before the relationship deteriorated any further. This wasn't just another difference in perspectives; this was a difference in ideology. Vansh hadn't slept at home last night, which signalled a breakdown to her.

She picked up the phone. It was Dr Shah who, after apologizing and confirming that he hadn't woken her up, gave her the good news that Baby seemed to be recovering well and that he would appreciate it if they could visit her at the hospital later that day because he wanted to examine Baby's response when she saw her family. He wanted to be present to supervise the visit should Baby have an undesired reaction. Priti promised to come by with Gayatri and Vamini later that morning and smiled: there was at least one rainbow to look forward to, at last.

Still in bed, she called Gayatri, and after the good-morning exchange, asked her to get some tea for both of them. 'Also, wake up Vamini and ask her to come here, I need to tell you something.'

Priti had to tell them about Maheep Singh now. In a few hours, they were to go see Baby, who might blurt it out involuntarily, and then it would be even more awkward to explain. She knew it would be a difficult conversation to tell Gayatri that her daughter had been assaulted in their home by someone they knew well, and it would be hurtful for Vamini to know that the attacker was one of her classmates who she freely mixed with, called a friend and who, in all probability, had come to their home to see her and had ended up raping Baby. How would she ever trust anyone again?

However, the trickiest part, she reflected, would be to convey the offer Maninder had sent via Vansh. While she completely disagreed with it, she didn't want to take any decision on Gayatri's behalf; she didn't want to fight someone else's battle without checking whether that someone wished to participate in the fight.

'Maheep?' Vamini almost yelled before her eyes welled up.

Gayatri didn't utter a word, but she slumped to the floor, her back against the wall, and put her head in her hands and sobbed.

'I'm terribly sorry, Gayatri. But I have some good news.' Gauging that the vibe in the room was already dismal and wet, Priti decided to have the balance of the conversation later, when she was alone with Gayatri. She didn't think it was something she should involve Vamini in. What if Vamini asked: *what does Dad think or say?* Or, worse still, *how could Dad even bring such an offer?*

Gayatri looked up.

'We can go visit Baby in a few hours. Dr Shah called and told me she's out of danger.'

'Thank God.'

'Why don't we shower, have breakfast and leave for the hospital?'

'Good idea,' Vamini exclaimed.

'Gayatri, please let Shiv Kumar know, tell him to get ready as he might be driving us around all day.' Priti didn't want to say that she had to go to see Akash Hingorani after the visit to Safdarjung Hospital. She had called Akash yesterday and asked to see him without telling him the reason for the visit, which, she thought, was best explained face-to-face.

Baby, given her age and the torment she had recently been through, was holding herself together extremely well. She was sitting up, reclining against the headboard of the bed, with a few plumped-up pillows supporting her when Gayatri, followed by

Vamini and Priti, entered the private room she was in. A smile broke across her face when she saw familiar faces, but it soon waned and morphed into tears. Priti could understand that she had attempted to be strong, but it was essentially a mask worn to display mental strength to the hospital staff, which, as expected, broke upon seeing the family, revealing the small, frightened child that she truly was. Tearful hugs ensued; the atmosphere in the room was sensitive, with no one either knowing what to say or finding themselves too choked up to open their mouths. The IV was still attached to Baby. If Dr Shah had to give her sedatives again, then it was the only viable method of nutrition.

Contrary to what Priti had expected, Baby didn't question whether the police had apprehended Maheep; she didn't even mention the attack. Priti knew, from Dr Shah, that Baby hadn't suffered any memory loss, so it wasn't a case of not remembering what had occurred. In any event, if Baby was being kept awake for two to three hours at a stretch now, it was possible that ASP Kapoor had already been asked to visit her. According to Priti, it was best if Baby gave the statement to the police and identified Maheep. They had another hour and Priti believed it would be better if she had a tête-à-tête with Gayatri and not involve Vamini.

'Vamini, why don't you stay with Baby? Gayatri and I need to talk about some other things … '

Vamini nodded.

Priti and Gayatri mutely walked to the café in the hospital grounds and ordered tea. Priti, obviously, didn't want to tell Gayatri all the details of her discussion with Vansh or his recommendation that Gayatri accept the offer made by Maninder Singh. Instead, she camouflaged the offer in a legal cape—she told her that Vansh had to ask Gayatri what she thought about the offer before refusing, though he couldn't imagine it was something Gayatri would or should accept. If Gayatri had overheard any of the heated exchange between her and Vansh before he stomped out into the night and did not return, she was magnanimous in not probing Priti about it. However, she made no attempt to disguise her disgust, her eyes contemptuous. The anger she exuded was on an industrial scale: cold, almost glacial. Potent and infectious. Priti got goosebumps as she watched the rage building within Gayarti. Vansh had grossly miscalculated a mother's wrath …

Over tea, Priti subtly, but candidly, told Gayatri that while it was good to believe that justice prevailed in this world, courtroom trials were prone to indeterminate results; a court verdict could go either way. History was awash with incidents where verdicts had gone horribly wrong. There was no guarantee that Baby would get justice. This wasn't some game where the best player or team won; once you took a case to court, it was the judge who called the decisive shot. Based on evidence, of course.

A cavernous silence ensued. It took a while for Gayatri to absorb Priti's blunt worldliness, but her anger did not dissipate. She was determined to go after her daughter's attacker. 'I will not give Maheep or his father a way out … ' was all she uttered before she broke down.

After they returned to Baby's private room, Dr Shah came around and asked Gayatri and Priti to step out with him. He told them that he had been observing Baby's activities through the concealed camera—he had already intimated to them that there would be one for medical reasons—and he believed that

Baby was recovering well. The tests conducted over the past few days had verified that her recovery was a hundred per cent as far as physical wellbeing was concerned, but he strongly recommended psychological evaluation by an expert, even though Baby's behaviour appeared apposite at the moment. There had been instances in the past where patients had not heeded their doctor's advice because everything seemed fine on the face of it, but the inchoate psychosomatic damage, albeit latent, certainly persisted and sometimes resurfaced in later years to cause mayhem in patients' lives. According to him, the probability of a shock like this causing long-term damage was about 50 per cent if left unattended. There was no way Baby would forget that she had been attacked and raped by someone known to her and her family. Dr Shah recommended the name of an expert who specialized in treating young adults after they had been through similar trauma.

Priti had initially assumed that the visit to Baby would be short, but given Dr Shah's encouraging summary, she was happy to leave Gayatri and Vamini at the hospital and go to her appointment with Akash Hingorani. She told them that she would send the car back to Safdarjung Hospital with Shiv Kumar after he had dropped her. She would take a cab back home after her appointment.

TWELVE

Shiv Kumar dropped Priti off and left. Akash's gleaming, midnight-black Jaguar XF was parked in the drive, announcing that he was home, as he had told Priti. Anyway, he usually worked from home, though he had an office in Saket, near the session courts. He only ventured out if he had an appearance in court or to play golf with his close coterie, which, despite numerous requests by him, had failed to interest Vansh.

Akash Hingorani lived in a 2,000-square-yard villa in Vasant Vihar, which had recently been valued at a little over ten lakh rupees per square yard by a reputed women's lifestyle magazine that had interviewed him. He was the perfect example of how the other half lived. He was one of the most eligible bachelors in the city. He was forty, had never been married, had had one failed romance when he was in his late twenties, and had never been known to be a womanizer. The magazine had given the best physical description of Akash: 'If you put the face of yesteryear's celluloid star, Feroz Khan, when he was younger, on the slender body of Chris Rea, you're looking at Akash Hingorani—the best, and the most expensive, criminal advocate in New Delhi.' He had presence: charm, looks, perfect articulation and magnetism, all blended in the right proportions.

Vansh wasn't bad looking either. A little shorter, a little chubbier, a great father and husband; Priti smiled, wondering why the sudden comparison had even strayed into her mind.

The front door opened before she walked up the steps to ring the bell, but there was no one at the door. The electronic gizmos in Akash's villa were a big part of the valuation of his property. He must have seen her arrive from his office, and had opened the door remotely.

'Come into the study,' he shouted from his study-office, which was an immediate right from the living room.

The door shut behind her automatically as Priti walked in. Akash's study was more like an atelier: his collection of over five hundred model cars, his floor speakers connected to a state-of-the-art turntable, vinyl records, and an assortment of tomes and journals in addition to the law books one came across in every advocate's office. Physics, chemistry, biology, mathematics, trigonometry, statistics … Priti remembered asking him once why he had such a varied selection of books and his response had been: *You never know when you might need a bit of science in criminal law. Sometimes science can provide an answer that is indisputable even in a courtroom.*

He sat at his vast desk, reclining in his leather chair, which was angled to the left to allow his feet to rest on the desk. He had a sheet of paper in one hand and a pencil between his teeth. The desk was clean except for his MacBook and a few scale model cars.

'Welcome, sweetheart.' Swinging his feet from the table, he rose, walked to Priti and gave her a tight hug. 'What is it that brings your gorgeousness here?' Akash. Funny and flirtatious.

Priti and Vansh and Akash had been friends for too long for her not to know that he didn't have any hidden agenda behind the comment.

Priti let out a moan. 'A lot.'

'Tell me everything, but first, what would you like to drink?'

'Coffee, if that's not a bother.'

Akash pressed a buzzer. A lady arrived, and he requested two coffees. Black, no sugar.

'You remember I have black coffee and no sugar?'

'It has nothing to do with memory, it's called deduction. How else can you maintain a body like that?' He winked.

'Thanks, and shut up,' Priti retorted.

'So what is it that you couldn't tell me on the phone?' he asked when the girl had exited the study after bringing the coffee.

'Where do I begin?'

'*Ab ovo*—from the beginning, it's always a good place to start ... '

Priti took the best part of an hour, with Akash interrupting and asking questions when he thought she might be skipping details. He didn't take any notes or record the conversation, but seemed to file it in his brain. He had heard of Maninder Singh, but didn't know him personally. He told Priti that whatever he had heard about Maninder was not noteworthy in a good way. And when Priti had finished her narrative, he sat chewing on the information for a while before he asked:

'This looks like a straightforward case to me, any public prosecutor worth his degree should be able to file this case, take it to trial and get a favourable verdict with the evidence the police already have, plus Baby's testimony that is yet to be provided. And if you need an opinion, Vansh can always step in to—'

'Vansh doesn't believe we should take the case forward.'

'Pray, why?'

'Maninder Singh is Vansh's biggest client … ' and Priti went on to explain the sickening offer Maninder had made to Vansh to be passed on to Gayatri and Baby.

Akash didn't say anything or flinch, but he smiled, confirming he had inferred the situation instantaneously.

'Vansh left home last night and hasn't been back.'

'Are you saying that Vansh has already signed up to defend Maninder's son?'

'I don't know, Akash.' Priti choked.

'Do you want me to speak to Vansh, sweetie?'

'I don't think he'll listen to you either, Akash.'

'Well, I won't if you don't want me to, but I don't think you two should fall out over something like this. You've been together for two decades, you have the lovely Vamini. Why can't you two talk it over?'

'He doesn't see any merit in taking Baby's case to court. I don't know how and when we moved apart in such different directions.'

'I can handle the situation outside court too, if you want.'

'What do you mean?'

'Anything can happen … an accident, encounter, kidnapping … no one would ever know how Maheep Singh vanished, I swear. Not even you.'

Priti knew he was kidding, but only just. She knew that Akash could be lethal. Somehow Vansh, despite his pedigree, or perhaps because of it, had never made those sorts of dangerous connections.

'I'd rather take the legal route.'

'I am ready to sign up to assist the public prosecutor, Priti, if that's something you want. Tell them they can seek my advice or support any time, including my presence in court at trial.' He got up from the chair just as Priti's waterworks were about to start.

Priti was aware that bringing Akash Hingorani on board was tilting the case in their favour. Akash was connected, he feared no one. Maninder Singh wouldn't dare fight him, at least not in the open. And Akash Hingorani couldn't be bought, not with any amount of money. If fear was the only factor that had dissuaded Vansh from standing up to Maninder, that was now gone.

'Thank you, Akash.'

'You don't have to thank me, what are friends for?' He embraced her. 'I love you both—you're my only living family now—and I can't let anything come between the two of you. Please go and sort it out with Vansh. Tell him to come and speak with me when you are comfortable, okay?'

Priti, tears still brimming in her eyes, just nodded. 'Could you call for a cab for me, please?'

'Where do you want to go?'

'Home.'

'My driver is around, he'll drop you.'

'Don't bother—'

'I bet he's tired sitting on his haunches all morning, he'll drop you.'

Priti reflected on her conversation with Akash on her way back home. What was it that some wise man had said? Yes, it was something like: *even a good player will someday become a ball for a better player to hit.* Well, well, well … Maninder Singh would finally meet his match. *This universe won't bend backwards to accommodate someone like you, Maninder.*

She knew Akash was right. She had to speak to Vansh, get him to understand the family's point of view.

THIRTEEN

Vansh was tired and miserable. Napping for an hour on the sofa during a stressful day was one thing, but spending the night on it, instead of in his bed, was something else entirely. He was hardly refreshed in the morning. The memories of the previous day had come calling without warning and everything annoyed him: Maninder's intrusive call early in the morning, which he hadn't taken, Priti's pig-headedness about not allowing him to talk to Gayatri and her subsequent decision to enrol Akash into the case. He didn't know what to do next. His office suite had a shower and a small wardrobe, which was a help. He was ready at eight-thirty, before the staff started arriving at work, since he didn't want his team to know that he had spent the night in the office. Then, leaving his iPhone behind, he ventured out for breakfast and returned to see three missed calls and voicemails from Maninder. He had no idea what had transpired at Maninder's residence the previous night, and had no desire to call Priti to check if she had any information.

Calling Maninder would be like walking into a lion's den empty handed. He contemplated calling ASP Kapoor but eventually decided against it because he didn't want to look desperate. He was certain his mien exhibited his anxiety, though he had had no visitors since the morning to tell him that. And if his anxiety levels were already so high, how would he handle the case or trial going forward? He looked at the missed calls on his iPhone again—none from Priti, and now five from Maninder—and called Maninder.

'Where the fuck have you been? I've been trying to call you since last night,' Maninder barked after he picked up on the first ring.

Vansh wanted to tell him that he didn't answer calls at seven-thirty in the morning, but he kept his thoughts to himself. 'I'm sorry. I dropped my phone somewhere last night and couldn't find it because the battery had drained. My driver found it in my car this morning and I've only got some charge in it now.'

'You should have called anyway. You didn't have to wait to know I called you so you could return my call.'

'I said I'm sorry, Maninder. What's the matter? How can I help you?'

'The police came around to my place last night ... '

Vansh patiently heard him recount what he already knew. That the E-FITs had been identified by sources as Maheep. Luckily, Maninder had not been told who had identified his son. 'I've asked the police to contact you before they come around again to see Maheep. I want your firm to get the paperwork ready in case the police have some evidence against Maheep. And please keep your phone charged, and with you at all times,' he concluded.

'You want me to represent Maheep?'

'Who else?'

'But why me?'

'Because I am your client and this is just another criminal case, one in which I want you to represent my son. Is anything the matter?'

'Do you realize that this incident happened in my home?'

'Yes, but it happened with a two-bit whore whom my son made the mistake of fucking so don't get all uptight with me. Young guys fuck such cheap trash all the time ... she should consider herself lucky that my son thought her worthy enough to poke. Did you speak with her mother, your maidservant?'

'No.'

'Why the fuck not? I pay you to do what I ask, not use your discretion in affairs that affect me. Do you want me to drive down to your place and have a word with Priti and that servant woman?'

'I don't think that's a good idea, Maninder.'

'Why not?'

'Because Priti is absolutely against the offer.'

'What's wrong with you guys? Do you want to be with us or do you want to support some wretched woman and her daughter?'

'It's not like that, Maninder—'

'I can wipe the two of them off the face of this earth and you know that goddam well.'

Vansh knew Maninder well enough by now to know that the threat wasn't idle. Maninder was capable of disposing of people who threatened him. And this was personal. His son's life was on the line. He would ruthlessly destroy anything in his path. People like Gayatri and Baby were too vulnerable.

'Listen to me, Maninder. I'm trying to work this out, please don't do anything dire. I'll ask my office to draw up the papers to be the advocate on record for Maheep, don't worry. Give me one more day.'

'Vansh, the police are not coming to my farmhouse without you.'

'Leave that—'

But Maninder had hung up. Gone was the paean to Vansh and his firm for standing by him for years. Maninder's earlier mellifluence—when he had first come with the offer—had morphed into menace, leaving Vansh with no alternative. He was now committed to defending Maheep. How would he explain that to Vamini? He owed it to her, at least. He called her, but his call went straight to voicemail. He left a message for her to call him back.

'Hi Dad,' Vamini called back at three. She had gone to see Baby and had switched her phone off while she was at the hospital. No, mum was not with her, she had an appointment somewhere else. Gayatri and she were heading home now. Baby was fine, recuperating well, and Dr Shah believed that she would be coming home very soon, maybe as early as tomorrow.

'Did ASP Kapoor visit Baby?' Vansh's mind was leaping ahead. If Baby was fine, it was logical that Dr Shah would have reported the fact to the police, too.

'No, Dad, but I think he's going to the hospital this evening.'

Shit! Vansh realized that he had lost his chance of convincing Gayatri or Baby. He didn't even know if Priti had asked Gayatri. 'Could I speak to Gayatri for a minute?' he took a chance.

'Hello, sahib, thank you,' were Gayatri's first words when she came on the line.

'For what?'

'For not taking Maninder ji's offer, for believing in me that I won't sell my daughter, and for agreeing to fight my case … '

Even more shit! What had Priti told her? He wasn't fighting for her. In fact, he had just signed up to fight against her.

Fuckety fuck fuck!

'It's okay,' he said and asked to speak to Vamini; he told her that he would be home that evening around seven and would talk to her then. It seemed there was an even greater mix-up to disentangle than he had first assumed when he made the call to his daughter.

ASP Kapoor and SI Verma were at Safdarjung Hospital at seven. Dr Shah wanted Baby to rest for a few hours after her first interaction with her family before the next set of visitors, however important, was permitted in. Talking to the police would dredge up memories she had bravely and consciously avoided thinking about. He had been clear that should anything upset Baby during the questioning by the police, she should press the red emergency button at her bedside and the interview would be stopped that very moment. He had deliberately chosen the evening for the interview; in case Baby reacted aggressively to the questioning, or if she exhibited behaviour that was even remotely perceived as something that could reverse her recovery, Dr Shah would give her a strong dose of sedatives, which would put her out for the next eighteen hours or so.

ASP Kapoor had been in similar situations previously and knew he had to tread carefully with a juvenile. The interview had to be on record and they had taken a miniature recorder for the purpose. Baby was coherent most of the time, but her breathing came in gallops when she narrated her story and hence they had to take several breaks during the course of the interview. There was not a moment's hesitation in identifying her attacker. She blurted out Maheep's name, unaided—the sketch wasn't even required. Maheep was known to her and hence she had opened the door. He had walked out when she told him Vamini jiji wasn't at home, but he had returned within seconds under the pretext of asking for cold water, followed her into the kitchen and attacked her. She knew Maheep was Vamini's classmate, and his parents were friends of Priti and Vansh. Nevertheless, to make the verbal testimony airtight, ASP Kapoor pulled out six E-FITs and showed them to Baby, who took less than a second to recognize Maheep from the line-up.

ASP Kapoor and SI Verma left the hospital at nine-thirty.

'What do you think?' asked ASP Kapoor as they sat in the jeep.

'It's him. What we have now is enough to arrest him.'

'I know, but we need an arrest warrant. If we go to Maninder's place now, we will have to speak to his advocate, Vansh Diwan, and he'll block our attempt to bring that brat in for questioning. But if we get the arrest warrant tomorrow morning, we can go to the farmhouse without the advocate and make the arrest. Vansh Diwan and Maninder Singh can come to see us at the station. What do you think?'

'I agree, sir. I'll do the paperwork tonight itself, and take it to a magistrate and get it signed first thing tomorrow morning.'

'I'm a bit baffled. The girl was raped in Vansh Diwan's house and he is the advocate Maninder Singh has chosen to defend his son … beats me.'

'It's crazy.'

'Mad world. It's good to know I'm not the only one confused.'

Vansh drove to Def Col. He didn't want the driver to know he might not be staying at home again tonight, which was possible if the tension between Priti and him wasn't resolved. He contemplated how he would face Priti, what he would tell Vamini to convince her, but he knew he could no longer avoid the discussion. He wondered who Priti had had an appointment with—it could be work-related—but it would be great, he thought, if she were not at home.

But that was not meant to be.

Notwithstanding Maninder's unruly conduct, his language and the grief he had given Vansh earlier in the day, Vansh still believed that the most pragmatic approach to the nightmare was to wake up and end it. And the simplest way to a cordial finish was to make peace, and make some money for Gayatri along the way. However, after meeting Priti, he got the feeling that she thought he had returned to admit that he had been wrong in siding with Maninder. Avoiding her glares and questions, he asked for Vamini.

'What for?'

'What do you mean what for? She's my daughter and I want to see her, I have a right to see her.' he didn't raise his voice, but the stress showed in it.

'Vansh, think again about what you're asking us to do—'

'I'm not asking any of you to do anything. All I'm suggesting is that we work together to make sure all this goes away.'

'And how do you suggest we do that? Should we all kowtow to your client, Maninder Singh and his son?'

'Can I see Vamini please?' Vansh changed tack.

'She's gone to bed.'

'It's only nine.' He raised his wrist and pointed at the watch, questioning Priti's explanation.

'She was exhausted after the visit to the hospital today, seeing Baby in that condition … '

'But I called and told her I wanted to talk to her.'

'But you said you'd be here by seven, didn't you?'

How convenient, he wanted to yell. Seeing that another debate with Priti was meaningless at this point, he went upstairs and collected some clothes for the next few days, packing them in an overnight bag.

'Are you leaving us?' Priti asked when he was back in the living room, a pained expression on her face, eyes moist.

'I don't know what else I should do. You tell me. Maninder has asked me to defend Maheep, and you're carrying the baton for Baby. We cannot live under the same roof till this goes away one way or another. He walked up to the bar and pulled out an unopened bottle of Jack Daniels and poured himself a drink. He carried the bottle and his glass back to where Priti sat solemnly.

'I spoke to Akash today.'

'And?' His heart sank. So he was the one she had gone to see.

'He's agreed to take the case.'

The earth started tilting under Vansh's feet and it wasn't the Jack Daniels.

The couple sat in silence for a while before Priti got up to go to bed.

'Promise me something, Priti ... '

'What?'

'When this is all over, nothing we do or say in the courtroom should break our home.'

'Vansh, if it was anything else, I would have promised, but this time, you are going against the very foundation of what a home is. Good night, and please ensure that the door is shut properly before you go.'

He refilled his glass and pondered a way out of this mess. He couldn't think of a way to say *no* to Maninder, but the price he would eventually pay seemed too high. Maybe Akash could help. His thoughts were interrupted by the sound of his iPhone vibrating on the dining table. He walked up to it and saw a message from someone who wasn't in his contact list. A local Delhi number though. As he typed in the four-digit passcode, he realized it wasn't his iPhone. Probably Vamini's, as Priti had a Blackberry. He knew Vamini's passcode but didn't think it was ethical to pry into his teenage daughter's life, particularly not when he was already in hot water with the family. How had he wandered so far from his own wife and daughter? He put the iPhone down and made himself another drink—his third, which was his usual limit on normal days, though he realized that he had started drinking a lot more in the past few days. He sat at the dining table and tried to think, but no coherent thoughts formed. Vamini's iPhone buzzed again as a reminder of the text.

FOURTEEN

11 JUNE

Aarti wasn't worried, but she was certainly uncomfortable. Maheep baba was being scolded a lot these days, for something she didn't know about, but she had never seen Maninder sahib so angry before. Even Jaya hadn't tried to stop her husband from lashing out. She reckoned it was to do with the accident Maheep had had when he had returned home, drunk, and had lied to her about not having left the premises. And then the police had come around. However, now with both Mrs and Mr Singh gone, she wondered if she should go up to Maheep's room, wake him up with breakfast. The young boy hadn't even come down for dinner last night and he would probably be famished. She worried over this thought for a while and then fried two eggs for him. Over easy; she knew Maheep was fond of the yellow being runny. She toasted the bread, buttered it well, filled a glass with orange juice, climbed the flight of steps up to his room and knocked gingerly. No response. She knocked again. Nothing. She looked at the time: it was almost 10.00 a.m. Dreading the thought of waking him up—she reckoned that he wouldn't be in the best of moods, considering what he had gone through the day before—she returned to the kitchen to carry on with her other chores. She could always cook breakfast again when Maheep baba woke up.

She made another attempt at 11.15 a.m. Same result. That was when she started getting edgy. It was unlike Maheep not to wander out for food or, at least, a drink, particularly since he hadn't had anything to eat since late afternoon of the day before. She sensed something was wrong, but she didn't know what it was and she didn't know how else to approach it but to call Jaya and update her.

'Is everything all right at home?' Jaya asked when she picked up the phone. She was probably sitting with her élite friends, and maybe a call from a servant in the middle of it all wasn't desirable. Aarti almost felt guilty.

'Sorry to disturb, madam … but Maheep baba hasn't woken up yet, so I was worried.'

'What time does he typically get up on holidays?'

'He usually wakes up and has his breakfast before ten, and it's past eleven now … '

'I know what time it is,' Jaya almost barked. 'Go, knock hard on his door, and then barge into the room if he doesn't respond. Tell him I told you to do so.' Then the line was abruptly disconnected.

What else could Aarti do?

She cooked breakfast again, arranged it on a tray and went up to Maheep's bedroom. Knocked once, knocked twice and getting no reaction or snappy comeback from within, she gently pushed the door. It was locked. She kept the tray on the bookshelf on the staircase landing and banged on the door with her fists. No response. She surmised something was amiss. The noise she had generated would have woken up Kumbhakarṇa—but Maheep baba didn't respond.

'Maheep baba's bedroom is locked . . . ' Aarti updated Jaya.

'Oh, Aarti, then let him sleep and please stop calling me for such trivial things, okay?'

Click.

Aarti tried calling Maheep's mobile. She heard it ring till it went to voicemail, which alarmed her even more. His iPhone hadn't shrilled inside the room. She was now convinced that Maheep was not in his bedroom, but there was little she could do. She had no intention of breaking down the door and facing the wrath of Jaya and Maninder in the evening.

It took the best part of the day for SI Verma to get the arrest warrant signed. ASP Kapoor wasn't pleased, but he knew there was nothing SI Verma could do to expedite it. Even an octogenarian tortoise in slow motion could beat the bureaucracy hands down in most instances. He didn't want to make any errors that came back to bite him later. A lot of convicts were let off on such technicalities—on an unlawful arrest by the police, on a coerced confession. The procedure had to be correct, done according to the book, especially in the case of someone important or their son or dog. He knew he had all the evidence, including the victim's statement and identification, so why ruin the case by making any pointless errors now? This would be his first big case and the impending arrest would make his seniors take note of him. He told SI Verma to confirm once again if Maheep was over eighteen, and then they drove out to Maninder's farmhouse.

Mrs and Mr Maninder Singh weren't at home, or so the housekeeper, Aarti, told them over the intercom. She also told them that Maheep wasn't at home either, which they knew was a lie, under orders from Maninder.

ASP Kapoor called Maninder several times, but it went straight to voicemail, and he didn't think it was wise to leave a message. He also tried calling Jaya, but she didn't take the call either. Perhaps neither of them took calls from anonymous callers. Given the police encryption, even Truecaller would have failed to identify the caller.

'Should we wait or come back?' SI Verma asked him.

'Call the station. I want two constables stationed here; they are to report to me as soon as someone enters or leaves this house.' He wasn't taking any chances. 'Tell them to come in plainclothes and keep out of sight.'

Aarti waited a while till she believed the police had driven away. She knew they had come to the house before to see Maninder sahib, but why had they come for Maheep baba again?

Maheep baba hadn't appeared for breakfast or lunch, and she was worried sick now. She resisted calling Jaya again for fear of being reprimanded for disturbing the madam for *trivial* matters, though they didn't seem trivial to her anymore. It was coming to thirty-six hours since the boy had consumed a morsel. Of course, Maheep kept some cookies in his room, but there was a limit to how many cookies one could devour before the baked glucose and lactose became nauseating. She had been up to his bedroom and knocked a total of seventeen times since she had last spoken to Jaya, and decided to give it one more try, but it didn't alter the result. There was still no response. And it would be at least another three to four hours, if not longer, before either Jaya or Maninder returned. She walked out of the house to go around the building, just in case she could detect something, but nothing struck her as out of the ordinary. Then she looked up, and saw that the windows of Maheep's first floor bedroom were open; this jarred her even more. From where she stood, she could hear the sound of the air conditioner purring, and a window left ajar in the June heat of Delhi negated the effect of any air conditioning.

Why would Maheep baba do that?

But what could she do except wait?

Aarti's anxiety got the better of her the moment she saw Maninder Singh walk into the house, although she didn't think it would be right to mention the little snooping around she had done outside the house.

'Maheep baba isn't at home, sahib,' Aarti uttered the moment he entered.

'Where has he gone?'

'I don't know. He hasn't been out of his room since the morning and—'

'He must be sleeping or ignoring you, go up and tell him I want him down right now.' Maninder was irritated. Another day had gone by and that bloody Vansh Diwan hadn't called. He had tried phoning him a few times, but the calls went straight to voicemail. He was furious at Vansh's insolence. He had spent the day asking around for another criminal advocate of repute in the city and his contacts had promised to send him some recommendations. He was determined to talk to someone better and then fire Vansh Diwan and his godforsaken firm.

'Maheep baba isn't opening his bedroom door.' Aarti returned to interrupt his thoughts, but before he could walk up to the first floor, the intercom connected to the main gate buzzed.

ASP Kapoor had arrived with his entourage.

When Maninder Singh had driven into his farmhouse a few minutes back, he had missed the presence of the two constables exactly like the police had wanted him to, but his car had been sighted entering the farmhouse by the constables stealthily keeping a watch on his place. They had relayed this information to the police station and ergo, ASP Kapoor and his driver, followed by SI Verma and a few constables, drove out from the Andrews Ganj police station to make the arrest. The cavalry was for the spectacle, just in case Maninder Singh made a scene, despite the paperwork. ASP Kapoor had anticipated the story Maninder would give them: *Maheep hasn't returned from his trip with friends*, and consequently, he had also arranged for a search warrant. He wasn't taking any chances: if Maheep was on the property, he couldn't afford to miss him.

'What is it now?' Maninder growled.

'We're here to see Maheep Singh, will you open the gates, please?' ASP Kapoor demanded, but politely.

'See him for what? Have you spoken to the advocate I told you to contact?'

'We don't need to call him. You're free to call him if you want, but we can't wait for him.'

'What the fu—'

'Mind your language, Mr Singh … you're talking to a law enforcement officer and not some employee of yours.'

Maninder's antennas went up. This same police officer had been courteous two nights ago. What had got into him that he was showing his teeth now?

'Will you go away on your own or would you like me to call someone higher up in your command chain to make you run, with your tail between your legs?'

'You can call anyone you want, but if you do not open the gate, I'll be forced to ask my men to break it open, as I have a search warrant for this place.'

'What?'

'You heard correctly, a search and arrest warrant for Maheep Singh, your son.'

Maninder realized this wasn't going away. 'Okay, give me a minute,' he said and hung up. He asked Aarti to open the gate after five minutes and he rushed to the first floor to wake up his son and make him flee. How and where should he send him, he tried to figure out. Maybe Maheep could slip out from under the barbed wire fence at the rear of the property, while he called and told one of his confidants to send a motorbike and helmet to take Maheep away? Five minutes before the gate was opened and then another seven or eight till the main doorbell chimed. So he had an approximately twelve- to thirteen-minute lead and it wasn't as if the police would immediately rush to the rear of the property to look for Maheep. So maybe another eight to ten minutes. They couldn't arrest someone they couldn't find. He dialled a number as he knocked on Maheep's bedroom door. It took him less than two minutes to instruct an associate to dispatch a motorcycle to pick Maheep up from behind the farmhouse, but what was wrong with Maheep, why the fuck wasn't he opening the door? Maninder was kicking on the door, but there was no response from the inside. His gut told him that something was amiss, that Maheep wasn't there.

Part Two

10 June

'Eye for eye, tooth for tooth, hand for hand, foot for foot,
Burning for burning, wound for wound, stripe for stripe.'

—Exodus 21:24 - 21:25

FIFTEEN

After the police had first come to their farmhouse, Maninder had stayed at home the following day, making calls to various people to save Maheep, before going to the club in the evening after dinner. Maheep had slipped out of his room around midnight of the day Aarti had discovered him missing at breakfast and had called Jaya. He'd had a tough day. While Maninder was his father, and he would do anything to protect his own flesh and blood, he had screamed at him, slapped him twice, taken his car away and decreed he couldn't leave the house without permission. He had been warned to stay away from alcohol and get ready to leave the country before anything dire happened. That little bitch—she had been in a coma and had come out of it and was apparently supposed to give a statement to the police shortly. He was suspected as the attacker and he was certain she would identify him positively. He had overheard his father speaking about the fact that Priti Diwan wasn't letting the maidservant and her daughter drop the charges due to some primitive principles. After the severe reprobation and sanctions, Maheep had stayed locked in his room the entire day on 10 June, not making any contact with anyone outside. He hadn't come down for dinner. Jaya, supportive of her husband in this case, did not insist that he did either. His father had declared that the boy had been totally out of line to abuse his parent's tolerance.

Skipping meals for a day or more wouldn't kill him, Maheep knew. In any event, what were the provisions in his room for? And he would shortly be sent to the US anyway.

His mom had also agreed with his father that it would be better to send him abroad. Better that than her card-playing friends coming to know what a monster one of their socialite friend's son had been, she had uttered.

He abhorred both of them for not understanding his perspective, despite his repeating that it was that servant girl who had lured him in.

He felt dejected, but not terribly concerned. He had more than a half-full bottle of Bacardi hidden under his bed for times like these. He had packets of Gold Flake too. No worries. His bedroom was on the first floor, but there was a guttering pipe next to his window that he had used multiple times to slip out and climb back in. He did the same that night and carried both his phones—just in case there was an emergency and his father needed to get in touch with him on the new unlisted number he had been given earlier that day—the bottle of rum and smokes. He walked past the swimming pool and into the vast tree-lined acreage. His plan was to go to the little pond at the end of the property, near the barbed wire fence. Easy to slip out if and when he wanted; he could always call or text some friends to pick him up, and slip back in later without his parents creating an unnecessary fuss.

He sent a few texts using the new unlisted mobile phone his dad had given him just in case the police were monitoring his number. Then he walked to the edge of the property and sat down against a tree, folding his knees so he could rest his chin on them. He looked at his watch and settled down to enjoy his alfresco drink and lit up, waiting for responses to his texts.

He thought he heard a noise behind him. His mind was a bit clouded as he had been sitting under the tree for an hour, consuming Bacardi straight from the bottle. He looked around but saw no one. His mind was probably playing tricks on him. Or was it the Bacardi?

He smiled and settled down again and sipped some more.

This time, he was positive he had heard a noise, as if someone was there. He wasn't that drunk, he knew. He discerned the sound of footsteps. He sat still, listening. Maybe some animal had slipped in through the fence—a stray dog?

As he turned to look up, he saw a figure.

He saw the figure towering over him, but he missed catching who it was or what the figure carried.

The hammer hit his cranium in the rear, precisely at the junction of the parietal and occipital bones. The impact crushed the skull; it caved in before Maheep could even let out a sigh. All he saw was a white light blinding him. Death was instantaneous.

The rum bottle in his hand rolled into the grass and slipped into the little pond, the half smoked cigarette fell from his fingers. His body fell forward with the blow and lay there.

SIXTEEN

11 JUNE

ASP Kapoor's initial mistrust was understandable. It had been all too convenient for Maheep to go missing at the precise time when the police had arrived with the arrest warrant. When he and SI Verma had been to the farmhouse two nights ago, they had been informed by Maninder that the prodigal son had gone out with friends and, on probing further, had been asked to leave the property. Now, two days later, Maninder's narrative had changed from the son not being at home to 'I can't find my son'. But as time rolled on, and Jaya Singh returned home and appeared genuinely shocked first, hysterical later, it became apparent that the parents and the housemaid, perhaps genuinely, did not know the whereabouts of the elusive Maheep Singh. His suspicion completely waned when Maninder—instead of attempting to stymie the search—started beseeching the police to find his son.

ASP Kapoor asked a few more men to be dispatched with lights to look for the boy in the vast property, and also ordered the control room to issue a search bulletin for Maheep. Maninder emailed the police the most recent pictures of his son. The tension in the household mounted with each passing second, then minute, then hour. The drama had begun with Jaya and Aarti playing the lead roles with tears. Maninder looked shaken, but he did not break down. Too much of a man. ASP Kapoor saw him making calls to his friends and associates for help, shouting, yelling, swearing, leaving messages. He certainly wasn't relying on the police alone for the job.

The search party—a jeep full of four constables with powerful searchlights—arrived at the scene by midnight. They were sent out into the wilderness behind the main building. The men were back by 3.00 a.m. with nothing. The police had sent pictures to all the exit points of the city—railway stations, bus stops, airport and taxi stands in the vicinity. Roadblocks were put in place. Traffic going out of Delhi towards Haryana, Rajasthan and UP was stopped and checked. Nothing.

Dogs were called in. Two German Shepherds arrived at 4.00 a.m. And it took the air-scenting dogs—trained to use airborne human scent to zero in on individuals—precisely an hour to find Maheep.

Maheep hadn't done the moonlight flit. His corpse was already twenty-four-hour cold.

By 5.30 a.m., the place was swarming with police.

ASP Kapoor was concerned. Just as he was about to close the enquiry into one of the first significant cases of his career, he had inherited another big one. Probably bigger. Murder trumped all. He had a bad feeling that it wasn't coincidental.

As he drove back to the station, leaving the police machinery to do its job, ASP Kapoor's mind went to the events of the past five days. As a human being, he knew that in the end, you could only reap what you sowed. Maheep had opened the wrong door, and no one could say it was accidental. In some perverse way, Maheep's untimely passing was tantamount to justice. It was a fundamental right, a core pillar of society in all parts of the world. If not for justice, human beings would be no better than millions of other animals: the mightier, like Maninder Singh, would always win. But ASP Kapoor was restive as a policeman: justice was never easy. It was seldom free and it was mostly painful. However, justice was above retribution, wasn't it? And if people started disposing of each other, wouldn't the society collapse?

What amazed him was the choice of weapon used, which the preliminary investigation had revealed to be a hammer. A hammer aka mallet aka gavel is one of the most fantastic tools ever invented by humans some thirty thousand years before the coming of Christ, which made it one of the oldest implements anyone had ever invented. No encyclopaedia records it as an invention, or describes who came up with the design, or when, or how, but it has largely stayed the same from the time it was first recorded: just a handle and a head. Thankfully, no one had tried to add a digital camera to it yet. It had been extremely efficient in delivering a blow to Maheep's head at a precise point, as if to the head of a nail. ASP Kapoor could visualize that it had been a big hammer for Maheep's head.

12 JUNE

Vansh Diwan was sure he looked way-worn when he woke up at 6.30 a.m. He hadn't travelled, but three consecutive nights on the office couch were no different than a red-eye. His sleep was sporadic, which was natural. Fear, anxiety, disbelief and uncertainty had drained him. And since the previous night, Maninder had been yelling at him that Maheep had gone missing. Maninder had ordered, not asked, him to drive to the farmhouse when he had called him at one in the morning to update him—and bark louder at him, maybe even bite him—that the police were all over his house looking for Maheep, and even they couldn't find him. Vansh had listened to him, then switched off his mobile, taken the office phone off the cradle, had a generous swig from the bottle of Jack Daniels he kept in his office and put his feet up on the sofa. The empty bottle of whiskey lay in the bin, reminding him that he had spent all of yesterday in a drunken stupor. What would his office staff think of him? Maybe he had been lucky and no one had come into his office the entire day yesterday, thinking he wasn't there at all?

Now at seven in the morning, reality started seeping into his brain again. *'You've got a daughter her age, Vansh. Remember, it's a heinous crime you're talking about, and not some game. Do you want to be an accomplice-after-the fact of a rapist?'* Priti's words echoed in his ears. He switched on his mobile. Eighteen missed calls, ten voicemails. All from Maninder Singh between 1 a.m. and 6.30 a.m. He listened to the first two only and that was plenty. Maninder was yelling expletives in Hindi: suggesting incestuous relationships and anatomical no-nos. In the first one he had growled: *'Maheep's missing so get your sorry ass to my residence as soon as you get this message*', and in the second one, which was peppered with swearwords, he had barked: '*I'll fucking fire you and your firm if I don't hear from you in the next ten minutes*'. The ten minutes long past, and disgusted by the first two messages, he deleted all the rest, one by one, without listening to them, and then called Priti. He knew he couldn't take it anymore.

'I want to come back home.' He almost choked.

'Are you okay, Vansh?'

'Yes. I'm sorry. I want to come home.'

'It's your home, come back.'

'Maheep's gone missing, Maninder told me.'

'Be realistic, Vansh. I'm sure Maninder's packed that beast off.'

'No, he sounded desperate.'

'I bet he's flown off to the US. Doesn't one of Maheep's sisters live somewhere on the west coast?'

'Los Angeles.'

'Can we not check with Immigration?'

'And how do you propose we do that? You think if you call them up, they'll run around and fax that info to you?'

'Can we not ask ASP Kapoor?'

'Why wouldn't he find out himself where to look? I'm tired Priti, why don't you call him up?'

'I'll do it straight away—'

'No, don't call ASP Kapoor now. He might still be at Maninder's farmhouse. You don't want Maninder to know you're actively going against him. Please … '

'Okay. We have to go and pick up Baby today. Come home Vansh, we'll all go together.'

'What have you told Vamini and Gayatri? What do they think of me, about what I suggested?'

'I didn't tell Vamini anything.' Priti succinctly told him how she had structured the conversation to make it appear as if it were necessary to tell Gayatri about the offer, as a legality.

'Thank you, Priti. I love you.'

'I love you, too. Are you okay?'

'I am. But I am very scared.'

'Maninder cannot harm us if we stick together, don't worry.'

'You don't know him.'

'We'll talk when you come home.'

Vansh decided he did not want to receive any more calls from Maninder and hence immediately switched off his mobile after the call with Priti. Then, leaving a note on his secretary's desk to cancel all his meetings for the day, he took the elevator down and asked his driver to take him home.

Everyone left for Safdarjung Hospital at ten to pick up Baby. Vansh drove, with Priti sitting in front next to him. Gayatri couldn't stop crying, and Vamini sat in the back seat with her, holding her hand, comforting her.

Priti looked at Vansh, said nothing. But with her eyes, she indicated to Vansh to glance in the rear-view mirror to see how much Vamini cared for her caretaker. She could see that that fact may have finally dawned on Vansh. When Vansh had come home that morning, they had had a tearful reunion—just she and him. He had narrated his fears. Even if they ignored the financial loss—Maninder would unquestionably take his business elsewhere, and that meant that Diwan-e-Khaas would lose close to 50 per cent of its Delhi office billings from its criminal practice—there was still the fact that Maninder wouldn't endure the unpleasant parting without fighting back. Vansh had told her about the nasty voicemails he had left for him all through the night and his intimidating tone since he had found out that Priti had stopped him from talking to Gayatri. She had asked Vansh to switch off his phone and leave it at home to avoid any calls from the big bully. They had enough phones in the car if he needed to make calls or if there was an emergency.

Baby was happy to see them all, excited that she was finally going home. Her lip had healed except for a slight incision that was still visible, but there was no longer any discolouration. They had shaved part of the back of her head, which was still bandaged although the sutures had now been removed.

Tears, smiles, hugs, kisses.

Priti and Vansh had a short exchange with Dr Shah, who yet again suggested that Baby be taken for a psychological evaluation. He warned that if she showed any unreasonable signs of anxiety or distress, they should call him immediately or bring her back to the hospital.

The plan was to drop Gayatri and the two girls at home and then to go see Akash.

Priti could tell that Akash was pleased to see Vansh alongside her when they sat in his study-office and thankfully, he didn't ask any awkward questions about the how and the why of it.

Instead, as they sipped their coffees, all he teasingly uttered was: 'So it seems I'm out of a job then?'

'We can still pick your brains, can't we?' Priti glanced at him and then squinted at Vansh, as if she were looking for his agreement too.

'No, I think it should still be you who works with the prosecution,' Vansh remarked.

'Pray why?'

'Because, though I haven't signed a contract to defend Maheep, I had worked out a strategy to save him, and I had shared bits of it with Maninder … to put certain things in place in time, to facilitate helping Maheep—'

'Do tell.' Akash looked askance at him.

'Honestly, there's nothing too far-reaching that any defence advocate worth his money wouldn't have thought of. The cold hard fact is that I got nervous when Priti told me that you might be advising the prosecution because I knew you would figure out all the defence strategies possible before you worked on your narrative.' Vansh detailed the exculpatory evidence he had commenced working on when he thought he was defending Maheep.

'So, you agree I'm better?' Akash got up with his palm raised high, to high-five with Priti.

'I have no shame in admitting that the best is one of my best friends.'

It was a truth that had proved itself. Priti knew Vansh was pedigreed while Akash was a prole; ergo, Vansh had an edge after he obtained his law degree. But now in legal circles, Akash Hingorani was a bigger name than Vansh Diwan. Akash had won more cases than Vansh had. Fortunately, they had never been pitted against each other, which was deliberate and not a coincidence. Both had consciously declined cases where they knew the opposing party's advocate was the other. If Maheep's trial had gone ahead with Vansh as the leading defence advocate, it would have been the first time the two friends had faced each other in a courtroom, and that was only because Priti had pleaded.

'If you still haven't signed with Maninder to defend his boy, then you should share everything with me. It's better not to let any detail slip, however trivial. As I promised my college sweetheart' —Akash winked at Priti— 'I have taken up the case already and now, more so with you not opposing me, I'll keep my promise. Any news from the police about new evidence or testimonies?'

'Maheep's run away,' Priti announced and told him about the calls Vansh had received as well as the copious obscenities showered. She also mentioned Vansh's dread.

'What exactly does this Maninder Singh do for a living anyway?'

'Everything that's flyblown or isn't legal,' she answered in a contemptuous tone before Vansh could sugar-coat it.

'He's not the world's most ethical businessman, obviously, if he is the biggest client of my firm's criminal practice, that's for sure. The issue is that he has odious connections, access to politicians and known criminals, which he doesn't flaunt, but I, being his advocate for years, know about, more than most people do.'

'I am intrigued already. More coffee, or is it time to open a bottle of wine?'

'Certainly wine for me,' Vansh exclaimed despite Priti glowering at him, which Akash caught.

'Come on, sweetheart, you only live once.'

'Yes, but he's been drinking quite a bit these last few days,' she protested.

'That was because he was making a new enemy; this is with an old friend. Coming back to our discussion about the mysterious Mr Maninder Singh, it seems he has his fingers in all the undesirable pies but has managed to stay away from the limelight. I checked him out since Priti told me about him, but he appears to be squeaky clean. Forget the palms that he or his clandestine friends might have greased well, what surprises me is how the media has overlooked him all along.'

'He is careful not to dirty his hands with anything that's too apparent, more a behind-the-scenes kind of guy for other behind-the-scenes guys. He's layered himself.'

'Flying under the radar, are we?' Akash gave a reptilian smile, raised his glass of wine in a toast. 'Well, you've come to the right place, I'll lower the radar's angle a bit.'

Vansh explicated the nuances of Maninder's businesses over the wine. Despite being too big to be missed, he had managed to fly under the radar. If Akash could—as he had said—lower the radar, Maninder was no Houdini. Vansh opined that Maninder lived in a secluded farmhouse that had no neighbours as they were usually the ones to point fingers and talk about others when they found something worth gossiping.

'But why has the media not highlighted his activities?' asked Akash. 'Hasn't the old neighbourhood role been taken over by the media, thereby increasing the reach of gossip exponentially?'

'Oh, Maninder Singh has for long remained an enigma for the fourth estate. It's not that they don't know something is amiss. Of course, they have an inkling that he isn't as straight and narrow as he pretends to be, but they have no evidence or stories to tell. I know that a decade ago a young and enthusiastic journo had written an unsavoury piece about him; he was sacked by his editor, allegedly for lack of credibility.'

Akash nodded.

'What are you thinking?' Priti asked.

'Nothing concrete at the moment, but I have a feeling this is going to be big. The media always loves to muckrake because people love to read stories that talk about bringing down empires. While the law of virtually every country wants you to believe everyone is innocent unless proven guilty, the media's belief—as you know—is quite the opposite. It presumes the guilt unless proven otherwise because guilty stories sell better.' Akash gave another reptilian smile. 'The media tries people even before the case reaches the doors of any courtroom. And the media continues to haunt and shame people even after someone has been found innocent and acquitted by the courts. I will find out which buttons need pressing to get Maninder Singh in line and get him off your backs. A deeper investigation into Maninder Singh's background might reveal all the other skeletons buried in his castle. Leave it to me.'

'Thank you.'

SEVENTEEN

Baby, the attack, the rape and the paying off of the victim, all were forgotten when Maninder Singh came to know that his only son had died. ASP Kapoor, already investigating a case in which Maheep was a suspect, was given an out of bailiwick responsibility to carry on with the investigation, based on the surmise that the two crimes might be related. Maheep's corpse was over a day old, the attending doctor declared after observing that the body was flaccid again—rigor mortis had come and gone. He also inserted a thermometer into the liver of the corpse and plotted the temperature reading against the outdoor temperature to confirm his deduction. When questioned, Maninder, Jaya and Aarti were definite that they hadn't seen Maheep since the evening after he had been reprimanded by his dad for misbehaviour. He had reportedly retired to his room after some harsh chastising by his father.

There was no doubt that Maheep hadn't died a natural death. It was a crime and as such, was being investigated as a murder.

The gash caused by the skull-breaking blow was approximately four inches wide and on the back of the head, which had ruled out suicide. Who could hit themselves so hard at the back of their own head that the impact could break their skull?

With all doors found bolted from the inside on the morning of 11 June, when the Singh household had woken up, ASP Kapoor guessed that the teenager had used the bedroom window to slip out of the house. Aarti added that she had seen Maheep go in and out of his bedroom using the guttering pipes before.

The police cordoned off the area around the pond where they had discovered the stiff and brought in equipment to collect evidence.

'Where's that fucking bitch?' yelled Maninder.

Priti and Vansh had returned home at eight in the evening and Vansh had only just switched on his phone to receive the notification of yet another ten missed calls from Maninder. Mercifully, there were no voicemails to listen to or delete. But his phone rang just then and he accepted the call.

'What is it, Maninder?' Vansh put him on speakerphone so that Priti could listen too.

Priti lanced him with her eyes. *Why did you answer*? She looked around to check that Gayatri were nowhere in the vicinity.

'I left a hundred messages for you, didn't you get any?'

Vansh kept silent. Priti could hear that Maninder's loud voice sounded as if he was choking, fire travelling through wires. She could also sense the anger building inside Vansh, his fingers clenching to make a fist as if he wanted to hit someone, something. She prayed that he didn't lose his cool while Maninder was on the line; it wouldn't be the best thing to do. She saw Vansh gritting his teeth, but he didn't say anything. It felt to her as if he was waiting it out to dampen his rage, distracting himself by shutting his eyes to the blatant insolence being meted out.

'Have you lost your voice, damn it?'

'Maninder, I am an advocate. I know you're a client, but I am not going to accept these obscenities showered by you. I'm not your servant, so stop dissing me. I don't appreciate this belittling. I know your son is missing, and I—'

'They found him, he's dead.'

'Maheep is dead?'

Priti looked at Vansh, mouth agape. Things seemed to have changed for the worse.

'How?'

'That bitch killed him.'

'What are you talking about? Who killed Maheep?'

'That hardscrabble woman who works in your house. Gayatri, who else?'

'That can't be true, it's not possible.'

'Are you crazy, Vansh? Are you now trying to defend the filthy whore who killed my son?'

'The woman who *you* think killed your son, that woman who is also a mother, however poor, that woman also happens to be the one whose daughter was brutally raped by your son … '

Priti felt a twinge of pride. There was something in Vansh's voice that reassured her that her husband hadn't rotted as much as she had earlier supposed.

'Stop that crap. My son would never have done such a hideous thing with a tramp like her even if she invited him to. He had better standards and an upright upbringing.'

'Then what's the issue here? If he didn't rape the daughter, then the mother didn't kill him.'

'Don't you fuck with me, I'll take my business away—'

'Hold on a minute, Maninder Singh. You cannot take business away from my firm because I, Vansh Diwan, dump you as a client. Ask your new advocate—whoever you sign up—to collect all your files from my office. I've had enough shit from you, and I'm in no mood to take any more. I'm sorry for your loss, but you know what? You reap what you sow.'

'Don't you fucking show me your teeth … remember, you are defending the killer of a member of my family, my own blood, how fucking dare you?'

'Mind your language, Maninder.'

'I'm sending my guys over to your place. I want that bitch and her daughter sent to me, do you get that?'

'You're doing nothing of the sort. Don't you dare send anyone to my place. If Gayatri has killed Maheep, then let the police conduct their investigation and we'll see you in court.'

'Vansh, I'll come at you with all I have. I'll bankrupt you, I'll destroy you, your business, your family—'

'Don't be so certain, Maninder. You dare point a finger at anyone in my family, I promise you that you will live to regret it.'

Well said, Priti wanted to say, maybe also applaud, but she could see that Vansh was quaking. He was only trying to put up a brave front. She knew Maninder was pure evil.

'You think you can stop me? I'll do what I want. I'll hire the best criminal advocate who has ever set foot inside a courtroom.'

'If we could agree on who is the best, you might find that he's already taken.'

'Your head is bloated beyond your talent; you aren't the best.'

'I know, and that's precisely why I won't be taking this job. Goodbye, Maninder.' Vansh ended the call.

The verbal scrap was over, but Priti could sense that the duel wasn't. It had only just begun.

It took ten minutes post the call for Vansh's breathing to return to normal. Priti gave him a glass of cold water and then made him a drink.

'Relax, Vansh,' she said, caressing his forehead with her palm, while he sat slumped on the sofa. He looked shaken, having taken Maninder head-on. 'What now?'

'I don't know.'

'You think he can actually send guys to our house?'

'I don't think so, but you heard him, and I can tell you he is crazy and pig-headed, and he's hurting at the moment. He is capable of any kind of stupidity.'

'What if he sends a jeepload of people to our house? Should I call Akash?' Priti suggested.

'And say what?'

'I don't have a clue, but I know he's equally connected. Maybe he can suggest something … '

Priti called Akash and updated him on the events. Maheep was dead, yes, killed. She didn't know how or by whom, but Maninder was pointing fingers at Gayatri and threatening to harm them all if they tried to protect her from him. No, Gayatri hadn't even stepped out of the house alone since the attack on her daughter. Akash told her to calm down; he would organize security for their house, but it might take a little while to mobilize things. He suggested that they pack some clothes for a few days and stay with him at his house. Maninder wouldn't know, and even if he did, he wouldn't dare cross Akash ... he might be dumb, but he wasn't outright stupid.

Twenty minutes later, Priti drove to Akash's house with Vansh, Gayatri and the two girls.

Priti sat admiring the paintings in Akash's open plan living room. The ceiling lights were off, all the lamps—floor and table—were on and lent a warm glow to the room. Some of the art he had collected over the years was astonishing, and the art included some of the lamps, either bought or created bespoke for him. A large red one standing on the floor in one corner, she figured, was actually fashioned using an antique fire extinguisher. There was a set of two portraits of women—charcoal on handmade paper—which he had once told her were by some American artist, who, when Akash had bought the portraits at an exhibition, was a nonentity in art circles, but he was so talented that he had gone on to receive some honour in France and his earlier paintings had skyrocketed in price. Meaning: the two Akash owned were worth a small fortune. Realizing that she was focusing on the artefacts in the house only to blank her mind to the misery they were facing, she consciously detached herself from the world of fine art to focus on the reality staring at them. She looked beyond the living space to see Gayatri assisting Akash's cook with dinner, the two women whispering to each other.

'You with us, sweetheart?' she heard in the background.

'What? Yes ... of course, I'm here,' she bounced back. Akash had poured some wine for her.

'Thanks, but I'm not sure I can take this tonight.'

'It will relax you.' He put the glass down on the table next to her.

She looked at Akash, murmured her thanks with a mirthless smile and then looked at Vansh who sat opposite her.

The grimness had pervaded since they had driven to Akash's home. Out of fear. She hadn't been frightened when Vansh had warned her, when he had proposed a compromise between Maninder and Gayatri. Maninder had been willing to pay whatever amount Gayatri wanted, and that had disturbed her; she couldn't bear that insult to Baby or Gayatri. That, to her, was a slur on womankind. But now she was scared.

ASP Kapoor had called to inform them that though he had yet to find any evidence that pointed towards Gayatri, he was duty-bound to interview her. He would be happy to come around to Akash Hingorani's house the next morning.

How had they gone from prosecuting Maheep for the rape of Baby to defending Gayatri for the murder of Maheep? She felt bad about a young life being ended. After all, he had been Vamini's age, he had had a life ahead of him. Kismet, for whatever righteous reasons, had upset the order of things; a father should never have to cremate his child. It wasn't natural. Maninder had every reason to lose it, but he was losing it on the wrong people: them, and that worried her.

The evening dragged on. The girls had dinner and went upstairs. Gayatri and the cook were sent to bed, too.

With no facts about how Maheep had died, there was little point in any discussion. It was plain conjecture on Maninder's part to believe that Gayatri was responsible for Maheep's death because she hadn't accepted his offer to retract the rape case.

Or, was there something that Priti couldn't remember?

EIGHTEEN

Akash was up early and in his study, reflecting on the entire episode. He knew how the proceedings ran for the indigent. Honestly, considering her financial and social background, if Gayatri had been on her own, she would have been taken to the police station—probably handcuffed—and intimidated, manipulated, maybe even coerced into admitting she had killed Maheep, and incarcerated. If she didn't admit to it, Maninder would have funded a way to incriminate her, to keep her locked up. The bureaucratic machinery would have provided her with a token advocate on the government's payroll who would have half-heartedly prepared a farce of a defence. Considering the wherewithal of Maninder Singh, Gayatri could have languished in prison for the balance of her healthy life as the trial would have been adjourned every single time, on one pretext or the other, before the allotted date. As for Baby, she would have been taken away by Maninder's goons to some place, gang raped and either sold into prostitution or worse, killed, her body dumped where it could never be unearthed. No better fate than Maheep's Honda Civic.

He had seen it all happen several times; obviously, no such case was in the records, but people had vanished throughout history without ever being found. Mostly, it was because no one went looking for such people. If Gayatri were jailed, who would ever look for Baby?

ASP Kapoor looked weary when he arrived at Akash's house at nine to interview Gayatri. The Diwans had been very specific that their whereabouts needn't be shared with too many people. Who knew who was on Maninder's payroll?

'Good morning, Mr Hingorani,' he said and offered his hand when Akash opened the door for him. He might have been only two years into the police service, but his conduct displayed that he recognized how eminent Akash Hingorani was as a criminal defence advocate.

Pleasantries out of the way, coffee served, they quickly established the course of play before Akash called Priti and Vansh into the room. Gayatri wasn't called in yet.

'I'm surprised you won't be representing Gayatri, Mr Diwan,' ASP Kapoor said when all of them sat down in Akash's study.

'I should have, actually. Given that it is so cut and dried. We certainly don't need the best of the best to mount a defence for Gayatri, but I am staying away to avoid the awkwardness. If this ever goes to court, it will be essential to call Priti as a witness,'

Vansh looked at his wife, 'and, maybe, Vamini too, so it's better for Akash to lead the trial.'

'And moreover, I think Vansh is too close to the defendant. Gayatri lives with us, she's family. It's better to have someone less subjective and detached,' Priti supplemented.

'Fair point.' ASP Kapoor nodded in agreement. 'Is it okay if I meet Gayatri to ask her a few questions?'

'Of course, my client will be here shortly, ASP Kapoor.' Akash looked at the Diwans who read him, got up and saying their goodbyes to the ASP, walked out of the study. It was now, strictly, a client and advocate meeting with the investigating officer where family and friends weren't welcome.

'Do you have any evidence against my client that I should know of, ASP Kapoor?'

'Not yet, Mr Hingorani.'

Gayatri walked in, as if on cue.

'Come, sit here.' Akash got up and offered her a seat. In that moment, it dawned on ASP Kapoor that Akash wasn't going to let anything slip. She might have been a pro bono case, but he was affording her every courtesy. 'Sorry, ASP Kapoor,' he said returning to his own chair, 'as I was saying, do you have any witness or witnesses who saw my client at or near the scene of the crime?'

'None that have come forward yet.'

'Any evidence?'

'Nothing yet.'

'I seriously can't understand why you want to question Ms Gayatri Yadav, if you have no evidence or witnesses.' Akash had pulled out a yellow pad and his Mont Blanc to jot down points.

'The father of the murdered boy believes that Ms Gayatri Yadav had a motive to murder his son.'

'And I believe the earth is flat,' he smiled. *He-said-she-said, he-believes-she-believes*: the nonsense every judge dismisses with a cautionary.

ASP Kapoor returned his smile.

'I'm not berating your investigation; that's not the idea and I'm sorry to come across as a bit sarcastic, but you have to appreciate that I have a responsibility towards my client.'

'Surely. Let me explain. Your client had said that she would kill the person who had attacked her daughter … ' Akash could see that the ASP hated himself for saying it, but he nevertheless had to, as the statement was on record.

'I'm sorry?' Akash looked at him, then at Gayatri and back at him.

ASP Kapoor explained that when he had gone to take Gayatri's statement after Baby's rape, she had said something akin to that. Twice. He promised to provide the verbatim statement to Akash later.

'Hmm … go ahead, ASP Kapoor. Please feel free to ask my client whatever you have to.' Akash seemed receptive to the idea of a police enquiry as the police had Gayatri's statement that explicitly recorded *mens rea*: malice aforethought—recognized by law as the state of mind indicating culpability as an element of a crime.

They spent the best part of the morning locked in Akash's study. ASP Kapoor wanted to be sure he got the answers to all his questions. Akash could fathom that Maninder Singh would definitely turn on the heat by calling some politician or high-ranking police officers, and ASP Kapoor was doing his job so that he had all he needed, on record.

Did you ever visit Maninder Singh's farmhouse?

No.

Did you see that there was a pond at the end of the property?

I've never been to the farmhouse, ASP sahib.

ASP Kapoor looked satisfied that he had the answers; he ended the interview, and Gayatri left the room, leaving him with Akash.

On enquiring, ASP Kapoor had to divulge the time and cause of death. It was early days and more details would follow, he elaborated. Akash would receive all the details about time and cause after the autopsy. And all evidence that the forensics team harvested from the crime scene. And any witnesses.

'I need to search the Diwan residence,' ASP Kapoor resumed his investigation.

'Pray why?'

'For the murder weapon.'

'Fair enough.'

'I'll need a search warrant if the Diwans aren't willing to cooperate in the enquiry, you know that—'

I don't see why they should object. I'll ask them anyway. Is it okay to invite Priti and Vansh in now?'

'Of course.'

Akash rang the buzzer beside his desk. They had agreed on that protocol; the Diwans walked in after a couple of minutes.

'What do you think?' Priti asked.

'I'm afraid I can't share that … ' ASP Kapoor replied.

'Do we take it that you have asked whatever you needed to and my client doesn't need to make an anticipatory bail application?'

'Mr Hingorani, I cannot answer that one either. If I were you, I'd definitely make the application.'

'Thank you.' Akash made a note on his pad. 'Priti and Vansh, the police would like to search your property for the murder weapon. As the advocate for Gayatri—who resides with you—I think we should cooperate with the police, arrange a time as soon as possible and let the police do their combing.'

'Absolutely,' said Vansh.

Priti nodded.

Another fifteen minutes, and ASP Kapoor got up to go.

'Thank you for your time, Mr Hingorani. If you or your client remember anything that might have a bearing on this investigation, please give me a call.' He handed his card to Akash.

'Likewise, ASP Kapoor. Thank you for coming over.'

The three were alone again in Akash's study.

Priti was eager to know what had transpired in the last two hours. Akash updated them on the lack of any evidence or witness at the moment. He also relayed the ASP's concern about Gayatri's statement regarding her desire to kill the culprit. He then left the room but was back in a matter of seconds.

'I wanted to check if Gayatri's gone up,' he explained.

'Yeah, I sent her up.'

'Guys, I don't need to tell you that all they need is one small fact to make a case. And the police and Maninder have the one fact with evidence: Gayatri declaring that she'd kill whoever had raped her child. An intent—nothing more—but it is on police records.'

Nods. The Diwans, of course, acknowledged that that had happened.

'On a scale of one to ten, how sure are you that Gayatri never left the house any time on the night of 10 June?' Akash asked Priti, now that he knew a few more specifics about the murder.

'Ten. She couldn't have. Did ASP Kapoor tell you how Maheep died?' she consciously avoided referring to it as murder.

'Someone crushed his skull with a hammer.'

'Oh god, no! Really?' Priti winced.

'Anyway, as I said, I don't think the police have anything on Gayatri so it might just go away. Maninder Singh, given the company he keeps and the dealings he has, won't be short of enemies, and none of them could be of the churchgoing variety, I'm sure. Anyone could have iced Maheep,' Akash shrugged.

'But the timing, it all looks quite contrived for someone else to have attacked Maheep just when he was being accused of rape, don't you think?'

'We don't know what we don't know,' Akash offered though he couldn't ignore the bad timing either.

'What do you think we should do?' asked Vansh.

'You heard what ASP Kapoor said. I think the first thing you should do is to ask someone in your office to file an anticipatory bail petition and take it for hearing to the division bench of Justice Prasad Kumar—I know him personally, so it's better your office files the application and I'll have a word with him.'

The lawmakers of most countries were a foresighted bunch. They provisioned for the fact that the need for legal protection could arise for themselves or their families and friends as much as for anyone else. Hence, under section 438 of the Criminal Procedure Code of Indian criminal law, they cleverly slipped in something they christened anticipatory bail, a way to release a person on bail; it is issued before the person is arrested on the charge of having committed a non-bailable offence. But it cuts both ways. It's as much a boon to the innocents as it is a cunning getaway for the guilty. But that has been the case throughout history: the bugs infesting the wheat always get pulverized with it. And the law has always been clear: it's tolerable to let a few guilty people escape, but it is not acceptable to let even one innocent person suffer. The truth, however, is that most innocents do not even know if something devastating is coming their way, they are not aware that they are being pulled down till they have actually sunk to the bottom. So, all in all, it is mostly a haven for the guilty.

Occasionally, as in the present case, some innocents like Gayatri benefitted from anticipatory bail. But it was only because kismet had provided her with a lifeline, the patronage of Akash Hingorani and the Diwans.

'Consider it done. I'll ask someone to file it today. What next?' Vansh asked.

'One thing before we proceed. If this case goes to trial and I'm leading the defence, I have a condition.'

Priti looked at Vansh who looked equally befuddled.

'You will have to trust me completely, and not question my strategy on this. I will ask when I need help, but the defence strategy will be mine. And the sole reason I mention this now is because, though we've been friends for decades, we've never worked alongside each other. I don't want anything to occur that jeopardizes our relationship. You are free to take the case to someone else, and I won't mind, I'll advise whoever and whenever you ask me. You two are more important to me than anyone or anything else, and I won't sacrifice my friendship for a case.'

Priti looked at Vansh once again who was already nodding in acquiescence. 'Agreed,' she said aloud.

'I hope you don't misunderstand me on this. We can go out and buy the services of any advocate and the three of us can advise her or him. We'll still win, there's no doubt in my mind ... '

'Priti has said she agrees and I nodded. Do you want me to write it on my forehead now?' Vansh quipped.

'Preferably in reverse, please, so I can read it in the rear-view mirror.'

'You're a close friend, Akash, and we are all camped here, at your place. We trust you with our lives. And even Vansh has now acknowledged that you're a better advocate than him.'

'But he has a better wife than I have.'

'You don't have a wife.'

'Even if I had one, she wouldn't be half as good as you.'

'Aye, stop flirting with my wife.'

'I'm not flirting with your wife, I'm flirting with my gorgeous classmate at the reunion, old man. Lunch anyone?'

'I'll make it today,' Priti offered.

'No, let the cook and Gayatri make lunch. We'll cook dinner together. Let's talk about the case for now.'

'Fair point,' Vansh chipped in. 'What next?'

'Let's hire a private investigator.'

'Why do we need to do that?' Vansh sounded curious.

'I want to unearth everything possible about Maninder Singh—his businesses, his liaisons, his friends, his associates, his rivals, everything. I have a feeling something might lead us to the murder of Maheep. I don't know what I might need when the time comes, so it's best to start digging now. The more dirt I find on Maninder, the better it'll play in court if and when we go to trial.'

'How?'

'Just trust me.'

'Okay.'

'And one more thing. In light of what ASP Kapoor has told me about the murder, I will need to take Gayatri to a doctor for some clinical tests—'

'What tests?' Priti asked.

'I know she has an alibi, and you'll testify in court, but I always keep a Plan B in my back pocket.'

'Sure.'

Akash Hingorani knew that this case would go to trial; he had no doubt about that. It didn't matter what he told the Diwans, there was no way Maninder would let his son's death go unavenged. Maheep might have been vile and disgusting, but he was his son. If Maninder Singh—from what he'd heard about him so far—did not avenge something this monumental, it would indicate that he was powerless, it would send the wrong signals up and down the chain. That was a strict no-no in his line of work. Being seen as forgiving meant he was no longer good at what he did.

Nineteen

Maninder was agitated. His henchmen had been in Def Col since the day before and had called to tell him that the Diwans were still not home. They hadn't even returned home the previous night, which made him more restless than worried. Where could they have escaped to? And for how long? No one could hide forever, it was said. He was at home, waiting for one of his influential friends to call him and give him the name of a noteworthy criminal advocate, now that Vansh Diwan was out of the equation. He was confident he would make Vansh pay for his backstabbing. If he could deliver no other blow, he would at least take gratification in destroying the advocate financially. He'd ask connections, too, to take business away from Vansh. Choke him dry. As he dwelt upon Vansh's devastation, his mobile pinged. The guy on the line—secretary to a political aspirant—provided him with the name and mobile number of a hotshot advocate and told him whose name to use for the reference.

Maninder dialled as soon as he disconnected. The phone was answered after three rings.

Akash was sitting in his study-office with Priti and Vansh when his mobile chimed.

'Give me a second, Mr *Maninder Singh*,' Priti and Vansh caught the inflection in Akash's voice, which they knew was a hint for the couple to not utter anything. Priti looked at Vansh, who shrugged. They kept quiet.

'How may I help you, Mr Singh?' Akash asked and put the call on speaker.

'I want you to represent me in a murder case … '

'Are you implicated in a homicide?'

'No, you got me wrong. I want to hire you to prosecute the murderer of my son.'

Akash looked from Vansh to Priti and then rolled his eyes. He pointed to his phone and silently mouthed: *how is that?*

'Are you there, Mr Hingorani?'

'Yes. Unfortunately, I cannot represent you, Mr Singh.'

'You haven't even heard me out.'

'I don't have the time to take on a new client or case at the moment. My hands are full Mr Singh, and I don't have a very large team.'

'At the moment, I am offering you just this case, but it could be the start of something big. I have recently fired my advocate and I am also looking for representation in a lot of cases. This relationship could be mutually beneficial, so to speak.'

There was not even a hint of agony in Maninder's voice. He sounded more like a businessman negotiating a deal rather than a pleading father.

Akash looked at Priti, then Vansh.

'As I said, I do not have the capacity to take on a new client, Mr Singh.'

'You're making a grave mistake, I was referred to you by Shri Jaswant Devgun, he's currently contesting the local elections for an MLA seat from—' There was a slight suggestion of irascibility in Maninder's voice.

'I know who he is, Mr Singh, and it is really nice of him to refer you to me, but unfortunately, he does not share my workload.'

'Mr Akash Hingorani, you don't know who I am.' It was obvious that Maninder was unable to hold his temper any longer; his voice had risen a couple of decibels.

'Wrong, I know exactly who you are.' Akash was still playing the guy, winking at his friends.

'You have to take this case.'

'Maninder Singh, right?' Akash conspicuously dropped the *Mister*, and confirmed Maninder's name patronizingly. 'There is nothing that I *have* to do simply because you tell me to do it … so let me explain something to you once again. I'll say it slow and in plain language so you can follow me: *I am not taking you up as a client*. Now which of those words are difficult for you to follow?'

'You will repent.'

'I've heard that plenty of times. I'm waiting for the day when I have to repent. And would you like me to also tell you why I declined to take the case you just asked me to represent?'

'Why?'

'Because I'm representing Ms Gayatri Yadav, who you are wrongly accusing of the murder of your son. Goodbye.'

Click.

The line was disconnected before Maninder could yell back any vulgarities. He was no longer merely restless, he was now worried. How could that penniless woman hire an advocate who was now declining his offer? It had to be that fucking Vansh Diwan who had engaged the criminal advocate. And instead of showing deference, that bloody advocate had insulted him. *Him? Maninder Singh?* Who did he think he was? He vowed to bring Hingorani to his knees to apologize. All he needed to do was to call in some chips. He went through his contacts to check who he could call to start the war.

An hour later, the situation looked bleaker than he had initially imagined. Whoever he had called—from hoodlums who collected hafta at roadsides to mobsters masquerading as upright businessmen to politicians in power—had counselled him against crossing Akash Hingorani. Apparently, Akash Hingorani had a bizarre collection of testicles—taken from each guy he had ever represented and saved—and though he held them safely in a concealed vault, there was no guarantee that he wouldn't take your set out and put pins in them if you tried to score against him. When Maninder asked the guys why they didn't simply eliminate him if he had become the proverbial sword of Damocles, the response was univariate and univocal: who would save them the next time? Summary: Akash Hingorani wasn't touchable; potentially lethal. Advice: stay away, make peace, be humble, make amends if possible.

That hurt.

That fucking hurt.

That little defeat hurt more than his son's death. A legal case was no less than a war: it had to be victory at any cost. If Maninder couldn't get the best advocate in Delhi, he wasn't going to hire some random loser. What would be the point of going into war knowing you would lose? He had an equally vile cousin who was based in Mumbai with connections there. He thought of calling his cousin.

'For a moment I thought he had somehow come to know we were staying here with you,' Priti said the moment Akash disconnected.

'You worry unnecessarily. No one knows you guys are here except ASP Kapoor and I told him that he shouldn't mention it for now. When he had Gayatri and I sign the statement, I saw that he had mentioned that the interview with the suspect had taken place at her advocate's office, not home, which is the truth. And for argument's sake, even if Maninder knows you guys are here, so what?'

'He won't come anywhere near Akash,' Vansh said confidently. Priti guessed that given Vansh's dealings with people on the wrong side of the tracks, he knew more than she did.

'Okay, it's quite late now, so who wants to come to the terrace with me for a cigar and who wants to retire?'

'Me.'

'Thank you, Akash,' Priti almost choked with emotion.

'Isn't that what friends are for? And quite honestly, I am enjoying living with and being part of a family, and I mean it.'

The anticipatory bail for Gayatri was issued in no time, without any unpleasantness or unnecessary questions. The magistrate made a show of sending it to his clerk for scrutiny, as people in bureaucracies routinely do, to rationalize their decisions, should an ombudsman come along with unsavoury questions or to point fingers later. In legal circles, this policy is branded as CYA—Cover Your Ass. The clerk added no value to the application except to follow the procedure of making an entry of date and time as receipt. He glanced at the documents for any errors. None. He looked at the person who stood in front of him with the application. No problems there either, as the application was made on behalf of the domestic help who lived with Mr Vansh Diwan and his family. No chance of the accused jumping bail or taking flight. Top it all with the phone call he had received from Mr Hingorani—not his office, or his assistant, the man himself had called. He was certain his boss, the magistrate, had received a call too.

Akash made the courtesy call to ASP Kapoor to let him know that the papers were in order, and thanked him for the useful counsel. Neither the advice from ASP Kapoor, nor the gratitude shown to him was required, but that was Akash Hingorani: build as many bridges as you can when you have the time and resources.

TWENTY

D.K. Pentium was a chronic drunk. His name was Dinesh Kumar, but he used his initials and added *Pentium* to emphasize that he was quick like one. And he was. When he was sober, which was occasional, or when he was challenged by someone. He was foul-mouthed, he was crooked; he had also been in prison for beating up two men so badly, they had to be admitted into hospital. He looked scary as some guys had set fire to his house late one night and therefore the right side of his face and right ear had been badly burned and scarred. As one of his eyebrows had been eliminated by the burns, he had shaved off the other one too, giving his mean eyes an even meaner look. The shaved head just added to his menacing looks. No one knew where he lived in New Delhi, as he wouldn't tell anyone after the arsonist got him. He had a mobile phone that he answered when he wanted and declined to answer when he didn't.

D.K. Pentium was the private detective Akash Hingorani customarily hired to dig up filth on people, and D.K. never declined a call if it came from an unknown number, disconnected after two rings twice, and then rang again. It was eleven in the morning and D.K. was slurring. Akash had called from one of his many pay-as-you-go burners, which could never be traced back to him. There were no pleasantries to exchange. Akash asked him if he was up to accepting a new assignment. He was. Akash gave him the name of the person and ended the call. Akash never asked for a rate or quibbled over expenses. And by the by, anyone working with D.K. knew that expenses included a bottle of expensive whisky a day, sometimes two. The next call from Akash, D.K. knew from experience, would be from another number. The advance was to be collected, in cash, from a PO box in Gole Market.

D.K. Pentium never needed any more details than the name of his quarry.

He knew his target: Maninder Singh. He picked up the news on the local channel: Maninder's son had died in suspicious circumstances. He had contacts in the local constabulary to provide him details—all expenses incurred on generous payoffs would be reimbursed. If Akash needed information on Maninder, D.K. knew from experience that his client wanted a complete dossier; it was never a single strand he was after, it was the total calculus. Family, friends, business associates, dealings, everything. He got up, took a shower and headed to the post office to collect the dosh first.

Security for the Diwan residence had been in place since the night before. The men had been provided with a set of keys to check and clean out anything suspicious, though after Maninder's conversation with Akash, he had been called by a few people—who Maninder had called to check on him—and had been assured that Maninder wouldn't do anything stupid that created problems for him or the Diwans.

But that did not mean he would drop the case or let Gayatri off the hook.

'You don't have to go back home for some time, you know that,' Akash told them over lunch.

'But we must,' Priti looked at Vansh, who just nodded. 'The longer we stay here, the more it reminds me that life has been derailed in some way.'

'I get that. Go tomorrow then, not today. Let me mentally prepare myself for your leaving.'

Neither contested that.

Later, when Akash, Vansh and Priti sat in the study, Akash shared his musings about the case. 'I believe the prosecution, in this particular case, will be working with a blank sheet of paper. The police have no corroborating evidence against Gayatri as ASP Kapoor told me, and I'll ensure he passes all the info from his further investigations and forensic reports to me. Currently, they don't have a single witness who can say that Gayatri was anywhere near the crime scene. Not just at the time of the crime, she was never there—she doesn't even know where *there* is. If nothing turns up, I'm thinking … the prosecutor will perform a tick-box exercise to try her. Maninder, I now know, has enough clout to file a case against her based on the statement that she made in the presence of the police—that she would kill whoever had raped Baby. That's enough, because the motivation and intent was there.'

'Can they actually try her, merely on that?' Priti revealed she was a corporate lawyer who had never set foot inside a courtroom.

'Oh, they've tried people for far less,' Vansh assured her.

'There is only one thing that you have to ensure. No one, not even ASP Kapoor, should meet Gayatri in my absence.' Akash paused; the eyebrows of his friends had risen quizzically. 'It's simple. You don't want her skin residue, her hair follicle, her fingerprints travelling through someone else.'

Vansh got it. Priti still looked at him questioningly.

'Priti, this is criminal law. Crime scenes are often contaminated after the crime has occurred. How difficult do you think it is to plant the DNA of an individual at a crime scene to implicate her? One strand of hair and she is placed at the crime scene and everything changes. Even ASP Kapoor, who today thinks it couldn't possibly have been her, would turn.'

'Got it. God, you're sharp.'

'Thank you. Though I bet your husband had thought of this, too.'

Vansh smiled.

'And I'll fix an appointment with the doctor and take Gayatri along. Remember, you won't question me, or Gayatri, after the appointment. As her advocate, I cannot let even my friends know about my discussions with my client.'

'I need Mumbai's best criminal advocate,' Maninder said, after conveying the news of Maheep's untimely death to his cousin, who voiced his disbelief and condolences.

'What happened to all the advocates in Delhi?'

Maninder succinctly told him his sob story.

'I'll sort something out. Give me a day or two, I'll call you back.'

TWENTY-ONE

D.K. Pentium collected the A4-sized sealed brown envelope from the post office and headed to Indian Coffee House in Mohan Singh Place. He couldn't count the cash, but he could clearly feel the two bundles of currency notes inside. Even if the stacks were of five-hundred-rupee notes, they added up to a lakh, which was a good start. Thousand-rupee notes would constitute two lakhs, but he wasn't expecting that, just as he wasn't expecting them to be stacks of hundreds. Too little. He knew that Akash knew better. He put the envelope in the simple Agarbatti-branded shoulder bag he carried everywhere.

Indian Coffee House wasn't the most happening place in town, but D.K. preferred it to the new restaurants with lots of youngsters floating around, white earphones blaring music in their ears. He hated noise on good days, and today he was barely over his hangover. The place brought back happy memories of his bygone days. The staff knew him and hence, despite his dipsomaniac state, welcomed him and gave him a table in the corner. He ordered a coffee, two mutton dosas and chips. He pulled out the envelope from his bag, opened it and took a peek inside after the waiter left him alone with his coffee. There was a lakh inside. He pulled out ten notes and kept them in his pocket for immediate use, put the brown envelope back in his bag and sat back to enjoy his meal and think about and plan his next move.

He left the Indian Coffee House, walked to Chandni Chowk, picking up a packet of Classic Milds on the way. He was a regular at Chandini Chowk for buying lost goods and untraceable pay-as-you-go mobiles. He bought three SIMs, a cheap Samsung phone and a camera. He still had a thousand rupees left from the ten notes he had taken out. Then he took the metro to Chhatarpur, and from there took a local bus to the Mehrauli police station. He called his source from outside the police station only to find out that he had miscalculated his first move. Despite Maninder Singh's son having been killed in Chhatarpur, the case had been registered at the Andrews Ganj police station. That miffed him. It was still only two in the afternoon so he decided to call a few of his other contacts.

By the time D.K. Pentium left the metro station in Chandni Chowk at eight that evening, he knew exactly what Akash Hingorani was after. Maheep Singh, the rape, Baby, the charges, the lynching, the Diwans, the whole nine yards. And he knew what he needed to do next. He picked up two bottles of whisky and walked to his shanty. He didn't need to fix himself a drink, he just opened the bottle of whisky and chug-a-lugged a few mouthfuls. The fire ran down his throat and settled down before he lit a cigarette. He purposefully upturned the brown envelope and let the contents fall on his bed. Not because he wanted to count the notes; he was certain that the stacks were complete, not a chance of there being a note or two less. Based on past experience, he knew that the envelope would have a contact number inside it. He shuffled the notes and out fell a piece of paper with the number. He opened his mobile phone and changed the SIM—there was no way he would call Akash with the same SIM that he had used all day to call his snitches.

Akash sat at his desk reading the reports. Forensic podiatry could tell you a lot if you could find a footprint or outsole print. The dimensions could tell you if it was a man or a woman. The length of the stride could help estimate the height of the person. On soft ground, the depth of the impression could give away the body weight. You could also tell if the person was walking, running, pulling something or walking backwards. But, the killer had attacked Maheep in a place overrun with weeds and shrubs, with no clear surface area at all on which the murderer could have stepped upon, the worst kind of exterior surface to lift outsole prints from. There was nothing that gave away anything.

Other police reports had found diddly-squat by way of evidence against Gayatri. There was nothing that pointed towards Gayatri ever being at the scene of crime. But there was nothing that pointed to anyone else being at the scene of the crime either, which reduced the lack of Gayatri's prints to a zero sum game. Though it did not necessarily prove someone's presence, evidence on the ground did usually suggest that an accused was at the crime scene. However, the inverse did not propagate the reverse. Most offenders attempted to obliterate all evidence against themselves; some succeeded, others didn't. Whoever had killed Maheep had definitely succeeded. Which obviously did not prove that no one had been there; someone had been there. And if someone had been there, it could well have been Gayatri. Why not? Her past folly of voicing her anger against her daughter's rapist revealed her intention to kill. Given the situation, Akash would have preferred if the police had found something that cleared her, but that was not the case.

The murder weapon was missing. Based on the caving of the skull, forensics had deduced the size and shape of the hammer used for the fatal blow. Calculating the arc, they knew the length of the handle too. Akash was certain that the police would never find the hammer unless they found the killer. The killer could lead them to it, not the other way round. It could have been dumped somewhere the police might never look. Or buried four feet under the ground, no way to find it then.

He examined the photos of the crime scene. Just as ASP Kapoor had described, Maheep's torso was at a right angle to his lower limbs, suggesting that he had been attacked while he sat on the ground with his back resting against the tree. When the skull cracked, his torso fell to the left, creating the angle, which preliminarily pointed to the fact that the attacker had been right-handed. The blood had flowed and coagulated solely around his head, which meant that Maheep had had no idea that he was about to be attacked, or else he would have fought back or fled. In which case there might have been some evidence of a struggle. No, he didn't get a chance to, Akash shook his head. Which also meant, Akash assumed, that either the person was a professional and had moved so cautiously that Maheep hadn't heard a sound or—and that was what confused Akash—someone had been really intent and had moved stealthily and silently. Another aspect that he couldn't fathom was whether the killer had known that Maheep would be in that exact spot at the time he was or had the killer planned to get into the house to strike, but had got lucky outside? That seemed a bit strange, considering the size of the property; it was too much of a coincidence that the killer had found Maheep sitting in the dark by pure chance. But stranger things have happened, he mused. However, if the killer's plan had been to get into the house, then there was no surety that he had intended to harm Maheep; maybe the killer had planned to harm Maninder Singh. It may be a moot point, but it was good to muddy the waters in court. He made a note.

Akash moved to witness statements. They were all ordinary and jejune. Just a chronology of events from the time Maheep was last seen by the family members and their caretaker, Aarti. Nothing inconsistent to work on, there were no gaps in the story to exploit or shoot holes in.

But there was nothing to incriminate Gayatri in any way either.

The interviews were theatrical, especially Maninder's, who accused Gayatri vehemently. She had vowed to kill his son because of a misunderstanding. Akash smiled. *Vowed? Misunderstanding?* What a flipping liar! He switched off the recordings and read the transcripts. Word for word, no deviation. No thoughts formed, nothing gave.

He was tired. The Diwans had left in the morning, and as the sun retreated and the day began to wind down, he missed the family atmosphere. He thought about calling them and asking if he could go over to their place for the evening when he heard a faint buzzing coming from the lower drawer of his desk. His burner phone was vibrating among the papers it was buried in. He knew who it was; he had given this number to only one man. D.K. Pentium used all the tricks—or only the tricks—in the book to scour for information, most of it illegally, and any illegally sourced information could only taint the cleaner-than-thou reputation of Akash Hingorani and he couldn't afford that. Hence, this was the first and last call this pay-as-you-go SIM would ever receive before its demise.

'How deep do you want me to go into this, boss?'.

'Bottomless. Take the carpet up and beat the last particle of dust and dirt out. I need a thorough spring clean.'

'Beyond the surface dirt then?

'Yes. I even want to know about it's previous owners and their previous generation.'

'I have reliable information that the old carpet has an extremely dirty past. And may be laden with virus.'

'Don't worry about the virus, I've taken the antibiotics. Collect all the dirt in the vacuum cleaner. I'd very much like to see it, just in case an odd jewel is still stuck there, which might come in handy.'

'Consider it done, boss.'

'Good, speak later.'

In case somebody heard their conversation despite the burner phones, the exchange was always kept cryptic; names were seldom mentioned, and the distilled essence of the call was jack shit. Nothing was said about anyone in particular. Nothing was meant for someone to decipher. Neither party said anything intelligible that any listener—however keen and able—could interpret. No evidence and nothing could be proven. Nothing whatsoever.

The conversation, in reality, meant:

How deep do you want me to dig, boss?
Bottomless. I want all the dirt on the subject—Maheep Singh.
Beyond Maheep Singh, then?
Yes. I want to know all about his parents too—Maninder Singh and family.
I have reliable information that Maninder Singh is extremely dirty. And dangerous.
I'm not afraid of him. Tell me everything, so I can use some dirt on him.'
Consider it done, boss.
Good, speak later.

Twenty-Two

The Diwan residence in Def Col showed no signs of being protected when Akash Hingorani's Jaguar rolled in, despite the four security personnel on the ground: two men on the gate, one on the terrace with binoculars and one guy constantly patrolling the property. Akash was convinced that the security was no longer required, but if it put the occupants at ease, and they were willing to bear the cost, he saw no point in starting a debate with his friends.

Priti seemed happy as she informed him that Baby was coming around to her usual self. She had undergone her initial psychological evaluation and the specialist did not foresee any long-term repercussions of the attack. However, he had warned them that sometimes the hurt was unwittingly concealed and didn't surface for years. It was advisable that she went for some therapy sessions by way of which a professional could look for subliminal symptoms. Bottom line: Baby would never be given a clean chit for life, but this was as good as it got, considering that other people in similar circumstances could become depressed, even suicidal.

'I need to talk to Gayatri,' Akash said when the three were alone.

'Now?' Priti asked.

'Now, yes, and alone.'

'Understandable.' Vansh got up. Priti followed.

The couple walked out of their living room. He heard Priti call out to Gayatri and Gayatri soon entered the room. She was a scared woman with not much in terms of weight: fifty-something kilos, maybe. Grey hair masked under a henna treatment, she wore a cotton sari and her eyes were still tired and wet.

'Sit down,' Akash pointed at the sofa, relieving her of the decision of whether to stand or sit and where.

She nodded, said nothing.

'Who am I?'

'Akash sahib.'

'No, I'm your advocate, Gayatri. Do you know what you are accused of?'

She nodded her head, which could mean yes, but it could well mean no, despite ASP Kapoor having spoken to her as a suspect.

'Okay. I am your advocate, and you are my client. Whatever we speak about should not be discussed with anyone. We have a legal relationship, which no one should be privy to.'

'Not even sahib and memsahib?' she asked innocently.

'No, not even Priti or Vansh or Vamini or Baby. No one, and that is why I asked them to leave the room. If they know what we discussed, they can be asked to come to court and repeat it under oath. They cannot say what they don't know. Is that clear?'

A nod.

'Okay. Maninder Singh has accused you of killing his son, you know that?'

A nod.

'And I will argue the case for you, to say that the charges brought against you are false.'

'It is a lie. I didn't do it. The police know that, don't they?'

'They might know it, but they also have a statement from you in which you voiced your wish to kill Maheep … '

Gayatri put both her hands over her mouth, her eyes widening.

'Don't worry, nothing is going to happen, but we will be required to prove your innocence in court.'

'Who killed him then?'

'I don't know yet. Maybe I'll find out, maybe the police will. Maybe we won't ever know, but that is not up to us to find or prove. We only have to prove that you didn't do it.'

She shook her head as if she had followed what he had just described.

'So, for my own benefit, I have to ask you this once. Did you kill Maheep Singh?'

'No.' She burst into tears.

'Gayatri, you have no need to be concerned, but I need to coach you.'

Her brows knit together. She didn't utter anything as she was still crying in response to the previous question.

'Don't worry. I won't tell you to say anything wrong or false; I'll simply coach you to make your point clear when we are in court.' Akash was aware how dreadful it could be for first-timers in a court. The prosecuting advocate would purposefully attack Gayatri to break her down, to make it look as if she was hiding something or being cunning or using theatrics to cover the truth. Of course, he could cry foul and object as often as possible, but it was best to coach the accused or witness ahead of time. Coaching also skilled people in keeping their answers succinct and to the point, and to not wander into explanations that weren't asked for. Often, when you put an untrained person on the witness stand, they unsuspectingly blabbered themselves into the opposing advocate's trap. 'Also, we need to go and see some medical experts before the case, just you and I. Is that okay?'

She nodded.

'Do you want to ask me anything for now, Gayatri?'

'How much will it cost, sahib?'

'Nothing.'

'Is Priti memsahib paying for all this?'

'You shouldn't worry about the finances. You know Priti, Vansh and I have been together since college, so if anyone attacks them, it means they've attacked me. We are family. And this is what family members do, okay?'

Tears in her eyes, Gayatri jumped up and walked up to Akash and bent down to touch his feet out of gratitude, but Akash caught her midway. 'No, please don't do this, Gayatri, we're the same age.' He held her arms, then bringing her closer, he pecked her on her forehead, and let her go. 'Now, smile and don't worry too much.'

'Thank you,' she said, turned around and left the room. He could still hear her sobs.

The Diwans came in five minutes later. Priti's eyes were moist. Maybe Gayatri had shared a part of the non-legal discussion—the fiscal part—with them.

'Can I have a drink in this house or not?' Akash asked, before either of the Diwans could say anything. 'And dinner too please …'

Maninder Singh was uneasy. What had been plaguing him since the discovery of Maheep's death was the missing mobile phone he had given to his son. The police had recovered only Maheep's iPhone when they found him. The one that everyone had the number for. The phone that Maninder had given him a few days prior to his death to keep in touch with him, should the circumstances require privacy, hadn't been found. Which could mean one of two things: either Maheep hadn't taken the instrument with him on the night, which meant it would still be in the house, and he had turned his son's room upside down but hadn't located the damned device. Or the killer had taken it with him after the murder. Why? Why would the killer leave an expensive phone and take the cheaper pay-as-you-go shitty phone? Maninder Singh's dilemma was—and he couldn't curse himself enough—that he hadn't bought a new phone and SIM for his son. He had taken a burner from one of his employees and handed it over to Maheep. He had called that number umpteen times, but it was switched off. He couldn't give that number to the police as he had called it enough times for his dodgy deals. Giving that number to the police would also give them insights into some of his other business dealings, which he couldn't bring into the open. He couldn't afford that.

His cousin called to say that none of the top criminal advocates that he knew had sounded keen to travel for a trial after they had been told the details. Nevertheless, a few of them had offices in Delhi, and one of the senior partners in Delhi could well represent Maninder or help the prosecution prepare a tight case. They recommended it was better that way, because though any qualified advocate in India could represent a client in any state, it was always better to fight on home turf: you knew the lie of the land, the subtle nuances of the system, the clerical staff, the media, the other influencers, the judges. After a lot of contemplation, Maninder agreed to take up the offer. He wasn't depending solely on the courts anyway. That was merely the first dice he had thrown. He had been a criminal long enough to know how many times Vansh Diwan had proved the right, wrong and the wrong, right. He had other aces to play once this was over. There was no way the Diwans would keep the security for the rest of their lives, there was no way Akash Hingorani would stay in the middle of this forever, and once that bloody Hingorani was out of the equation, his connections would not restrain him from making Gayatri and Baby and the entire Diwan clan pay. He'd see to it. He only needed to bide his time till the court case was over. In fact, he believed it would be easier for Gayatri if she were convicted and sentenced by the court rather than his people getting to her and her daughter.

He reckoned that it would be asinine to show impatience. He stopped squawking in public and to his circle of connected people.

Gayatri's coaching commenced almost immediately. Akash advised, and Vansh agreed, that she needed a lot of preparation. Her nods and barely audible responses had to be tuned. Given that the police had nothing from the crime scene a week after the murder, there was slim chance of something coming up later.

In the month that followed, Priti went back to work. Vamini had got admission in Lady Shri Ram College, and Baby had gone back to school in the next grade. Both girls were clandestinely watched by the security firm, so as not to draw attention. Though Vansh would not be an active counsel on record for the reason they had agreed upon previously, they knew that two brains were better than one. As such, the two friends spent a lot of time together to prepare the case. But Akash refrained from discussing some salient points—anything that was strictly an advocate-client conversation. Whenever needed, Akash spoke to Gayatri alone. As decided before, he had taken Gayatri for a full medical check-up, which, according to him, was satisfactory for the purpose of the detailed examination.

Leaving Vansh out of the equation, Akash spent time with Priti and Vamini individually. He didn't want their testimonies—providing alibis for Gayatri for the night of 10 June—to be contaminated in any way. He told them as emphatically as possible not to discuss anything about the night with each other or with Gayatri. The two testimonies should match, but they shouldn't appear to have come from the same hymn book. He knew that Priti, being an advocate herself, would keep it airtight.

Twenty-Three

D.K. loved dirt more than a doggone mite. And he loved digging more than a rabbit. He had the one quality any investigator worth his profession must have: patience. He could sit for hours with his camera for a shot. If D.K. was asked, he could procure anyone's DNA without the subject even knowing. Cigarette butts thrown carelessly, chewing gum spat out, drinks discarded at a bar … he'd put on his gloves and scavenge in trash bags if required, collect a target's piss by installing a slightly inflated condom under the steel drain cover in a public urinal, retrieve hair from a public handbasin that a subject had stood over while combing his hair in a public restroom. He staged accidents in restaurants: pretend to slip when he got close to someone and then hit his head against the target's nose, profusely apologize and then offer his kerchief to blot the blood. He had never failed Akash. Akash's only worry was if D.K. was someday hired by someone against him. The thought always made him shiver.

However, Akash Hingorani was hardly concerned on this particular occasion. D.K. Pentium had kept abreast with the police investigation. At times, D.K. had called him before the news had travelled from an investigation to police headquarters. And D.K. hadn't restricted himself to procuring what the police had already obtained. He found out all about Maninder and Maheep. He took pictures of Maninder Singh with despicable crooks and bent politicians. He shot Maninder with the rubes who actually carried out his dirty orders on the ground. And he shot Maninder knocking young, underage women. He even found the charred and trashed Honda Civic. He made the field trip to see the remains of the chassis and snapped pictures. From trustworthy sources, he dug up the fake pre-dated First Information Report on Maheep's car, which proved that it had never been stolen. He knew which police station it was reported stolen at, he knew which station house officer (SHO) had taken a backhander, and he knew exactly how much money had changed hands. He even knew the time and place of the deal. He got orders from Akash to retrieve that FIR. People forget that what can be inserted in the police files with influence and money can also be removed with greater influence and more money. All one needs is a room full of temporarily blind people while the page in the file is torn off and shredded. With the FIR being deleted, the file on Maninder and Maheep was nearly complete.

The defence didn't have to share all the research they had carried out on the case. If questioned, they could always blame the prosecution's slipshod search. Even better. It always scored points with the judge to show any weakness on the prosecution's side—be it investigation or arguments.

However, a lot of the dirt D.K. had dug up by unscrupulous methods couldn't be presented in court. The law, unlike the mantra that numerous management gurus have started repeating like a broken record these days, does not permit you to *think outside the box*. It always stays inside the fence. It is either said or written or it has precedence. Outside the box might constitute breaking the law, the tradition; it's an altogether different way of thinking or doing things. You do something out of the box, the judge could put you inside the witness box to explain. And Akash Hingorani wasn't dim, he would use only some of the information provided by D.K. The law, he knew, was clear and ambiguous at the same time. A murderer is guilty. Clear. How to prove who's the murderer? Very ambiguous, till proven beyond a reasonable doubt.

Two of his juniors worked full-time on preparing Gayatri's case. Documents were typed and filed. Reports were analysed. Evidence was scrutinized. All transcripts of witness statements were read and re-read. Reports from the prosecution were checked against D.K.'s investigation—only the selected pieces that Akash had shared with his colleagues.

Moreover, D.K. Pentium had left a dossier on Maninder Singh, his various businesses and criminal connections, which, Akash reckoned, would give him enough to raise reasonable doubt in the mind of the judge about other individuals who could have had a motive to punish Maninder.

Akash Hingorani didn't need proof. It was enough to point fingers.

'Akash.' Vansh cleared his throat. 'I'm scared, Akash. For the first time in my life I'm scared about a criminal trial.' Vansh and Priti had come to Akash's house.

'Why? You are neither the advocate nor a witness … '

'That's not the point.' Vansh looked ashen, the colour gone from his face.

'So you think I might get sloppy and mess up?'

'Not that, I'm only worried because Priti and Vamini are witnesses, more for Vamini … '

'You don't need to be concerned at all.'

'Is there no way you can appeal not to put Vamini on the witness stand, excuse her from the court proceedings? My alibi should be enough, don't you think?' Priti requested.

'Vamini is over eighteen, so it will not be possible, Priti. I promise I won't let the prosecuting advocate ask Vamini any questions about Baby's rape whatsoever. I'll object, stop the testimony. Leave it to me, don't worry. She's as much my responsibility as yours.'

'Is Baby going to be a witness too?' Priti asked.

'No. I have arranged for her testimony to be on affidavit. If required, it will only be between the judge and us advocates, not for public consumption. Baby being a minor, it was simple. Is that all?'

'Yeah, Vamini is the bigger worry. I'm a qualified legal head, so I'm sure I can handle such matters professionally. Plus, you've coached me.'

'Mum's the word … ' Akash put his finger on his lips and smiled.

'Have the police got any evidence against Gayatri?' asked Vansh; he looked more nervous than Akash had ever seen him.

'None, but the murder weapon is still missing,' he paused and smiled. 'My gut feeling is that ASP Kapoor is an honest guy and he would have certainly informed me if they had discovered it, but you never know ... I have been let down by my gut a few times before.'

'But you don't think that—even if the police found it—it would carry any evidence against Gayatri, do you?' It looked as if the approaching trial date had really got to Vansh, making him edgy, anxious, scared.

'Oh no, not organically. But you know as well as I do how incriminatory evidence can be planted.'

'And what if ASP Kapoor springs a last minute surprise ... ?' It was Priti this time.

'Priti, stop hyperventilating. What is it with you two today? I have all the answers, but I can't tell you two. Trust me.'

'How does it matter if you tell us the strategy now?' asked Vansh.

'Oh, what if you are Maninder's decoy?' Akash winked. 'And besides, I cannot break my client's confidence. I told you I have a plan B, which will work with or without the murder weapon. Gayatri will get a clean chit the day I get my first or second witness on the stand.'

'I like your confidence. You know I haven't watched you in court for years now. I'll watch the trial. How many witnesses do you think the prosecution will have?'

'Six or seven, but they might send me a bigger list.'

'And you?'

'Three, but I might only need two on the stand.'

Both Priti and Vansh, being advocates, stared at him, mouths agape. Just two witnesses.

'Close your mouths before a fly dives in, my friends.' Akash raised a glass to toast.

'I have just one more concern, Akash.'

'Go on Priti, what is it?'

'We can't have security around the house and the girls twenty-four/seven for the rest of our lives; besides the expense, it's also an infringement on our privacy ... '

'You worry too much. By the time I'm finished with Mr Maninder Singh, his steel balls will have been swapped for plastic ones; he will be powerless to do anything.'

'How?'

'It's actually quite simple and I'm sure you guys would have worked it out too, but because you're emotionally involved, you've missed it.'

'Is that part of your strategy too or can you tell us something to relieve us of our fears?'

'Priti, the only reason Maninder's business thrives is because he is the squeaky clean façade for those who aren't so clean themselves. He has no police file, no awkward or malicious media mentions, nothing that says he's a dirty bastard. Once I blow his mask in public court, those giving him business will think thrice before letting him carry on as their front guy, don't you think? If the media and authorities are watching him, it will be in their interest to cut him loose. Now I know a lot of people he does business with—I have photographs of them with him, and I'll send those pictures to them after the trial, advising them that the spotlight on Maninder means he could lead the police and media to them. Those who are dirty need a clean veil; if the veil is soiled, it is of hardly any use.' Akash stopped and took a sip of his drink.

'No one wants to be on a sinking ship with sharks circling around.'

'How do you have these pictures of Maninder?'

'I told you I hired a private investigator.'

'Thank you, Akash.'

'He came too close to my friends, Priti. His mistake. He won't have the clout or the connections to do anyone any wrong after this trial.'

Akash was confident. He had realized, early in his career, that there were good stories and average stories, good screenplays and average screenplays, but if you convinced Big B to accept the lead role, even an unexceptional film had a chance of bringing in the money; and, if you had an amazing story and an equally remarkable screenplay, and then you signed up Big B, well, then you had a blockbuster on your hands. In this particular circumstance, he already had a winning case—what with the prosecution and the police having no evidence against Gayatri—and in addition, not only was he the best criminal advocate in the city, but they had also ensured that the second best criminal advocate in the city—Vansh Diwan—was out of the race, out of reach of the opposition. The odds were stacked against the prosecution. Mounting a defence would be child's play; an oneiric opportunity for any defence team. He realized he was grinning like a dog now.

TWENTY-FOUR

The theoretical beginning of any case, before it is tried in court, is with the police investigation. Once the police discover evidence incriminating someone, they are required to take the supporting evidence to a public prosecutor who then files the case in court. But that is all academic; the practice varies. There is the letter of the law and there is its spirit. And there are a million loopholes in the law, which can provoke and entitle a public prosecutor to file a case and the magistrate to accept the same. With no murder weapon or any other possible suspects, besides Gayatri, ASP Kapoor felt it was a little premature to take the case to trial. Despite ASP Kapoor's convincing resistance, Maninder's money and influence saw him overruled by his own superiors in the police force. The flimsy and laughable evidence was presented to the magistrate who had already been briefed by some high-ranking police officer. If a magistrate accepts the validity of the existing evidence, he has the power to issue an arrest warrant, but thankfully, Akash Hingorani had already secured anticipatory bail on behalf of his client.

And thus, a criminal case was filed against Ms Gayatri Yadav.

Nothing, they say, is ever lost in the universe. All information is stored somewhere in the clouds, but not everyone has access to it. However, that didn't deter ASP Kapoor from digging. He discerned something wasn't right, but he didn't know what. What didn't sit right with him was the prime accused: Gayatri. To add to his misery, the murder weapon, now established by forensics and the morbid pathologist who had performed Maheep's autopsy to be an iron hammer with a diameter of eleven inches, was still missing. He hadn't found it in the search of the Diwan residence and was under no illusion that he would ever find it. It would have been different, and perhaps easier to find the murder weapon, if Maheep had been killed with a gun. A gun wasn't as ubiquitous as a hammer. This wasn't America, this was India. By contrast, a hammer, even a heavy industrial-sized hammer such as the one that had crushed Maheep's skull, was available with every roadside mechanic, every labourer, practically anyone who worked with stones or metal. How could he ask every Tom, Dick and their hammer-owning cousins? Moreover, no one would have informed the police about a stolen hammer, while a missing gun would have been reported at a police station immediately by its owner. And save for the blood or any other forensic evidence still on the head of a hammer, there seemed no way to identify a particular hammer. A gun was distinct. Of course, no doubt the serial number of the gun used in any cold-blooded crime would certainly have been filed off or burnt away with acid, but in most cases, the fired bullet—if they could find the casing—

could lead you back to the gun it was fired from should the police discover the weapon.

The thing that bothered ASP Kapoor the most was something that would be difficult for any policeman worth his salary to come to terms with: a guy accused of the rape of an underage girl dying a few days after the incident, under mysterious circumstances. What were the odds that the two incidents were totally unrelated? How was it even possible? Did someone take advantage of the situation? Take out Maheep to make it appear like someone else's work? He had to find out who else knew about Baby's rape. All murder investigations were a story in reverse. The police had to work back from the crime scene to build what could have happened before the crime. It was twice as hard, if not impossible. And unless you had evidence, everything was conjecture or circumstantial—a puzzle that only revealed itself after it was solved. There was no illustration on the box to follow to put the pieces together. The only other way—and the one that good investigators followed in the absence of concrete evidence or witnesses—was to look at people known to the victim directly or indirectly and establish which ones had some motive. Who had something to gain from the crime? Once that was evident, eliminate the ones with alibis, and those who did not have the opportunity.

Based on the information that his parents had provided and Maheep's contact list on his iPhone, which had been retrieved from the crime scene, ASP Kapoor had contacted several of Maheep's friends, especially those whom Maheep had called frequently or in the last few days. His efforts revealed a normal—if it could be called normal—rich, spoilt teenager's life. Some were his friends; some were friends of his money. What ASP

Kapoor uncovered was no more than typical teenage bickering, envy and bantering; nothing that could possibly be a motive for murder. None of the friends' backgrounds suggested they could kill. The only gross misdemeanour Maheep had committed was Baby's rape, a few days before his unnatural death.

Nevertheless, in his investigation into Maheep, ASP Kapoor predictably came across the dark world Maninder Singh operated in: a nexus of duplicitous individuals, shell corporations and secretive partnerships. Maninder Singh came from a not-so-privileged background, unlike his son, Maheep. Maninder's father was a schoolteacher, his mother a full-time mum in East Delhi—'Yamuna-paar' as everyone termed it. He had very humble beginnings. Maninder was a good student in school, but by the time he got to college, he was attracted to insalubrious company that met with the disapproval of his parents: he was smoking, drinking and doping with the rich, misguided youth who were more interested in university politics than studying for honest careers. But his parents' disapproval didn't keep Maninder from venturing into that murky world to make a fast buck. With no background or family in politics, he soon grasped that he could make easy money operating on the periphery of politics, feeding the appetites of wannabe or manqué politicians and their powerful mentors in the kakistocracy. Maninder began by luring young university girls into politicians' beds and then became a full-time pimp. Prostitution wasn't a novel idea or a new business, but he was able to viciously wipe out the other players that competed with him in the market. He took over their businesses and girls. People who opposed him simply vanished overnight. Others became his subordinates, partners or employees. But that was over a quarter of a century ago.

Even if he had bankrupted someone, or besmirched someone's daughter or sister back then, who kept a grudge for so long? Who waited for twenty-five years for an opportunity to strike back? And what ASP Kapoor didn't know was if some people had attempted previously to strike at him and failed.

Maninder went on to discard prostitution in favour of drugs. His viciousness and the clout he now had eliminated competition yet again. Over the next twenty years, Maninder Singh collected friends and favours, but he also made a lot of enemies. And every single one of them had the wherewithal to carry out a hit. But there was an unwritten, unspoken understanding of sorts: even the most abominable of men didn't indulge in causing harm to other vile men's families as they, too, had families and it wasn't a war any of them wished, or could afford, to start. That said, it could well have been a grudge held by someone who couldn't care less. Or the person who had been hired to strike had mistakenly hit Maheep instead of Maninder. There were various possibilities, numerous questions, but no answers.

After burning enough resources for a couple of months, the bureaucracy removed manpower from—what they disgruntledly referred to as a witch-hunt—the ongoing investigation. The people higher up in the police hierarchy saw no point in continuing the investigation when the magistrate was convinced about the evidence against the accused. Ongoing investigations were not only a drain on resources, they also tainted the department's reputation, as they showed incompetence, and that resulted in a lower allocation of funds to the department. Closing a police case was a positive statistic. More closed cases meant a proficient team, which meant more funding flowed in to help catch more criminals and keep the streets of Delhi crime free.

ASP Kapoor and SI Verma carried on their bare bones investigation till the very end, but even they knew it was inadequate.

The first jury trial that took place in India in the late seventeenth century was academic as it was nothing more than a mockery of justice. A British woman was charged with the murder of an Indian servant girl and tried. The verdict: not guilty. It was ridiculous to expect any other verdict. But that wasn't the only case. Over the years, all-white juries returned numerous such perverse decisions when it came to trials of charges against British subjects. Given this baggage, juries did not find a place in the Indian Constitution in 1950 and a majority of the states in the Union shunned them from the beginning. In 1958, the Law Commission of India eventually abolished juries and moved wholly to bench trials, which wasn't the best solution because judges became the single entities who checked that procedure was followed by the book and also decided the credibility of the evidence. But it was what it was. Rules were rules and no advocate or any citizen of the country could influence that.

The case of National Capital Territory (NCT) of Delhi v Ms Gayatri Yadav was assigned to the court of Additional Sessions Judge, Ms Shilpa Singh. Given her diary and existing commitments, the first date for the trial was set for 3 October. Vansh was sitting with Akash in his study-office when they were informed of the same. Judge Singh had asked for all the documents and filings to be completed two weeks prior to the start of the trial. The prosecution was supposed to provide all the evidence collected by the state to the defence. With an abundance of machinery at their disposal, the state bore the burden of the entire investigation and then passed on all that was uncovered to the defence. The prosecution and the defence also exchanged witness lists. It was akin to a game of chess. Both players had the same set of pieces; it was how you played them. And of course, while unethical, a lot of salient evidence was always withheld by the investigators under one pretext or another—they wanted to win, didn't they, and the defence team was the opposition.

A day before the trial was to commence, Maninder called up Vansh Diwan with an offer. He was willing to drop all legal charges against Gayatri and reinstate Diwan-e-Khaas as the criminal defence advocates for Maninder's business empire. For once, he wasn't as offensive as he had been the last few times he had spoken to Vansh.

'That's quite a change of heart, Maninder,' Vansh said, after he listened to his erstwhile client, knowing well that the offer wouldn't be without a caveat.

'Well, I realized that whatever the court's verdict is, it will not provide me the solace I'm looking for.'

'What are you looking for?'

'I'm willing to drop the charges if you hand that bitch and her daughter over to me. I'll—'

'Wait a minute. What do you mean, hand them over to you?' asked Vansh, his voice an octave higher.

'You know what I mean, Vansh, so don't pretend you don't.'

'Oh, I know exactly what you mean, Maninder. And who do you think you are to dispense justice?'

'Don't you talk to me like that, okay?'

'No, it's not okay Maninder. You think you are some priest on higher ground who can mete out justice? Is your method of justice to let your goons rape and kill two women who have nothing to do with your vile son's untimely death—'

'Murder. You mean murder.'

'Yes, murder. But you know as well as I do that that poor woman had nothing to do with your son's death.'

'She killed my son.'

'So why don't you let it be proven in court? What are you afraid of?'

'I am not afraid of anything. If she escapes the law, how long can you afford to keep her from me?'

'As long as it takes.'

'You will repent. You know I'm not used to losing, Vansh.'

'Then get used it.' Vansh, not wanting to carry on the conversation even one second longer than he needed to, hung up and dialled Akash.

Akash was seated in Vansh's chair in Diwan-e-Khaas sipping Vansh's whisky when Vansh walked in.

'No one told me you were in,' he said when he saw his friend.

'That's because I charmed your secretary.'

'Charming my secretary *and* palming my drink?'

'I hope you don't mind—'

'Not at all Akash, not at all. Fix me one too.'

Akash poured a sizeable drink and slid the glass across the desk. He was in no mood to vacate Vansh's seat.

'The trial begins tomorrow. I thought I'd come over to discuss the prosecution's advisor with you,' Akash said. 'I've never had any dealings with R.P. Lohia. Care to advise?'

If and when the State brings charges against an accused, a public prosecutor tries the case. However, there is no reason why a public prosecutor cannot take advice and direction from a private and reputed advocate or the client cannot hire a private advocate.

Which is why Advocate Raunak Prasad Lohia was hired by Maninder Singh via his cousin's connections in Mumbai.

Vansh gave him a rundown on R.P. with Akash stopping him intermittently and processing the information.

Mr R.P. Lohia was almost fifty, a rotund man, probably overweight by thirty kilos, with a few meagre strands of silver hair remaining on his shiny, watermelon-sized pate. And as if that didn't make him look comical enough, he wore round John Lennon glasses. But he was bright, and had a résumé that was hard to beat. He was a senior partner and headed the Delhi legal practice of one of the most reputed law firms in Mumbai. R.P. Lohia was to advise the public prosecutor, Advocate Puneet Mathur, who was the antipode of Lohia. Thin, frail, a full head of jet black hair—the wonders of Godrej Kali Mehndi—that he kept long enough to cover part of his ears, à la the Amitabh Bachchan coif of the seventies. He usually wore short-sleeved shirts, showing his hirsute arms, which were unappealing, to put it mildly. Akash smiled at the description of the two opposing advocates provided by Vansh as he pulled out pictures of the two men from old files.

'Laurel and Hardy,' Akash jibed.

'Exactly.'

'My learned friends, so to speak.'

However vile or funny opposing advocates were, you still referred to them as 'my learned friend', which, both men reflected over their second drinks, was so old a practice that everyone had forgotten how it had come about. It probably arose during the time of British rule when all the advocates were British, all expats, living and socializing within their own little community, which warranted that they maintained amicable relations amongst themselves. What was the point of severing relationships in the courtroom over some plaintiff or defendant when you inevitably returned to dine with your learned friends at the end of the day or on Christmas or on another occasion? Courtroom battles were only professional arguments so why put a longstanding friendship on the line? They didn't care who won or lost. They'd win the fees in any case.

'I guess if we are honest with ourselves, not much has changed since then. We've argued and won cases against opposing advocates and then dined with them at weddings, public functions or clubs, haven't we?'

But both understood that this case was different. This was pro bono. They were doing it to right a gross wrong.

Akash got up, gave Vansh a hug, then picking up his big briefcase, said, 'God, it is becoming heavy.'

'What are you carrying?'

'Everything I need for this case,' he smiled. 'This case is personal, Vansh, but don't you worry, nothing will happen to Gayatri or Baby. Maninder is not stupid enough to do anything till the trial is on, in any case. And I've already promised that I'll destroy him in court; by the time I finish with him, he won't have any support from the people he thinks he can bank on.'

'You sure?'

'Trust me.'

'I do.'

'In any event, why don't all of you come to my place for a sleepover, as once the trial begins, I won't have time to meet … '

True that. An advocate defending someone accused of murder—however frivolous the charge may be—hardly had time to socialize.

'Good idea. I'll check with Priti and let you know.' Vansh let out a sigh.

Part Three

3 October

'You shall not bear false witness against your neighbour.'

—Exodus 20:16

Twenty-Five

The universal symbol of justice—Lady Justice aka Goddess of Justice—hadn't always been blindfolded. No one knows the precise moment when the blindfold was added, but it first appeared somewhere around the fifteenth century. The blindfold symbolizes objectivity and impartiality in delivering justice regardless of money, power or the person's identity, to let those who deliver justice do so without any fear or favour. Lady Justice carries scales in one hand to symbolize that justice would be granted after weighing the pros and cons, after listening to both sides of the story—the support and the opposition. And she also carries a sword in her other hand to represent the power she holds to see that justice *is* carried out. But is it?

Saket is an upmarket residential address in south Delhi. Though not common knowledge, it is also known as Ayodhya, though the ancient city of the same name, which is the birthplace of Lord Rama, is located in Uttar Pradesh. Nestled in this posh locality of New Delhi is the Delhi District Court.

Contrary to the photographs of courts you see in films or on book covers: old structures supported by big columns, this is a modern building. It stands tall like any other contemporary corporate office tower, built in sandstone with its windowpanes wearing blue sun-reflecting film.

All things considered, it is a handsome building and if it were a shopping mall, it would bring joy to the customers that visited it. But, it is a place of justice and unfortunately, that never brings any cheer to any person present there. Happy customers never go there. No one willingly, in their right minds, ever becomes a customer there. Some go because they, or someone they love, has suffered some atrocity and the court is their last hope; others are dragged there because those aggrieved presume that they have been wronged by them, and the court is the place where a third party determines if those accused of wrongdoing have truly committed the said nefarious act.

Ergo, it is easy for the common man to be misled that justice will be sound and that truth will prevail, but truth is a promiscuous word; it is a perspective, at best.

The media was there when Vansh and Gayatri, accompanied by Akash Hingorani, arrived at the court in the morning. Akash was dressed to the proverbial nines in black Armani—with a young and smart twenty-something assistant, Sonia Pahwa, in an equally snazzy black skirt suit, carrying their robes, which they would only don once they were inside the courtroom—well aware that the media always papped and videoed a big defence advocate going into the courtroom, first thing in the morning. Then, if nothing else, they had that clip to play whenever they reported on the case. It authenticated their presence: *their* press cameras were there. A few microphones were switched on and the usual questions were hurled at Akash:

'Is your client innocent?'

'Why does she need one of the city's leading defence advocates if she's innocent?'

'If she's innocent, who murdered the boy?'

However, the questioning was lackadaisical, just for show. For the camera, for the television audience to hear that the questions were voiced. No advocate—prosecuting or defending—ever answered media questions before the case. Most said 'no comment', but Akash did not voice even that.

Their heads down to avoid excessive photographs, Vansh walked with Gayatri behind the advocates till they were inside the court.

'Did you get any more info from your private investigator, D.K.?' asked Vansh.

'Shhh … don't ask what you should not know.'

'Is he around?'

'Pentium is on standby mode, no pun intended.'

All courtrooms are cookie-cutter similar. The judges sit in front, facing their courts, on a higher desk, which signifies their superior position in court. That isn't something that was planned or designed for modern courtrooms; it is a throwback to the olden days when kings and queens held courts to run their states, and one of their tasks was to dispense justice. The legacy carries on. There are slight variations in the respective seating positions across courtrooms in various states and countries, but generally the court clerk sits in front of the judge, albeit at the ground level, not on a raised platform like Her or His Honour. And on the other side of the court clerk is the witness box. In this court, presided over by Judge Shilpa Singh, the clerk sat on her right. Opposite the witness stand was the prosecution's table with Laurel, Hardy and a gofer; the defence table was fronted by the court clerk: Raj Kumar.

Laurel aka Puneet Mathur looked every bit the public prosecutor. Fiftyish, with a scrawny build, attired in a black Jodhpur suit that was one size too big for his frame, jowls with a day's growth, cheeks sunken in by the early loss of teeth, glasses in a thick wire frame large enough to cover the eyebrows that needed trimming, and hair oily and combed back. Sitting alongside him was Hardy aka R.P. Lohia, who was the complete opposite of his co-advocate, which made Vansh smile. If someone pushed Lohia off when he sat on the wall, he surely wouldn't know how to get back up. He was dressed in a wool-silk suit like Akash. Only his was not as well-fitting as that of his adversary. He was bald and wore rimless glasses. He turned and gave a glad-handed smile to Akash and company. Professional courtesy. The gofer who sat alongside them was definitely Mathur's junior—dressed in an equally ill-fitting, un-ironed suit, and every bit as shabby as Laurel. He sat shuffling files and papers and didn't look up; he might have been faceless. A budding state prosecutor sitting next to his idol—Sir Laurel Mathur—who himself, at fifty plus, was most probably still struggling to keep his family afloat and nourished. Maybe the prosecutor's assistant had it in him to break free of the month-end salary addiction, take a risk, go against the tide and become a force in New Delhi's legal playing field. Maybe he was happy subsisting for the rest of his life: a creaking boat in a safe harbour that would never sail.

This wasn't a trial the country was waiting for and as such it was held in one of the smaller rooms. Most present were either media or trainee advocates or people who had nothing better to do than watch other people's miseries.

Maninder Singh, his wife Jaya, Priti and Vamini Diwan were not present in court. Judge Shilpa Singh was clear that if they were on the witness list, then they weren't privy to the discussion or the statements other witnesses provided before them. She didn't want testimony contamination—where people observe other witnesses talk and then change their versions accordingly to fit.

'All rise,' called Raj Kumar. 'The court is now in session; Judge Shilpa Singh presiding … '

Shilpa Singh was young. Still in her early forties, she had a reputation of being fair. A tall, Sikh lady from Punjab, she had a heart-shaped face and long dark hair. Though she was in her black court robe, you could easily picture her in a little black dress at a cocktail party. She wore a massive crimson bindi on her forehead, à la Usha Uthup. 'Proceed,' she murmured to Raj Kumar as she sat down.

'Judge Shilpa Singh is here to preside over the case of National Capital Territory of Delhi v Ms Gayatri Yadav. Could both the advocates introduce themselves to the court please?'

The prosecution always went first.

'Your Honour', began Laurel Mathur, 'I am Advocate Puneet Mathur and this is my co-advocate, Mr R.P. Lohia and together we represent the State.' He sat down. That was it.

Akash kept his own introduction as clipped as his opponent's.

'Are there any motions or appeals that the two parties or their advocates would like to bring to my notice before they proceed?' Albeit posed as a question the subtext to the two advocates and their teams was, *'don't test me'*. And it was a fact. Anyone with a law degree knows the consequence of throwing a spanner into a judge's schedule last minute. Caution: don't. If you needed to discuss anything last minute, you should have gone to see the judge in her chambers before she stepped out for the proceedings.

The unified response echoed in the courtroom from both parties: 'No, Your Honour.'

Akash had expected the prosecution to appeal against Gayatri's anticipatory bail, but that didn't seem to be on their agenda. At least, not at the moment.

'Proceed with your opening statement, Mr Mathur.'

Hardy Lohia stood up. It was apparent who was calling the shots here: Maninder's money and clout. Mathur was a minion, a non-playing captain. 'Your Honour, this is a cut and dried case of first-degree murder. We have evidence that the defendant—' Hardy looked over at the defence's table where Gayatri sat between Akash and Sonia; Vansh sat immediately behind them in the first row— 'had a bona fide intention of carrying out the murder of an innocent young man. On the night of 10 June, she mercilessly carried out a heinous act that I used to earlier believe could only be done by dreaded killers in horror movies ... '

The guy was good, mused Akash. He knew how to shape a descriptive story. Shilpa Singh, he wagered, could already picture the blood flowing between the sentences, see a demoness going around killing teens.

'... she hammered the skull of an innocent boy who was about to embark upon college life, to accomplish his dreams, to fulfil his parents' vision. But she,' Hardy pointed at Gayatri again, 'ended those aspirations when she ended that young life.'

Akash turned and winked at Vansh. In pure appreciation. R.P. Lohia was a truly accomplished actor who, despite his girth, didn't just stand behind the desk and deliver the opening statement in a monotone. He was up and moving about, his face emoting every word that left his throat, his eyes moving from the judge to the defendant to the media present in the court. He was impressive, to say the least. He was impossible to ignore, and difficult not to admire.

'... the defendant misjudged Maheep Singh as the man who attacked and raped her daughter and hence, this was a murder for revenge ... '

Akash could see that everyone else in the courtroom was equally wrapped in admiration when he heard Hardy concluding his statement.

'... and in the next few days, we will provide evidence and witnesses to the court and prove that under that brilliant guise of a humble mother is a cold-blooded killer ... '

Akash looked at Laurel who looked as if he was about to doze off. Suddenly, he heard: ' ... that's all Your Honour.'

'Thank you, Mr Lohia. Mr Hingorani?' It seemed Justice Shilpa Singh was a fan of American Westerns and Clint Eastwood; why use ten words when two were sufficient to invite Akash to speak?

Akash didn't get up; he looked towards Sonia who, on cue, stood up. He heard Vansh writhe behind him as if someone had injected liquid nitrogen straight into his spine. He tapped Akash on his shoulder and with his eyebrows and hand gesticulated: *What are you doing? Letting Sonia open the trial, and not you? Are you in Maninder's pocket too?*

Akash just looked at his friend, smiled and gestured to him to calm down. Then he turned, scribbled a line on a piece of paper and handed it back to Vansh: *'Don't play the game; play the opponent.'*

It seemed that Vansh grasped what he was doing.

Akash wanted to shock Laurel and Hardy that despite the heavyweight opening of the trial from their end, Akash had let a junior do the honours; it was a master stroke. Maybe it would work in dampening them, maybe it wouldn't. He was always there for back up when the time came. He thought he saw a slight smile in Judge Shilpa Singh's eyes. Was that in admiration of Akash's confidence or was her appreciation because he, as an established advocate, was mentoring a junior in a real trial, and a female mentee at that. Opening statements were pure theatrics. The advocates didn't have to present any evidence. Seconds ticked by slowly as Sonia got up and took the stage. She looked stunning. She was twenty-seven. This was her first real murder trial, but she exuded nothing but self-assurance. Tall, slender, tailored suit, and tutored by him, no less.

And to be fair, Mathur had *apparently* let his co-advocate, his assistant on the case—albeit a better advocate—handle the opening statement. Akash was giving him the proverbial tit-for-tat.

'Your Honour,' started Sonia. 'My learned friend has presented the prosecution's perspective, and I have to admit, their enthusiasm to convict the defendant should be admired, even though every word was spoken only to besmirch my client.' Sonia paused, turned, looked at Gayatri, pirouetted and carried on. 'With no evidence whatsoever, they have managed to mount charges against an aggrieved mother. However, considering the location and the circumstances in which this particular crime was committed, it was beyond the art and science of the possible for Ms Gayatri Yadav to have murdered Mr Maheep Singh, and during the course of this trial, we shall provide you with enough evidence and rationale to ascertain that ... '

'She's good,' whispered Vansh.

'Of course, she's my protégé.'

'That's all, Your Honour,' concluded Sonia. Short, precise, to the point, and minus the histrionics. She turned, glanced at the prosecution's table, gave an earnest smile that would surely have made Laurel's or Hardy's heart skip a beat.

Judge Shilpa Singh looked at her wrist. A few minutes past eleven. The better part of the morning was over.

'Who is your first witness, Mr Mathur?'

'Dr Anil Mehta, Your Honour—he's the senior morbid pathologist who led the autopsy on the victim, Mr Maheep Singh.'

Old school, but a rock-solid approach. Display the pictures of the murdered victim to the judge to invoke sympathy. Make the judge witness what the unfortunate victim went through in the final few seconds of their life, make them feel the pain, absorb the hurt. A conventional strategy, but the reality is that—despite most judges having seen it all before multiple times in their careers—it does influence their decision more times than it doesn't. Even death by natural causes stops life, and it gives people pause from thinking about anything else, captivates them, instils fear, makes people realize how transient their own lives are. The photographs prove nothing except the brutality of the crime. Add the blood and the gore and you add an additional layer of compassion for the victim. One emotion they always invoke is: *it could have been me*. Deep breaths, sighs, exhalations, throat constrictions ensue. Judge Shilpa Singh, it appeared, sensed that the visual display of the brutality wasn't something the prosecution would like to accomplish in a rush.

'How about we continue post-lunch?' It might have sounded like a question, but it was rhetorical. Shilpa Singh wasn't seeking the advocates' permission. 'Court to reconvene at 2.00 p.m.'

'All rise … '

Twenty-Six

Akash couldn't plumb what had happened during the two-hour recess, but the crowd had increased considerably for the afternoon session. The rear benches in the courtroom, which had earlier been scantily filled, were all occupied now. As the defence team walked in, it was apparent that media interest had been kindled. Perhaps the few scribes present in the morning had seen the potential of the case per se or had done some research on Maninder Singh and had realized that the case could possibly extend beyond the murder. Perhaps the mention of an *aggrieved, merciless, cold-blooded* mother had ignited their curiosity. Or was it that the two best defence advocates in the city were both present in the same courtroom? Baby's rape and trauma hadn't been in the public domain. Before the police could file charges, the prime accused, Maheep Singh, had been murdered and hence, the news had never made it into the eager auricles of broadcasters and editors. Murder to avenge rape sounded plausible. Maybe the grieving mother was the slayer; the murmurs had started.

Judge Shilpa Singh was seated on her throne at one minute past two and ordered the proceedings to begin.

'The State calls Dr Anil Mehta as its first witness.' Again, it was Hardy Lohia leading the trial with Laurel Mathur sitting beside him doing, well, nothing. Akash couldn't imagine Mathur providing little pearls of wisdom to Lohia or Lohia even accepting any advice from Mathur. It was evident that Maninder had paid Mathur to sit quietly and not interfere.

Dr Anil Mehta was short—five feet five, if that—of average build, no muscles, no flab. His features were fairly inconspicuous, nothing too long or too round or too short to catch anyone's attention; just another unassuming face in a crowd. He had wavy black and white hair that he had coiffed with a parting on the left. He was wearing navy trousers with a grey acrylic sweater with navy and white argyles—the all too common Indian barfi design—over a white shirt with an open collar. His eyes looked weary even through his tortoiseshell glasses. The doctor was in good shape for his forty-plus years and it appeared that he did reasonably well financially too. His countenance had an air of confidence and his gait professed a certainty of purpose. He was there to deliver justice, whatever that might be. He walked into the witness stand and took the oath.

The usual questions regarding Dr Mehta's résumé were asked and answered to establish his credentials to ensure that Judge Shilpa Singh grasped the fact that the State hadn't brought in a locksmith or a geek from Apple's Genius bar, but a reputed, qualified, experienced morbid pathologist to certify the cause of the unfortunate incident.

'Dr Mehta, have you ever testified in a court before?'

Akash noted that this was the first pointless question from Hardy. A morbid pathologist who carried out post-mortems only did so to verify the cause and time of death. He didn't visit his patients—who were incidentally dead—to prescribe them cough syrups. And morbid pathologists were pulled in if there was an untimely, unnatural death in which the police were involved. This, by inference, meant that the autopsy report would be documented for the police and, if required, the same would need to be elucidated in court. Dr Mehta did not look wet behind the ears, but Akash waited for the doctor to confirm.

'Yes, I have.'

'How many times have you testified in court?'

Where was this headed?

'About forty-fifty times?' Dr Mehta shrugged.

'This is your fifty-third appearance in court, so you are quite experienced, I must say … ' Lohia had done his homework.

Okay, so Hardy had established a fact that was apparent in any event, that Dr Mehta had not just fallen from a green mango cart a few minutes ago. So?

'Dr Mehta, in the previous fifty-three times that you have testified for the State, how many times was the accused convicted?'

'Objection, Your Honour. Irrelevant statistic.' Akash cried foul.

'Sustained. How is the past record of Dr Mehta's testimonies leading to successful prosecutions relevant to this case, Mr Lohia?'

'Your Honour, I was only establishing—'

'Objection … ' Akash sprung up again.

'Your Honour, I haven't even described what I was establishing ... ' Hardy almost pleaded in the tone of a schoolboy complaining to his teacher that the other boy was bullying him for no reason.

'You're quite right, Mr Lohia. Mr Hingorani, wasn't your objection a little over-enthusiastic?'

'Your Honour, my learned friend is attempting to establish something that is beyond this witness's area of expertise. Even if in all of those fifty-three previous instances where Dr Mehta testified, the accused was convicted, it is still an irrelevant statistic for this case. Dr Mehta's area of expertise is to enlighten the court on how the victim died, not who killed him. I'm happy for my learned friend to essay the point—if Your Honour permits—on how many times Dr Mehta has been correct in establishing the cause and time of death, which is his true specialization.'

'Sustained. Mr Lohia, please progress the case.'

Hardy looked back and glared at Akash who just shrugged.

'Let me rephrase the question for you, Dr Mehta. On any previous occasion, has anyone ever contested your testimony?'

'No.'

'Not even once?'

Akash turned to Vansh and rolled his eyes.

'Not even once.' Dr Mehta's response was filled with pride.

Another few circuitous questions later, Mr Hardy Lohia finally brought up the topic of Maheep Singh. He made a huge fuss about the unlived, unfulfilled life of a bright youth who had the world at his feet, blah, blah, blah ... Then: 'From the post-mortem that you performed on the young corpse, what, according to you, was the cause of death, Dr Mehta?'

'The death was caused by a severe blow to the head by a hard metal object. On analysis and comparisons, we eliminated all articles that do not have a handle—'

'Handle?'

'Yes, it would have been impossible to cause such an injury by hitting the head if the metal block was held in the assailant's palm; the heavy metal with something that the assailant held in his or her hand. The metal object would have had to be attached to a handle or an arm to enable the assailant to swing it down from the top to hit the head with enough force to crush the cranium—'

'I'll have to stop you, Dr Mehta. Could you, for the benefit of the court and my understanding, explain how such an action could have crushed the skull please?'

'Yes, of course.'

'Your Honour, if you would allow us to indulge, I'd rather let Dr Mehta enact the action sequence.'

Judge Shilpa Singh glanced at Akash who didn't offer any reaction. Not that his objection would have mattered here. 'Go on, but keep it short,' she said.

Lohia gestured to Mathur's junior, who was sitting meekly at the prosecution's desk. The guy walked out from behind the desk with a heavy hammer in his hand and stood next to Hardy Lohia. Dr Mehta walked out of the witness box. He asked Mathur's junior to sit on the floor as he stood over the young man with the hammer, which was about eleven or twelve inches in diameter with a foot-long wooden handle.

'So our victim, Maheep Singh, was sitting when the assailant attacked him?' Lohia asked. All rehearsed beforehand, but everything was required in a courtroom drama.

'Yes.'

'Objection.' Sonia stood up.

Akash had read the autopsy report submitted by the prosecution before the trial. There wasn't any point in arguing with science. The analysis had unequivocally proved that the heavy blow that had crushed Maheep's skull and killed him instantaneously had been delivered from above the victim's head, which, most logically, was the result of Maheep sitting and the assailant standing over him. But Akash also knew that this drama being enacted had been rehearsed without any interruptions. This was the defence team's way to interfere with the flow, and they had orchestrated it such that Sonia objected this time. Teamwork.

'State your objection.'

'Your Honour, how does Dr Mehta know that the victim was sitting on the ground while the assailant was standing?'

'Physics, Your Honour,' Dr Mehta elucidated without being questioned directly. 'To build the requisite force, we calculated the hammer had to travel a certain distance to generate the velocity and create the impact required to crush the cranium. If the killer's arm had been any closer, the hammer could not have travelled at the speed needed to crush the skull.'

'But,' Sonia continued, 'even if we allow for the distance required between the two points—the starting point of the hammer's swing and the target—to create the force, there is no way that Dr Mehta can comprehensively prove that the victim was sitting on the ground. Let's say, for argument's sake, that Maheep Singh could have been standing under the very tree that Dr Mehta, in his analysis, said he was sitting under, and his attacker might have been up in the tree, concealed by its foliage.

When the victim was under the tree, the attacker could have jumped with the hammer and struck the fatal blow to Maheep's head. Wouldn't that have also cracked Maheep's skull?'

Akash glanced at Vansh who looked as if he wanted to give a standing ovation.

'That's not likely because Maheep Singh was hit on the back of the head—at the junction of his occipital and parietal bones.' Dr Mehta pointed towards the precise junction on the back of the junior prosecutor's head, who was still sitting on the floor. 'And anyone jumping from above—' Dr Mehta once again gesticulated with the hammer in his hand, 'would have probably hit the top of the victim's head and not the back where I just showed you.'

'But—'

'Ms Pahwa,' Judge Singh stopped Sonia, 'you will get a chance to cross-examine the witness. Could you please resist posting your doubts during the prosecution's demonstration? Your objection and your hypothetical alternative of how the victim could have been attacked have been duly noted by the court.'

'Thank you, Your Honour.'

Sonia didn't lose her composure on being stopped mid-sentence by the judge. The girl was a keeper. She was the full package: looks and performance. Like a Ferrari. For whatever it was worth, she had broken the drama with her aside.

'Continue, Mr Lohia,' said Judge Shilpa Singh to Hardy.

Dr Mehta dramatized the whole scene, analysing the momentum, the arc of the swing, the size and weight of the hammer and the total force it had delivered. The electrifying performance by Laurel and Hardy Productions Limited took twenty minutes before Dr Mehta walked back to the witness box and the nameless junior assistant prosecutor dusted his trousers and returned to his table.

'Thank you, Dr Mehta,' Hardy recommenced. 'Your Honour, based on the description provided and enacted by Dr Mehta and Mr Rahul Singh'—the nameless junior prosecutor had a name, after all—'I would like to ask the court for permission to further prove Dr Mehta's conclusions with pictures of the victim.'

Akash stood up without saying anything.

'Do you have an objection, Mr Hingorani?'

'No, Your Honour. But, I would like to save the court's time. After consulting with my co-advocate, Ms Pahwa, we waive the right to contest the exact positions of the victim and the murderer, which should eliminate the need to display the pictures, I think. We acknowledge that Maheep Singh sat under the tree and his assailant struck a blow while standing over him.'

'We would still like the court to see the pictures so there is no doubt whatsoever,' Hardy jumped in. He wasn't going to let the opportunity to display the gore slip away. No sir.

'Overruled. You may continue, Mr Lohia.'

Akash sat down without any further protest.

'Could we see exhibit A, please?' Hardy requested.

The court clerk, Raj Kumar, opened a brown manila envelope marked exhibit A, extracted a DVD and inserted it into the player below the television, which was on a tall stand next to him. The first gory picture came up on the forty-two inch screen for all in the court to see. As expected—and for the very reason they were being displayed—gasps were heard around the courtroom. Lips quivered and a wave of faint murmurs ensued as the screen changed from one picture to the next, each one ghastlier than the previous one, the grisliness only marginally reduced by the absence of sound and smell; the sight more than compensated for the other two senses. The police photographers had used no soft lenses or Instagram to embellish the pictures. No mortal human ever becomes accustomed to pictures of death. They make hearts skip beats and eyes flinch, they dehydrate throats; people swallow hard. Some people merely mask it well. Like the judge was attempting to. She picked up the glass of water from her desk and took a sip. Purely by reflex.

'Silence, please. If you find the pictures disturbing, you are free to leave the courtroom silently,' ordered judge Singh.

A legal case is no less than a war: victory at any cost. Deceit, ambush, lies, threats, grim pictures displayed to incite sympathy; it didn't matter. Only victory did.

Ten photographs later, the show finally came to 'The End'.

Hardy Lohia then questioned and established the time of Maheep's death. Close to midnight on 10 June. The same had been determined by the condition of the body when it had been discovered. The defence didn't object. Why would they when they had the alibi for their client for the said time?

Lohia then threw in some ancillary questions to confirm that everything testified to by Dr Mehta was correct and beyond any scope of doubt.

'That's all, Your Honour,' he finally pronounced.

'Does the defence want to question the witness?' queried the judge.

'Yes, Your Honour.'

'Will it take long?' the judge questioned further, looking at her watch. It was already past four.

'No, Your Honour, just a few questions,' replied Akash and then he whispered something to Sonia, who nodded and stood up as if Akash had made an impromptu decision to let her question the witness. It had already been decided who would question the doctor, but they had to put up a fine act.

As Sonia cat-walked to the front, Dr Mehta sat up ramrod straight as she approached him. Maybe she had fluttered her lashes at him, but there was no way for anyone else to see.

'Dr Mehta, apologies for my interruptions during your demonstration earlier. I am Sonia Pahwa and I represent the defendant, Ms Gayatri Yadav.'

'It's okay.' Dr Mehta's voice was mellifluous, honey dripping from the corner of his mouth.

'Dr Mehta, my senior colleague and I conferred on your demo, and we acknowledge that the attack on Maheep Singh was carried out with the attacker standing above him, no doubt about it now. Now, the hammer that you used for the demonstration in the court, is that the hammer that was used for the attack?'

'No.'

'No?' She fussed as if she had actually believed it was the murder weapon. 'So the hammer you used was similar to the one used in the attack?'

'Yes, ma'am.'

'The same size, the same shape, the same weight ... ?'

'We cannot say ditto, but similar. Our analysis of the depression on the bone and the size of the wound told us the size of the murder weapon used, which was very similar to the one we used in the demo.'

'How similar?'

'Sorry, I do not understand.'

'How similar would the hammer used in your demo be to the actual weapon used on Maheep Singh's skull?'

'Very similar.'

'Could you compare the similarity in terms of percentage?'

'Err … almost 99.99 per cent, I would say.'

'Thank you,' she said and turned to the judge. 'Your Honour, could I ask the court to keep the hammer Dr Mehta used to re-enact the murder for the record please? We might need it later.'

Judge Shilpa Singh nodded.

'Dr Mehta, considering the deep analysis you have done on the case, would it be possible for you to ascertain if the attacker was left-handed or right-handed?'

'Oh, right-handed, most certainly.'

'And you can say that with such confidence because … ?'

'The indentation on Maheep Singh's skull had a slight gradient that established that the swing came from the right side, and not the left. It would be impossible for someone who is left-handed to generate such force with their off-hand.'

'But the attacker could have used both hands to generate the blow?'

'Not possible.'

'Why not?'

'Because it would be quite impossible to use both hands and hit the spot where Maheep was hit. If both hands had been used, the wound would have been higher than it was.'

Sonia was so good that Akash had started visualizing the swing of the hammer in his mind. She seemed content that the expert was confident that the attacker was right-handed and had struck the blow using his or her primary hand.

'The defence wants the statement of the State's expert witness on record that the attacker was right-handed, and could not have struck the blow using both hands.'

All such statements were recorded by law, but Sonia and Akash were making a point that might have escaped a few people for now.

'No further questions, Your Honour,' Sonia said and retreated to her seat.

'Does the prosecution want to ask any further questions of their witness?'

'No, Your Honour.'

'Thank you for your testimony, Dr Mehta. You are free to go now,' sounded the day-tired voice of Judge Shilpa Singh. 'The court adjourns for the day. We shall be back to further the case tomorrow at 10 a.m. Any appeals or motions that the two advocates want to raise may please be brought to my notice in chambers by 9.30 tomorrow morning. Any questions?'

None.

'All rise ... '

Twenty-Seven

'What do you think?' asked Akash as he sat in the car with Vansh at the wheel and Sonia in the back. Gayatri had gone home with Shiv Kumar.

'I can't say as I don't know the whole game plan, but Sonia was good.'

'Thank you, Mr Diwan, it was all Mr Hingorani's training.'

'So, when are you taking me under your tutelage, Akash?'

'Ha-ha,' Akash faked a laugh. 'Who do you think Laurel and Hardy will bring in next?'

'My money would be on ASP Kapoor.'

'I think so, too.'

There was no further discussion. Then:

'You know,' Akash began, 'something tells me the prosecution in this case will lose without much effort. I have a feeling Judge Shilpa Singh might dissolve the case and give a verdict of acquittal after listening to the phoney case mounted by the prosecution. They have no evidence, but … '

'But—?'

'But, we're prepared, aren't we Sonia?'

'Yes sir.'

'Also, I want to put my witnesses on the stand.'

'Why, if I may ask?' asked Vansh.

'Because that is the only way to destroy Maninder Singh. That is when I plan to provoke the prosecution or Judge Shilpa Singh to ask me questions regarding any alternate theory or conjecture. It will be a logical question: "If not Gayatri, then who?" And that is when I'll smash Maninder's face into the cold granite. Otherwise, he will forever remain a menace to us.'

'Gotcha.'

'There you go, now you know my strategy.'

'Nope. I know your post-defence strategy, not the actual defence strategy.'

ASP Kapoor was the next State witness. Hardy might have been a good actor, but he wasn't an original director. His case seemed to follow a standard template used by the prosecution. The same set of witnesses in the same order.

Laurel did not even make the pretence of being the captain of the ship any longer. He looked content to be in the shadow of his co-advocate's commodious girth.

ASP Kapoor was called and sworn in after Judge Shilpa Singh took her seat.

'So ASP Kapoor,' commenced Hardy, moving his bulk out from behind the desk and pulling up his trousers. 'Am I correct in understanding that you were the chief investigating officer in the murder of Mr Maheep Singh?'

'Yes, Mr Lohia.'

'It's strange.' Hardy paused for effect. 'Isn't it?'

'What is?'

'The crime, Maheep Singh's murder, took place in Chhatarpur, which is certainly out of your bailiwick, so why were you appointed as the chief investigating officer?'

Akash looked at Sonia and then turned around to Vansh and smiled. Hardy was coming straight to the point. And it was very smartly done, too.

In chess, the tactic is called a fork. Two of the opponent's pieces are simultaneously threatened by one piece. In the end, one of those threatened has to be sacrificed.

In a courtroom, the strategy is called a double attack. And Hardy was playing it well.

The only evidence the prosecution had in this case—if it could be called that—was Gayatri's outcry on record that she would kill Maheep, and that was linked to the crime that was not being tried here: the rape. To make the crime look like an act of revenge, Hardy had to introduce the attack on Baby. He would use the opportunity to slander Baby and incite Gayatri, who was sitting at the defence's table between Sonia and Akash. And God help her if at any time during the session, she had a similar outburst threatening to kill her daughter's rapist. And though Akash had told her that this could happen, and had coached her to stay calm and she had promised that she would, there was no surety that she, as the mother of the girl being maligned in an open courtroom, would not react violently.

Akash looked at Gayatri, who sat stoically. Maybe she was putting on a brave front, maybe she didn't know Hardy was about to blow crap at her. It was more the latter, Akash assumed, and gesticulated to Sonia to focus on Gayatri in the event that the discussion turned ugly; he would take care of the objections while she should deter Gayatri from any adverse knee-jerk reactions.

'It was my superior officer's orders, Mr Lohia.'

So far, so good. Question deflected.

'But why would your superior want to add to his workload when the location of Maheep Singh's murder falls in another jurisdiction? Is that police station short of staff or is your police station overstaffed?'

'Objection, Your Honour.'

Judge Singh smirked. She knew it was a pointless objection, albeit legal and within Akash's rights.

'Is that one question or two or three questions, Your Honour?'

'Apologies, Your Honour,' Hardy didn't lose time in coming back. 'I'll repeat the question. ASP Kapoor, why do you think your superior would want to add to his workload when the location of Maheep Singh's murder fell in another jurisdiction?'

'Objection.' Akash stood up again. 'My learned friend is asking the witness to speculate by asking him what he thinks about why his superior took a decision.'

There was no way Akash could stop Hardy from gently coercing ASP Kapoor into a corner where he would have to mention the rape—and he didn't want that either—but he wanted to make Hardy work hard for it, reminding him constantly that the defence would get fiercer with every question. Under the law, advocates have a right to object to their opponent's questions whenever the other side steps out of line. The judge can decide whether to sustain the objections or overrule them. However, the more objections an advocate can slip in and get a judge's blessings, the more it shows shoddy work by the opposing advocate. Not unlike a bad student versus a good student in the eyes of a teacher. And Hardy, at the moment, was coming across as the sloppy one.

'I'll rephrase,' Hardy sounded miffed. 'ASP Kapoor, did your superior officer provide you with any reason why he was giving the investigative responsibility of Maheep's murder to you when it was not in your bailiwick?'

'Yes.'

'And would you care to share it with the court, please?'

'We had an arrest warrant for Maheep Singh and—'

'An arrest warrant for Maheep Singh? The same Maheep Singh who was murdered?'

Oh, the acting; Akash wanted to put the tips of his fingers under his tongue and whistle loudly in adulation: *the same Maheep Singh ...*

'Yes.' ASP Kapoor answered.

'Why? I mean, why did you have an arrest warrant for Maheep Singh?'

'He was accused of a violent attack on a minor girl.'

'By attack, do you mean he slapped her, punched her?' Hardy was crossing the line to the dark side now. He was dredging for dirt, but he was playing it well. He was building up a story that would be difficult not to believe. And that was the whole game in the courtroom. The advocates were actors performing their parts. One would outperform the other; one's narrative would be more believable than the other's.

'No. Maheep Singh was accused of the rape and assault of a minor girl, Mr Lohia.'

'But these assault and rape charges, they are unproven, aren't they?'

'That's because—'

'Yes or no, ASP Kapoor. The response to my question is a simple yes or no.'

'Yes, they are unproven.'

'So he was accused, which could be a lie or a misunderstanding?'

'The victim identified him, Mr Lohia.'

'So it's her word against his, and unfortunately, Maheep Singh is no longer available to voice his side of the story.'

'Objection, Your Honour.'

'What is the objection, Mr Hingorani?'

'Your Honour, we get it, the court gets it. The deceased, Maheep Singh was accused of the rape and assault of a minor girl—accused, not charged or convicted because unfortunately, he passed away prior to his arrest. I don't comprehend where my learned colleague is headed with this testimony.'

'I'm as curious as you are, Mr Hingorani. Why don't we wait and find out? Could you please advance the case, Mr Lohia?'

Okay. Objection not sustained, but not overruled either. Zero-sum.

'Yes, Your Honour,' Hardy said and immediately resumed his questioning. 'ASP Kapoor, who was raped? Is the girl in court?'

'Objection, Your Honour. The witness has just stated that the victim was a minor, and this is not the trial of her rape where she has to be present. In any event, her testimony is in the documents already filed by the defence in the docket provided—the prosecution may please refer to Exhibit 23.'

'Sustained. Mr Lohia, could you move on with the case at hand please?'

'I apologize, Your Honour.' Hardy's flabby face was scarlet. His strategy might have been correct, but somehow he had drifted too much. He was sweating. He looked like someone who had recently had a heart attack. Or at least severe palpitations.

'Are you okay, Mr Lohia, do you need a break? Judge Shilpa Singh wanted to know.

'No, Your Honour, I'm fine. Thank you for asking.'

'Continue when you are ready, Mr Lohia.'

'ASP Kapoor, did anyone, besides the victim, accuse Maheep of raping the minor girl?'

'Yes, Mr Lohia, there were a number of people who identified Maheep Singh as being in the area when—'

'But surely, they weren't present at the scene when the incident took place?'

'No.'

'So who reported the crime?'

Hardy was nonchalantly guiding the ASP towards Gayatri.

'The minor girl stays with the Diwan family, and they filed the FIR.'

'She stays with these Diwans, but she is not their daughter?'

From the corner of his eye, Akash saw that Sonia had put her palm over Gayatri's. Support, comfort. The bullet was about to be shot.

'The girl is the daughter of a domestic helper who lives with the Diwans.'

'A maidservant?' Hardy did not let contempt show in his voice, but he made the point.

'If you say so.'

'What else would you call her, ASP Kapoor?'

'Objection. Argumentative and inconsequential to the current case.'

'Sustained.'

'ASP Kapoor,' Hardy carried on without letting his flow break, 'was anyone from this minor girl's family informed of the rape?'

'Yes.'

'Who was it?'

'The girl's mother.'

Hardy paused as if he was pondering something. 'Is the girl's mother here in this courtroom?'

'Yes, Mr Lohia.'

'Could you identify the lady for the benefit of the court please??'

'Ms Gayatri Yadav.'

'You mean Ms Gayatri Yadav, the defendant?' Hardy turned to look at Gayatri who, on prompting from Sonia, stood up for everyone to see.

'Yes,' ASP Kapoor acknowledged her as the one.

'And what did she say when she was informed of the rape?'

'She said she would kill whoever had raped her daughter … on record.'

'What were her exact words?'

'She said *"If I come to know who did that to my Baby, I'll kill him … "* in her statement. She said it twice.'

'Twice? And what did you think of her statement at the time?'

'I obviously hadn't expected that kind of rage, but she was pretty upset and—'

'That's all, Your Honour.'

The ASP may have added that the mother was upset and she had blurted the statement out without thinking, but Hardy deliberately cut him short. That wasn't something he wanted the judge to hear.

'Do you want to cross-examine this witness, Mr Hingorani?'

'Yes, Your Honour.'

'I don't need to ask you to know that it won't be a quick round,' Judge Shilpa Singh said with a smile. 'Why don't we meet after lunch? 2 p.m. sharp.' Then, without wasting another minute in waiting for anyone to respond or acknowledge, she got up and left the courtroom.

'All rise … '

ASP Kapoor was cautioned after the lunch break that he was still under oath, though being an officer of the law, who had been in courtrooms before, he did not require any reminders.

'Good afternoon, ASP Kapoor,' Akash stood up, buttoned his jacket and moved into the ring. It was time to fillet the prosecution. 'I heard the testimony you gave to my learned friend that my client—the defendant in the murder trial of Mr Maheep Singh, Ms Gayatri Yadav—when giving her statement to you after you informed her that her minor daughter had been brutally raped, in an agonized state said: *"I will kill him"*, referring to the rapist of her only child, is that correct?'

'Objection.'

Judge Singh looked at Hardy.

'Maheep was only accused of the rape, he wasn't convicted, so it is not correct to refer to him as a rapist, Your Honour.'

The judge's eyes swept over her courtroom, took in everything and gestured to Hingorani to explain.

'Your Honour, nowhere in my last question to the witness did I say that Maheep Singh was the rapist. I asked if the mother, Ms Gayatri Yadav, had said the words, *"I will kill him"*, twice, referring to the rapist of her child. Is my learned friend contesting *corpus delicti*—that the said crime was never committed, that my client's minor daughter was never raped and assaulted? Guilt is a very consuming emotion—'

'Overruled. And Mr Hingorani, please refrain from philosophizing.'

Philosophizing about guilt; he recognized he had been caught out.

'My sincere apologies, Your Honour.'

'Apologies accepted. Now, please proceed.'

'ASP Kapoor, do you want me to repeat the question?'

'No, it's okay. And yes, Ms Gayatri Yadav did say she would kill the person if and when she found out who had violated her daughter.'

'However, at that time, did she know who the culprit was?'

'No.'

'As a senior police officer who has attended numerous crime scenes and taken statements from victims and aggrieved parties, was that the first time someone had expressed themselves so harshly, ASP Kapoor?'

'No.'

'Does it happen often—I mean such outbursts from aggrieved parties?'

'I wouldn't say often, but yes, it's happened before.'

'And in your experience, how many such people who declare in your presence that they will kill their attackers, actually carry out such attacks?'

'None that I know of.'

'Your Honour, if I have the court's permission, may I ask my next question, which is not for evidence from the witness, but only to ask if he has any knowledge of it.'

'Keep it short, Mr Hingorani.'

'Besides your own cases, have you heard through your colleagues in the police force of any such incident actually happening?'

'Not that I have any knowledge of.'

'Thank you, ASP Kapoor.'

The ploys of a courtroom trial. Akash had tricked everyone by asking and making the ASP answer a question that could probably have been objected to as hearsay, but he had hinted that such practice of taking avenge by killing the perpetrator oneself was more filmi than real.

'What do you think was my client's frame of mind when she said those words?'

'Objection. The witness is not an expert in psychology—'

'Your Honour,' Hingorani slipped in his explanation before Judge Shilpa Singh could sustain or overrule Hardy's objection. 'The witness is a police officer who has attended to more victims than any of us, maybe all of us put together. He is trained to assess people and their temperaments.'

'Overruled. You can answer that one, ASP Kapoor.'

Akash knew that Gayatri's statement was on record. She had said those words and there was no way he could get them struck off the evidence register. The next best thing was to slant it, taint it.

'Would you say, ASP Kapoor, that my client wasn't in her right mind when you interviewed her—that she might have been in a state of shock?'

'She was, indeed, not in her senses. Her daughter had been raped, and if that wasn't enough, the girl had gone into a coma, and was in the ICU at Safdarjung Hospital. It was an emotional outburst.'

'Moving on from there, ASP Kapoor, does this murder look like a crime of opportunity to you? Does it look as if someone just walked in through the fence and found Maheep sitting alone, waiting to take the blow to his head?'

'No, our informed opinion is that the murderer had recced the property.'

'And my client, Ms Gayatri Yadav—in your investigation, did it come up whether she had ever been to the property where the murder happened?'

'She said that she hadn't.'

'Objection. Her daughter had been there. She could described the property to her mother.'

'Doesn't it sound very far-fetched for a mother to have had a conversation with her teenaged daughter to describe a property because she was going there to murder a teenage boy?'

'Objection. Speculation.'

'Withdrawn.'

The point had been made. The judge had followed the logic.

'ASP Kapoor, physical evidence is gold dust in police parlance, is it not?'

'It is, indeed.'

'So did you or your team find any physical evidence that Ms Gayatri Yadav had been at the scene of the crime?'

'No.'

'Any eyewitnesses who saw Ms Gayatri Yadav at the scene of the crime?'

'No.'

'So there's no physical evidence, none whatsoever—DNA, fingerprints, hair, fibre, skin, toxicology—or even a single pair of eyes, to support the fact that the defendant was ever there at the scene of crime?'

'None, whatsoever.'

'Hmm ... ' Akash let the answers sink in. 'The police records show that Maheep Singh was murdered close to midnight on the night of 10 June; is that correct, ASP Kapoor?'

'Yes, it is.'

'How convinced, would you say you are, that the date and time of Maheep's death, as established by the autopsy, are correct?'

'Absolutely convinced that they are as close to the exact date and time as we will ever be; we have no doubt that the report is correct.'

'Thank you, ASP Kapoor. Your Honour, my learned friend, Mr Lohia, has presented an abstract theory. The so-called threat was made by a mother in circumstances where her emotions were running high. That was it. A cry for help, a lash out at her own soul for leaving her daughter alone at home, at the wrong time, nothing more. To presume that she actually carried out the heinous act is not just a margin outside conventional thinking, it's a conceptual leap, Your Honour, and it's a ridiculous leap. A non sequitur. I don't deny that the police have on record what Ms Gayatri Yadav said, and even if—purely for hypothesis—we take it that the muttering came from a rational mind, all we have is Gayatri's statement to the police that she would kill whoever had raped her daughter. That only supports malice aforethought: *mens rea*, a motive to kill, but there was no opportunity. No evidence, no witnesses. Moreover, history can prove that women usually poison to kill. Of course, there are exceptions, such as when it's a crime of passion, which, may I add, is hardly the case, if the murder took place days after the violent sexual attack—'

'Objection. Historical data on women killers is not evidence ...'

'Sustained.'

'I'm sorry, Your Honour, I got carried away.'

'Do you have any more questions for the witness?' the judge asked.

'Just a few.'

'Can we sum up for the day quickly then please?'

'Yes, Your Honour.' Pause, then: 'ASP Kapoor, does the defendant look as if she could kill someone in cold blood?'

'Objection, Your Honour ... ' Hardy's mien exuded contempt now.

It was an open-ended question, asking the witness to opine and it was refuted as such by the prosecutor. Nevertheless, Akash knew he had sown the seed of doubt. He followed Judge Shilpa Singh's eyes as she looked from him to Gayatri and then back at him. Even if she did not intervene or say anything at that moment, she would reflect on it. Mission accomplished.

An infinitesimal victory.

But a victory nevertheless.

'I apologize, Your Honour,' Akash said before Shilpa Singh sustained the cry from Hardy. 'I have no more questions for this witness. Thank you.'

'Thank you, ASP Kapoor. You are free to go for now, but as the chief investigator, I'd request you to keep your diary free for the duration of this trial, in case we need to call you back for some clarifications. Court is adjourned for the day,' the judge announced.

'All rise … '

TWENTY-EIGHT

Priti sat, sipping wine, looking gorgeous as ever in a figure-hugging black dress, not short, just knee-length, but the hem of the tight number had climbed up as she was sitting on a low sofa, knees bent sideways. Perfect legs, thought Akash for a moment; Akash had always thought that she was blessed with equal measures of seductive charm and girl-next-door attractiveness. Age has always been biased as to whom to bestow its generosity upon.

'How did the day go?' she asked.

The Diwans had gone over to Akash's house for the night. Vamini, Baby, Gayatri and Akash's cook had turned in. The trio had descended into the large games room in the basement, which also had a pool table. The guys stood with cues in their hands, their drinks precariously balanced on the raised edge of the table. Akash was on his second glass of wine, taking it slow as he had to be in court the next day. Priti was merely a social drinker—she was still on her first glass, which had been served before dinner. Vansh Diwan, on the contrary, was on his fourth—or was it fifth?—glass of Cognac, Rémy Martin XO, no less, from Akash's bar.

'The day was … good, good.'

'Stop it Vansh,' Priti chastised. 'You've had enough to drink tonight.'

'It doesn't matter now, does it?' Akash could tell that Vansh would have to skip the courtroom the following day after that many drinks, so he wasn't asking his friend to either slow down or stop now.

'I know, but still … '

'You know Priti, I'm en-envious of Akashhh … he'ss very good.' Vansh hit the cue ball, but instead of it hitting the striped one that he was aiming for, it shot straight to the opposite side of the table, ricocheted and rolled into a side pocket. Foul. Eight-ball pool was something he was definitely better at than Akash, but he was clearly out of focus.

'And I'm envious of you, my friend.'

'Why? I just fouled.'

'It wasn't the game I was talking about; you stole the prettiest girl in class, didn't you?' Akash winked at Priti, indicating that he was taking the piss now.

'That izzz trooo … ' Vansh uttered before something seemed to click in his Cognac-clouded brain. 'You flirting with … mai girrlll, again?' He walked back to the head of the table, where he had placed his drink.

'I always fancied her, you know.'

'Really?' asked Priti.

'No, what are you guys? Teenagers?'

'I'm hurt now,' Priti feigned being let down. 'What's the plan for tomorrow?'

'I don't think the defence will be able to present the case tomorrow. Hardy is going to continue with Maninder.'

'What can Maninder say about the murder?'

'Oh he'll attempt to push the emotional pedal as much as possible: *my young son, I'm a father who's had to cremate a son …* I can't think he'll provide any evidence, per se.'

'Are you going to cross-examine?'

Priti was keen to know. Vansh had slumped on to the sofa next to her, his eyes glazed and out of focus.

'Of course I will. Not his grief, but I need to show his true colours to the judge, and I also want the media to pick up a good story to start dismantling his holier-than-thou mask. Another drink for you, Vansh?'

'Stop it,' Priti sounded stern.

'Just teasing. But, whatever happens, do not let him come to court tomorrow—he's in no shape and the last thing we need is the media picking up anything that can tarnish his rep. An advocate, even if he isn't trying a case, shouldn't be found inebriated anywhere near a courtroom.'

'I know,' she responded, looking at Vansh who was almost comatose now, his eyes shut, his mouth slightly open. 'Can I ask you something?' she almost whispered.

'Of course.'

'Did you … ?'

'Did I what?'

'Remember, when I came to see you the first time regarding Baby, you had said that you could make this whole problem go away, disappear. Did someone bump Maheep off on your orders?'

'Of course not, Priti.'

'Are you sure?'

'Don't be crazy.'

'It's too much of a coincidence, isn't it?'

'It is, and maybe that's precisely why the word coincidence exists in the dictionary.' He winked again.

Maninder was at his farmhouse with his advocate, R.P. Lohia, who updated him on the day's proceedings.

'The ASP's testimony wasn't helpful for us then?'

'I wouldn't say it wasn't helpful, I'd say it didn't go as well as expected. He did put across the defendant's intent to kill,' Hardy told him. 'That Hingorani sidetracked the questioning, going into pointless hypothetical territories, claiming that women normally poisoned, and did not batter their victims and some crap, but I objected and the judge sustained it. I don't think he earned many points there. However, he did manage to make the defendant look like a grieving mother for a minute or two.'

'Why is she grieving? Her daughter isn't in a coma any longer.'

'She was raped—'

'No. How come you're speaking the defence advocate's language, Mr Lohia? She wasn't raped, she pulled Maheep in for consensual sex, remember?'

'Considering her age, it cannot be consensual, Mr Singh, and you should know that.'

'Oh I forgot. Let's rewind and practice all over again for tomorrow. Remember, Maheep did not have sex with her. Let's go with the initial narrative that Diwan had prepared. Maheep was driven there, my driver was with him, the servant girl fell, but she grabbed Maheep's arm at the last minute … correct?'

'Yes.'

'Okay, let's split now and practice our respective parts.'

Twenty-Nine

Hardy Lohia took the best part of the morning asking Maninder Singh questions that didn't shed any light on any evidence against Gayatri. Maninder Singh was maudlin over his son, which was expected, pointed repeatedly towards Jaya, who sat in the courtroom and emphasized her grief, which, at least, appeared genuine. Akash and Sonia alternated in calling out objections as and when they thought the melodrama was getting unbearable. Hardy made it a point to run Vansh Diwan's story on how Maheep, who had only saved Baby from a fall, became the accused because her memory had played tricks on her—the shock of the near-fall and the shock of the attack had mixed things up in the poor girl's memory. Hardy pointed to exhibits in the dockets provided to the court and defence team pertaining to patients in such conditions. Maheep was deceased; it wasn't that this was his trial on the rape charges. The whole smokescreen was to cover up Maheep's brutal action, in case the judge thought that as a rapist had been murdered, it was justified and therefore, would dismiss the case.

A whole nine yards and some change later, Hardy declared that he was done with Maninder Singh. 'Your Honour, the grieving parents want justice ...'

Akash had switched off.

'I'm not asking you how much time you require for questioning this witness, Mr Hingorani, I'm breaking for lunch. I have a motion to hear in another case, so I won't be back before three,' Judge Shilpa Singh informed.

'Then 3.00 p.m. it is, Your Honour.'

'Mr Maninder Singh,' commenced Akash, post lunch, 'my sincere commiserations to you and Mrs Singh. Losing a child is never easy, and any amount of words cannot provide any solace, but I am really sorry for your loss. Believe me, like you, I want those guilty to be brought to justice.'

'Thank you.'

'Mr Singh, besides the emotional outburst of my client to the police when they came to question her regarding her daughter's rape, is there any other evidence you possess that Ms Gayatri Yadav murdered your son?'

'Isn't that enough?'

'Mr Singh, I'd prefer it if you did not answer my questions with your questions.'

'No, but I think—'

'The court does not need to know what you think, Mr Singh.'

'Okay, as you wish.'

'As I explained when I questioned the previous witness, ASP Kapoor, my client wasn't in the right frame of mind when she uttered this, but nevertheless, even if we, for a moment, discount her mental condition, all Ms Gayatri Yadav said was "*I will kill him*", correct?'

Maninder nodded.

'Mr Singh, could you please verbalize your response since nods are not sufficient in the court of law.'

'Yes, correct,' Maninder looked annoyed, braced for a fist fight. Aching for it, but chained by the rules of a courtroom, with the judge watching and the police around.

'But your son, Maheep Singh, according to you, couldn't have been at the Diwan's house alone to rape Baby because he was there with your driver, correct?'

'Yes, I just told Mr Lohia that in this court before lunch.'

'And Maheep Singh wasn't there alone because his car was stolen on the 4th of June, two days before Baby's rape, correct?'

'Objection, Your Honour, the defence advocate is only repeating the testimony the witness provided to the State before lunch. It is a waste of the court's time.'

'Your Honour,' Akash spoke before Judge Shilpa Singh could decide to overrule or sustain. This was the important bit. 'Please indulge me for a few more questions. I promise to keep this succinct.'

'Overruled. You may answer the question, Mr Maninder Singh.'

'Can you repeat the question?' Maninder swallowed. Akash could see that the witness wasn't dumb; he didn't have a choice but to respond. Amending a testimony already given in court and filed in the records is tantamount to discrediting your entire testimony. Vansh Diwan's game plan had been to defend Maheep. Hardy had needlessly turned it around to play it for prosecution, without thinking if it was required. They had desperately tried to make Maheep look the opposite of what he actually was: a brute, and it had come back to bite them now.

'Was Maheep's car reported stolen by you on the 4th of June?'

'Yes, we filed a report on that day.'

Akash asked Maninder which police station it had been filed in and Maninder told him.

Akash walked back to his desk and Sonia offered him some sheets of paper.

'I have photocopies of the police register from the same police station that Mr Maninder Singh just mentioned. The copies are of the entries from 1 June till 6 June. The register does not have a record of any such FIR being filed.'

'There must be some mistake,' Maninder cried out.

'On the contrary, what we discovered were the charred remains of Maheep's car in a field. The investigator confirmed that the VIN number on the burnt heap matched the number on the papers of your car. Here's the Transport Department's confirmation.' Akash passed both papers to the court clerk and then walked over to leave copies on the prosecution's table.

'What does all this prove, Your Honour?' Hardy shot up from his chair.

'What it proves, Your Honour, is that Maheep Singh's car was neither stolen on 4th June nor was a police complaint filed by Mr Maninder Singh. Maheep Singh had possession of his car, which was spotted in Defence Colony on 6th June, and he was driving it himself when he went to the Diwan residence. The State's version of events that Maheep was not alone when he met Baby is hogwash.'

'That is not correct—' Maninder barked.

'I'm suggesting it is. Can you prove otherwise?'

'We just told you the truth, we cannot provide any other evidence except—'

'So it is correct then. Moving on … ' Akash could see that Maninder's sanctimony had been shattered in the eyes of the judge. That's all that mattered. He had provided enough doubt that neither Maheep nor Maninder were as clean as they pretended to be.

'Your Honour, the defence advocate is accusing a deceased teenager of charges that have not been proven. That's not fair.'

'I didn't say it was fair. But how is it fair to beat up, rape an underage girl and leave her in a pool of blood to die? How an act of the good God in Heaven—' Akash looked up, theatrics, of course, 'saved the little girl is beyond any of us. It's nothing short of a miracle … '

'Enough, gentlemen, please … ' roared Judge Singh. The 'please' didn't sound like a plea, it sounded more like a warning. She must have realized that the argument was spiralling out of control, and besides the fact that the State had presented the background and the rape only to circle it back to Gayatri seeking revenge, it was of little relevance to the trial at hand. 'I understand. I have read the subtext, and I need to hear no more. Now, Mr Hingorani—do you have any more questions for this witness?'

'None, Your Honour. No more questions for this witness.' Was this witness a zero-sum testimony too, Akash wondered? He believed he had drilled at least one hole in the State's case. That they were liars, that Maheep *might have* raped Baby. That was enough.

'Who is the next witness for the State?'

The next three witnesses that the State brought in were unexciting.

Mrs Jaya Singh repeated her husband's testimony word for word. Her grief appeared genuine, and she wasn't loud and brash. Sonia did not cross-examine her.

The driver—who had allegedly driven Maheep to the Diwan residence on 6 June—was next. He was prepared to the T, but caved like a house of cards when Sonia asked him to describe what Baby looked like. He had never seen Gayatri's daughter and he developed amnesia. Hardy protested that it was normal for someone not to be able to describe a person they'd only met once in their lifetime. The driver should have been pulled up for perjury and though it was evident that the driver was lying, Akash and Sonia had no way of proving it.

The police officer who had filed the report of the stolen white Honda Civic couldn't attend court as his grandmother had conveniently passed away and he had gone to the funeral. Judge Shilpa Singh must have come across several such instances in her career. She simply smirked and let him off the hook on compassionate grounds. Akash let it go too—there seemed little point in humiliating an officer of the law in an open court, or forcing him to commit perjury. As for his reputation, that had been besmirched already.

Hardy gave a gratuitous, long drawn out oration on how the State had nailed the defendant with ironclad testimonies and evidence. Akash wanted to get up and ask what evidence, but he controlled himself. After almost thirty minutes, he heard Hardy concluding: 'The prosecution rests, Your Honour.'

Good riddance to bad rubbish.

'Mr Hingorani, the defence can present their case from tomorrow morning,' announced Judge Shilpa Singh.

THIRTY

'Good morning, Your Honour,' Akash started the session the next morning. 'Considering the farcical case the State has presented, with no witnesses or any evidence that implicates my client, Ms Gayatri Yadav, in the murder of Maheep Singh, the defence appeals to this court to dismiss the charges … '

'Objection,' shouted Hardy.

'Sustained,' shouted the judge, with almost the same ferocity. 'Mr Hingorani, evidence and witnesses decidedly incriminate an individual; however the lack of them does not exonerate someone. Please present the defence.'

It was anyway a half-hearted attempt by Akash. He looked at Sonia and smiled. 'Your Honour, unlike the State, we do not have a long list of witnesses prepared to tell stories … '

'Objection,' Hardy was loud enough to be heard outside the courtroom.

'Gentlemen … a word of advice: don't test me.' Judge Shilpa Singh smiled. She hadn't been made a judge simply for her looks.

She had grasped the jibe Akash had made at the prosecution in his inaugural remark, despite him having carefully articulated it as a characteristic opening statement. 'Sustained. Mr Hingorani, take this as the last warning from me to curb your witticism and sarcasm, please.'

The judge's 'please' sounded like a warning this time.

'Apologies, Your Honour, but I was only—'

'Please progress the case, Mr Hingorani.'

'Prepared' to tell 'stories', what was he thinking?

'As I mentioned, we have only three witnesses. Two who can provide an alibi for my client for the time of Maheep's murder. The time was specified by the State witness in court. The defence's first witness is Mrs Priti Diwan—a member of the Bar Council of Delhi and a respected advocate.'

Priti was called to the witness box and sworn in. Without any superfluous histrionics, Akash took Priti through her credentials and her relationship to Gayatri and Baby.

'So Mrs Diwan, on the night of 10 June, where was my client?'

'She was at home, sleeping.'

'Did she leave the property at any time during the night?'

'No.'

'Mrs Diwan, you don't live in a one-bedroom apartment. If I'm not mistaken, you live in a sprawling mansion, so to speak ... how can you be sure that Ms Gayatri Yadav did not slip out in the middle of the night, travel to Chhatarpur—the scene of the crime—avenge the attack on her daughter and return without your knowledge?'

'That is impossible ... '

'Why impossible, Mrs Diwan?' Akash was ensuring he didn't leave anything uncovered for Hardy to explore. If he asked all the pertinent questions, the prosecution would be left with nothing on the cross.

'Because of the recent attack on her daughter, Gayatri was in a state of shock. I arranged for my daughter, Vamini, to sleep in the same room as Gayatri. If Gayatri had left the room, Vamini would have called me.'

'Maybe Vamini didn't wake up when Gayatri slipped out. Is that not possible?'

'Sure, anything is possible, and she could have slipped out, but how would she have re-entered the house? She doesn't have a set of keys to the front door to let herself in. She would have had to ring the bell or ask someone to open the front door. Also, Gayatri does not know how to drive and hence, she couldn't have taken one of the cars. It's difficult, at least for me, to imagine she took an auto-rickshaw to Chhatarpur in the middle of the night, and maybe asked the auto driver to keep the meter running while she ran in to see Maheep, don't you think ... ?'

Hushed laughter ensued in the courtroom. Even Judge Shilpa Singh let out a measured smile. Priti Diwan had been a great witness.

Akash questioned her some more before telling the judge he was through.

Surprisingly, Hardy did not cross-examine the witness. Akash could see it was a smart move. Asking Priti Diwan, another advocate, questions, wouldn't yield much benefit; he would rather grill Vamini. It was time to change the order of things.

'The defence would like to call Dr Javed Khan as their next witness.'

Akash could see Hardy conferring with Laurel for the first time, before both the advocates, and their gofer, sneered.

'Your Honour, I must clarify for the court that I believe witnesses don't necessarily lie, but they can surely misinterpret, some of them may have biases, others can misconstrue or miscommunicate, and correspondingly their advocates can misunderstand and therefore, their advocates can misrepresent a fact. It's all possible without anyone—witnesses or advocates—deliberately attempting to mislead the court. Fortunately, science does not give us that latitude. It either is, or it isn't. Physics doesn't have many grey areas.'

There was a faint murmur around the room. In the ensuing silence, Akash could hear scribbling: scribes diligently jotting down the explanation. It made good reading, if nothing else.

Akash introduced Dr Khan and gave his credentials after the witness was sworn in. Dr Javed Khan was an eminent physicist at Delhi University. He had a doctorate and had published several papers nationally and internationally. In the past decade, no candidate in India had completed their doctorate in certain areas of physics without a reference to some work by Dr Khan. A learned man in his late sixties, he came dressed in khadi trousers and a white, full-sleeved cotton shirt. He looked as simple as he was. Clean-shaven, silver hair, square-framed glasses, a slight stoop, and a self-assured expression.

In their discussions about the case earlier, Akash had discovered that Dr Khan had never been inside a courtroom, let alone provided testimony as a witness. He was a widower who had lived his entire life on the university campus, and post-retirement, had taken a two-room residence near it.

'Your Honour, we've heard the cliché repeated numerous times, "it doesn't require an Einstein to solve this case", but in this case, I will do precisely the opposite. I will use science and

Dr Khan's testimony to prove that my client, Ms Gayatri Yadav, is innocent.'

'Please proceed, Mr Hingorani, you've got me very curious now.'

'Thank you, Your Honour. Dr Khan, could you please tell the court what you do?'

And Dr Khan went into a monologue on physics and his papers and achievements, ' … and then I was invited for a seminar at Christ College at Oxford … '

'Dr Khan, I'll have to stop you there,' Akash intervened. People only become experts in a chosen field when they dedicate and focus all their efforts on that particular chosen field. They sacrifice a lot of other interests that normal people waste valuable time on, which also means that in the pursuit of achieving their desired result, they starve themselves of other interests that can waylay them. Sachin Tendulkar was a genius batsman. It didn't occur by chance. Imagine the sacrifices he made when his friends might have been flirting with girls or watching movies. Similarly, a PhD academic in physics has little interest in cabaret dance or bungee jumping. He is focused on physics. Invite him to talk about physics in a witness box where his knowledge could actually make a difference to the verdict in a capital murder case and you could be listening to his soliloquy till the rooster crowed the next morning.

'Of course,' the physicist politely agreed.

'Physics is a large field, Dr Khan, in which aspect of physics do you specialize in?'

'Newtonian physics.'

'And how would you describe Newtonian physics to a novice like me?'

'To keep it really simple,' Dr Khan smiled, 'I'd say it is a branch of physics that deals with acceleration and momentum.'

'Hmm … ' Akash nodded, and decided to further explicate for the benefit of the court. 'So it covers velocity, acceleration, motion, force, mass … ?'

'Yes.'

'How are all these relevant?'

'Mr Hingorani, momentum is mass in motion. Mass times velocity equals momentum; p = m x v—'

'Objection,' Hardy stood up, 'Your Honour, it seems that my learned friend is providing a physics lesson to the court. I'm sure Dr Khan is an eminent physicist, the best of the very best, and he can teach us a lot about Newtonian physics, but at this time, I think it's a sheer waste of the court's time … '

'Why don't we listen to Dr Khan and find out?'

Subtext: Shut up Lohia!

'Please continue, Dr Khan,' Akash requested.

'As I was saying, momentum is a vector quantity, which means to calculate momentum, you need magnitude and direction. I have read the autopsy report, and my surmise is that, in our case, the two variables—mass and velocity—in generating the momentum required, should both have been large … '

'I'm sorry, Dr Khan, but for the benefit of the court, could you explain that in layman's terms, please?' Akash intervened.

'I'm sorry, I get carried away.' Dr Khan looked at Judge Shilpa Singh.

'No issues Dr Khan, carry on.' The judge sounded interested.

Good, very good.

'Sure, madam. What I mean is that I have measured and evaluated the muscles in Ms Gayatri Yadav's right arm, and from the autopsy report I have studied the wound inflicted on Mr Maheep's cranium. The two don't corroborate each other.'

'How is that, Dr Khan?' asked Akash.

'Ms Gayatri Yadav could have carried a small hammer and generated the requisite velocity to cause a fatal wound, though the probability of killing someone with one hit of that small hammer is miniscule. Nevertheless, she could have caused some damage, maybe even incapacitated Maheep, and then attacked him repeatedly, till he passed away.'

'But we know that did not happen, Dr Khan.'

'Of course not, there was only one indentation, indicating one hit on Maheep's skull and that was much bigger—if I remember correctly, it had a circumference of about eleven inches, correct?'

'Yes sir—the hammer on display here … ' Akash pointed to the hammer that the State had used for demonstration earlier in the case, 'has been recorded as being 99.99 per cent similar to the one used as the murder weapon, and it has a gross weight of 5.1 kilos.'

'Given this heavy hammer, and my calculations based on Ms Gayatri's arm, there is no way for her to lift this weight and swing it in an arc,' Dr Khan simulated a hit with his right arm, 'to generate enough velocity to create the momentum required to deliver a fatal blow.'

'For the benefit of the court, could you say that there is no way Ms Gayatri Yadav could have killed Maheep Singh with a large hammer in a single blow, Dr Khan?'

'Objection, Your Honour, that's a leading question.'

'Overruled, Mr Lohia, I'd call it asking for an expert's opinion.'

'The only way she could have managed it was if she was atop a tree and jumped on the victim, and with the force of her body weight behind her, hit the top of the head with the hammer.'

'Thank you, Dr Khan. Your Honour, the State's expert witness, Dr Anil Mehta, vehemently disagreed with my co-advocate, Ms Sonia Pahwa, when she suggested that Maheep's Singh's attacker could have possibly jumped from a tree. His words were,' Akash collected a sheet of paper that Sonia handed over to him: "*That's not likely because Maheep Singh was hit on the back of the head—at the junction of his occipital and parietal bones.*"'

There was whispered, but animated discussion at the prosecution's table. Hardy Lohia was seen consulting Laurel Mathur. Their faces had the same expression; they realized that they had messed up.

'Thank you, Dr Khan. No further questions for the witness, Your Honour.'

'Does the prosecution want to cross-examine Dr Khan?'

'Yes, Your Honour,' said Mathur. It was strange, as he had hardly spoken a word since he had introduced himself at the beginning of the case.

'Really?' whispered Sonia to Akash.

'I think Hardy has conceded defeat, and rather than taking it on the chin, he's letting Laurel take the fall.'

Advocate Puneet Mathur walked Dr Khan through his entire analysis again, asking pertinent questions about the detailed equations used to determine and establish if physics could even prove such a thing. It was a losing battle. Dr Khan had asked Akash if the advocate wanted him to show the calculations to the court. Akash had deliberately asked the physicist to keep them as a backup, as he had anticipated that someone might want to see them—irrespective of whether they could follow the sums or not.

'I have all the calculations here, Mr Mathur,' Sonia offered when Mathur had gone quiet. She walked up to the court clerk, handed him a copy and then gave one to Mathur, who was standing beside the witness box, mouth agape and befuddled.

Mathur looked at the papers for a minute. You could see the lights flashing above his head. Reality was dawning. 'No further questions for the witness, Your Honour.'

'Is your next witness ready, Mr Hingorani?'

'In light of the testimony of Dr Javed Khan, and a solid gold alibi from an advocate—a preponderant of law herself—the defence does not see the need to produce another witness only to provide an alibi for my client.'

'That's your call, Mr Hingorani, but I will not allow introducing that witness later, should you ask for it.'

'I understand, Your Honour. As I said earlier, the prosecution's case was total cockamamie. They presented no microscopic evidence against my client and the only shred of evidence they had was that in a moment of frustration and agony, she had cried out that she would kill whoever had raped her daughter. We all know elapsed time changes feelings, emotions and perspectives—what you believed in yesterday, you might not believe in today. We all once believed there was a Santa Claus, didn't we? Does my client, Ms Gayatri Yadav, still think the same way she thought when she learnt of the injustice done to her daughter? Not at all. Besides, based on the unquestionable science Dr Khan has provided us with, there is no way my client could have murdered the young man. She could not have been at the scene of the crime. How did she get to the Chhatarpur farmhouse? How did she get back? We know she cannot drive. How did she leave home without Mrs Priti Diwan and Ms Vamini Diwan knowing? And where is the hammer, the murder weapon? I, yet again, request the court to acquit my client. That's all, Your Honour.'

'Anything you'd like to add, Mr Mathur, before I adjourn this session? I'll be giving my verdict later in the afternoon, after lunch.'

'Your Honour, I'm perplexed.' It was Mathur again. Hardy looked sombre. 'How can the defence ask for an acquittal without providing an alternate theory of what caused Maheep's Singh's death? After all, the young man did not strike his head with the hammer, we know that.'

Mathur's inexperience in courtroom trials shone like a polished diamond. He had ignored the basic rule of never asking a question in the courtroom that you didn't know the answer to. It's almost a mantra. And Mathur had just asked a question that was akin to taking a selfie with a shark.

'Incorrect, Mr Mathur,' Judge Singh responded before the shark jumped. 'The defence *can* provide an alternate theory, but they are not, by law, obliged to. The defence only has to provide evidence that the charges brought up against their client are not enough to prove the guilt beyond a reasonable doubt. And I haven't given my verdict yet if that was enough in this case.'

'Your Honour, if you indulge me for five minutes, we have an alternate theory, and I'm willing to provide it to the court right now.' Akash Hingorani was waiting for the opportunity.

'Let's hear it, then.'

'Your Honour, it's a strange reality: when people don't care and tell the world to go to hell, the world generally turns around and comes back at them to give them a piece of hell. When the defence ran its own investigations, we came across a lot of skeletons buried in Mr Maninder Singh's past, so if you really want me to guess, it could have been anyone. Mr Maninder Singh isn't the squeaky clean farmer he wants us to believe he is, he's got more enemies than I can count on my hand—'

'Objection, Your Honour. Mr Hingorani is slandering a respectable individual with no evidence whatsoever.'

'You asked for a theory, now we let them furnish the theory. They do not have to substantiate it, we do not have to believe it. So, however ridiculous this court, you or I may find it, I suggest let's listen to it before we discard it.'

Laurel Mathur sat down, deflated. Hardy Lohia looked away as if he wasn't paying attention to the futile discussion. Maybe he was already strategizing for his next trial.

'Thank you, Your Honour. Who killed Maheep Singh is a valid question. As a matter of fact, our hypothesis,' Akash pointed towards Sonia to include her in the conjecture he was presenting, 'is that anyone could have killed Maheep Singh. Any one of Mr Maninder Singh's enemies—considering the fact that he has a lot of illegitimate businesses—could have taken the opportunity to strike. Another theory is that Maheep came across something that his father didn't want him to know and thus, confronted Mr Maninder Singh. He had kept his life of lies and deceit concealed for years only to be challenged by his own flesh and blood. Filicide, Your Honour, might be taboo, but it isn't unheard of, people have done far worse crimes for self-preservation—'

'Objection, Your Honour,' Hardy had woken up, it seemed.

'The truth is, the State never looked for another suspect—'

'Sustained. Enough of your alternate theories, Mr Hingorani,' said Judge Ms Shilpa Singh. And please strike the two alternate theories, so kindly dispensed by the defence team, from the court's records,' she decreed to the court clerk.

But the damage had been done. The media had already noted it all down. The news would certainly carry it. Maninder's reputation would take a beating, and his so-called important clients, who needed anonymity above everything else, would undoubtedly find a new courier. Akash stole a glance at Maninder, who sat shaking his head, glowering at him, eyes red. Akash could tell that Maninder had also gathered the immense ripples this gentle dip into his character would cause.

Based on the testimonies and evidence—or the sheer lack of them—a not guilty verdict in favour of Ms Gayatri Yadav was delivered by Judge Shilpa Singh post lunch. She was succinct in her verdict and did not mince her words in highlighting that the defence had a more scientific and much weightier preponderance of evidence while the case presented by the State seemed more agenda driven rather than led by any significant evidence. Following the usual courtroom etiquette, she acquitted Ms Gayatri Yadav and apologized for the unnecessary inconvenience and stress the trial had caused. As a goodwill gesture, she also commiserated on the assault on Gayatri's daughter, and asked if Baby was fine now. Likewise, she paid her condolences to Jaya and Maninder Singh before she adjourned the court and left the courtroom.

Wow, good-looking, brainy and compassionate—wasn't she worth dating, Akash thought. Was there a law against an advocate romancing a judge? A conflict of interest of some sort? He had never met her or seen her before this trial despite them both being in the same profession in the same city for years. He knew he would give her a courtesy call, maybe ask her out for dinner and see if things progressed from there.

Maninder hadn't expected it, but his loss had been of more than his son. All the powerful contacts he called for favours when he got home, weren't available. None of them returned his calls either.

His phones hadn't stopped ringing since he left the courtroom; the media wanted his statement regarding his various businesses. No one, even for a second, may have believed that he had killed his own son, but the ramifications on his business were dire, beyond his expectations. What had happened to his venal, vile contacts that they did not want to do business with him any more just because he had been all over the news?

Thirty-One

'Thank you, Akash,' Priti congratulated him when all of them met at Akash's place in the evening.

'I didn't realize you'd conclude today,' Vansh, who had only just brightened up after the pervious night's Cognac, expressed his surprise.

'It was a cut and dried case from the beginning, I told you. And I think I achieved what we set out to do—I've had calls from a few so-called influential people to confirm they will never do business with the high and mighty Maninder Singh. He's a celebrity now—the media are hounding him.'

'You missed a good physics lesson, Vansh. And now I know why Akash has all these books in his study. He actually reads them.'

'Thank you.'

'You know, one thing bothers me ... '

'Pray, what?'

'Your alternate theory was good—but that was presented to thwart Maninder's infamous powers; so there is one thing that still remains unanswered, isn't there?'

Akash and Vansh looked at each other. They could sense what Priti's apprehension was.

'I'm sure neither of you can argue that someone did kill Maheep.'

'Not at all, but why should we be concerned?' questioned Vansh. 'That's for the police to investigate.'

'But they haven't been able to figure it out.'

'That's simply because, as I said in court, they never looked for anyone, thinking Gayatri was the murderer. In fact, for all his affability, ASP Kapoor didn't do a diligent search for the real culprit. He did a better investigation into Baby's rape, but not a very good job in the Maheep case.'

'True, but maybe your investigator—what's his name?—could dig up something to help find the real murderer?'

'What's the motive here, Priti? You are not the police and you are not the aggrieved party anymore, as Baby's rapist is dead. In fact, you guys are the farthest from Maninder Singh. You just won a courtroom battle, which he had brought against you and Gayatri on the flimsiest grounds possible. Why scratch an itch that's about to go away?'

Priti didn't look convinced.

'Maheep was disgusting. I am not condoning his death, and if he had lived, he would have ruined more lives and his equally filthy father would have protected him from being convicted—you know how hard he leant on Vansh, and Vansh was his advocate for years. Maheep raped an underage girl at his school friend's house, how reprehensible is that? He had no morals, no remorse, just like his father. What next—he might have murdered someone. In any event, he pretty much left Baby to die, didn't he?'

'Akash is correct. We should leave it at that, not pursue something that we have no reason and no wherewithal to.'

'Both of you promise me one thing. If you inadvertently came across anything that even remotely points to Maheep's killer, you will inform the authorities.'

'No question about that,' Vansh said.

Akash nodded. 'Should we have a drink now?'

'I'm not having any. I should go home with Gayatri and the girls. I don't think Vansh should have any tonight either, considering he drank like a fish last night.'

'Aye ... don't insult the fish, they don't drink. And Vansh rested all day. I'm pretty sure he's ready to have a couple of drinks with me. A boys' night?'

'You'd better stay at Akash's then. I don't want the girls seeing you returning sloshed again, please.'

'You have my word,' Akash smiled.

'What about the security at home?'

'I'd keep it for a week and see what Maninder does before we take any decision on that,' Akash looked at Vansh, who nodded in acquiescence.

THIRTY-TWO

'What drink can I fix for you?' Akash closed the door after the women had left. He had even sent his own cook-caretaker along with them: a total boys' evening.

'What are you having?'

'Today deserves a Macallan 25, don't you think?'

'Of course, my friend, and thanks for everything.'

'You should only thank someone for doing something that you wouldn't do if the roles were reversed. I bet you would have done the same for me if I was in your place.'

'No doubt about that.'

'No thanks required then, Vansh. Cheers!' Akash filled two short crystal glasses with ice and topped it with Macallan. 'Here's to our friendship. Let me put on some music; any preference?'

'Jazz, please.'

'*Love Supreme* okay for you?'

'Certainly, it's a milestone.'

John Coltrane's '*Acknowledgement*' came to life through the speakers. Awakening. Emotional, like the darkness was lifting.

'Will you ask your investigator to look for Maheep's killer as Priti wants you to, or are you sure it's not our problem and leave it to ASP Kapoor and the police to find whoever it was?'

'Their problem really, not ours, although I know they'll never find him.'

'*Him?* You are so sure it was a male?'

'Vansh, I don't pay D.K. Pentium top dollar for shoddy work. I already sussed out who it was before the trial.'

Vansh was in the middle of taking a sip of his whisky, but the colour drained from his face as if he'd been hit by lightning.

'Who was it?'

'Don't fret, the secret is safe with me, it will go to the grave with me.'

'How did you … ' Tears rolled down Vansh's face. His throat suddenly seemed parched and no words came out.

'How did I know?'

Vansh nodded; he did not make any attempt to talk with the lump in his throat.

'Pentium visited the murder site a day after I hired him. Of course, he didn't have the right to enter Maninder's property legally, but he is sharp, he knows his way around. He figured out where the intruder had slipped in through the wire fence to get into the property. It was obvious no one could have travelled on foot to that godforsaken wilderness, so he looked for activity around the place. And guess what he found?' Akash took a sip.

'What?'

'Tyre prints half a kilometre down the road. It's a single-lane road, so his guess was that there was no way the intruder would have left the car on the road to block the traffic—not that there would have been any traffic close to midnight, but would anyone take that chance? What if a truck came along just then and started blasting the horn? So, the person who was driving the car left the road and parked the car on the unpaved track. Only for a short distance, but the tyre tracks were there in the sand. Pentium found the tracks made by the car as it left the road, and then reversed—maybe post the event—to make the three point turn back on to the road. That was enough for him to identify the prints and hence, the make of the tyres.'

Akash looked at Vansh who had upended his drink and sat motionless, expressionless.

'Won't you ask which tyres they were?'

'Could I refill my glass first?' Some colour had started returning to Vansh's face. He no longer pretended that he was listening to a story about a third person. He knew who the driver of the car was.

'Sure, go on.' Akash chugalugged his own drink and handed the glass over to Vansh. 'We are in no rush, are we?' He grinned. 'It's not like you have to go home tonight.'

The hard-swinging bop of Coltrane's '*Resolution*' had begun; the rage was evident in the music.

'What tyres were they, then?' asked Vansh, settling on the sofa with his drink. He had kicked off his shoes.

'Pirelli Tubeless,' Akash pulled out his wallet, extracted a thin sheet and read: 'Pirelli ZERO 245/45 R18 100Y XL Tubeless—to be exact.'

Vansh didn't say anything. Maybe he didn't want to acknowledge any awareness of the specifics of tyres, maybe he wanted Akash to carry on without unnecessary interruption.

'Expensive tyres. The last time I checked, they were around twenty-five grand each and ergo, normally they are used in luxury marques. Incidentally, I have them on my Jag XF, and hence I noticed you have the same on your BMW. And by the by, those prints in the sand—they're gone now. D.K. erased them, so there's no need for concern. As I told you, the police did a shoddy job … fortunately, they didn't look beyond Gayatri because, if they had, they might have looked harder.'

'But how do you know … I mean, there must be a good number of BMWs and Jaguars in the city, not to mention those coming in from Gurgaon and Noida or anywhere else.'

'Yes, and to add to your point, most of Maninder's friends and foes might own luxury cars.'

'Indeed.'

'Because I don't believe in coincidences. The odds of someone targeting Maheep Singh, merely a few days after the incident in your home, driving a BMW 5 Series or a Jaguar XF with that exact make and spec of tyres, was something that set me thinking. I took the info from D.K. Pentium, and stopped him from probing any further.'

Vansh sat like a statue, not moving, not blinking even. He looked at Akash, his eyes glazed as if he was visualizing the scene from memory.

'Remember I dropped by at your office unannounced one day?'

Akash could see Vansh look skywards, trying to retrieve whatever he could about that day.

'Yes, the day you *charmed my secretary and palmed my whisky,*' Vansh made a meagre attempt at humour, but his nerves showed.

'Correct.'

'Did you check my car in the basement parking when you left?'

'I didn't need to.'

'Why not?'

'Because I found the hammer in your office.'

'My god, how did you? It was locked in my drawer, how did you even know that?'

'It was simple deduction, Vansh—please grant me some credit, I have a decent IQ. The hammer was certainly not in your home—the police searched the premises for it, and I imagined they did a good job of it. The only two places it could possibly be were either your office or your car.'

'I could have thrown it away ... '

'Not a chance. You did not have enough time to dispose of it safely on the night you went to Maninder's farmhouse. You're a lawyer, you wouldn't have just flung it out of the car window on your way back. You would have kept it somewhere safe to be disposed of at some later date, which you did—you concealed it. We've known each other long enough to know how the other one thinks, don't we?'

'I need a drink.'

'Bring the bottle and ice bucket here, and I think we should order some food too.'

The blues of '*Pursuance*' had started up. Coltrane was progressing towards the attainment of goal.

They ordered pizza. The ultimate man-food after a long drinking session. Bread, cheese and meat—everything they wanted, and nothing they didn't.

'I carried it away in my briefcase. Remember I said it was heavy?'

'Yeah and I asked: *What are you carrying?* And you replied: *Everything I need for this case*. Of course, I remember.' Vansh slapped his forehead with his fingers to acknowledge his slip. 'I've been such an idiot.'

'I also connected the timing of your change of heart from supporting and abetting Maninder Singh—even agreeing to defend his despicable son—to jumping ship and turning hostile to the point that you were willing to lose 50 per cent of your firm's business. That tied it up for me.'

'I can't thank you enough ever, Akash,' Vansh's voice was on the verge of breaking once again.

'Stop that overemotional drama, you nitwit. I heard this in one of those Swedish television series, I think it was *Wallander*: "We protect those we love, even when we know they are wrong." You just admitted that you would have done the same for me if our roles were reversed.'

'Indeed, I would have.'

'You could have asked me to get it done. Honestly, you didn't have to carry out the job yourself—do you even comprehend the magnitude of the risk you took, the ramifications that it could have had for you and Priti and Vamini?'

'I wasn't left with a choice.'

'What happened? What made you change your mind from defending the bastard to knocking him off?'

The doorbell chimed.

'Pizzas, yoo-hoo!' Akash jumped up and bolted to the door, returning with three boxes in his hands. 'I don't think we need plates and cutlery, do we?'

'Definitely not.'

'So, care to tell me what changed your mind?' Akash took a meaty bite into his pizza.

'Initially, I didn't think it was a big deal, honestly, and that was my fault. Don't misunderstand me, I didn't share Maninder's view that as Baby was a girl from an underprivileged background, so what if his wayward son had sex with her despite her refusal … '

'Vansh, even if she had said yes, it would still not be consensual, considering her age.'

'I knew that, but I was thinking from a father's perspective. However vile Maninder was, it somehow didn't feel right to let his son go to jail for five, maybe six years. The boy's future would have been ruined, and if there were any chance of him regretting his actions or becoming an upright citizen, unlike his father, it would have been lost. Six years for someone his age is a lifetime, he would have returned to life damaged. And, Maninder wanted—at least I thought at the time—to compensate for the atrocity.' He paused to take a bite of the pizza.

Akash refilled their drinks.

'Drink number three?' Vansh asked.

'Who's counting?'

'Psalm'—free, lyrical, slow and exceptional—the last part of Coltrane's genre-defining album, had commenced.

'The crime had happened, Baby had recovered from the physical damage,' Vansh continued. 'The psychological damage would remain whether Maheep was jailed or beaten or hanged, but the money I could have wrangled out of Maninder could have gone a long way for both Gayatri and Baby. In my mind, it wasn't a price for being raped; I was only being pragmatic, though Priti was very against it, and now, when I look back, she was right, as always.'

'Then what happened? What changed your mind?' Akash asked again.

Vansh took a sip, swallowed hard.

'It's okay if you don't want to share, Vansh … '

'Now, don't be a nitwit. It happened the day I went home to see Vamini, the day Baby came out of the coma—'

'The day Priti came to see me for the first time regarding the case?'

'Yes, it was that very day. I had been living in the office for a couple of days by then, if I remember correctly, and I had called Vamini, told her I'd be coming home that night and I wanted to see her, talk to her. But when I got there, Priti wouldn't let me see my own daughter. She told me Vamini had gone to bed, and it was only nine o'clock, but she was adamant. She told me you had agreed to take the case and then she stomped off, leaving me in the living room.'

Akash could see the latent regret building in Vansh.

'Are you okay?'

'It was a mistake, even the thought of shielding Maheep was a mistake. While I sat there drinking, I thought my iPhone vibrated, but it wasn't mine. It was Vamini's. I saw a text, but it was not from someone known to Vamini, as the number wasn't stored in her contacts. I didn't check whom it was from at first, even though I knew what her PIN was. But my curiosity got the better of me when it vibrated the second time. It was then that I read it.'

'Who was it from?'

'Maheep Singh. His father had given him a new phone and he had sent a text from that number; that's why it wasn't in Vamini's contacts.'

'What did it say?'

'I think Maheep had found out from Maninder or Jaya that Priti and Gayatri were determined not to drop the charges.' Vansh's eyes were welling up, surpassing the rage, remembering the night perhaps.

'It's okay, Vansh, I get the essence. You don't need to tell me any more. It must have said something harsh to offend you so much to—'

'Harsh?' Vansh smiled derisively. 'Maheep, in his text, after cursing Gayatri and Priti, also said that he would do to Vamini what he'd done to Baby. He admitted he had, in fact, come to our place to make out with her, not Baby. Heartless bastard. He mentioned he was sitting outside, behind his house and he'd think of her as he—'

'I don't think I want to hear any more, Vansh.'

'I erased the text from Vamini's phone. I knew where he was, I'd been to Maninder's farmhouse plenty of times. I went into the garage and picked up a hammer—remember we had some construction work done a couple of years back? Well, the workers had left it behind and never came to collect it. I then drove to Chhatarpur, despite my drunken state. The rest happened as D.K. put it together for you: I parked on the side and slipped into the property. I found him where he had said he would be and smashed his skull ... and took away the phone that he had texted from. Maybe it was destined, maybe I lost it, but I could barely think at the time, let alone reason.'

'I hear you, my friend.'

'I drove straight back to my office, removed the SIM card from Maheep's phone and flushed it down the toilet. Smashed the instrument against the wall and threw the unrecognizable splinters of plastic into various garbage bins across the office. Then I drank till I lost all senses. I think I woke up the next evening, I can't remember. I fully expected the police to come looking for me. I still can't comprehend why Maninder never reported Maheep's missing mobile phone. The police could have traced the text he had sent to Vamini an hour or so before the time of his death, and that would have certainly led the police to our house, and then to me. Maybe it was a number Maninder couldn't disclose for whatever reason.'

Coltrane was almost at the end of '*Psalm*': ... *the will of God* ... *thank you God.*

Akash didn't say anything; he just sat and sipped his drink. Despite his making it known to Vansh, twice, that he didn't need to hear any more details, he realized that Vansh had wanted to talk, to get it out of his system; it must have been eating him up.

'I was ridden with guilt. That bastard had actually come to our place looking for Vamini, and poor Baby had taken the brunt ... '

There was silence in the room for a few seconds.

'And you know what the worst, the saddest part was, Akash?'

'Tell me.'

'I knew Maheep would get away with Baby's rape, and—even if I ensured that rascal never came within a mile's radius of my daughter—he would ruin someone else's life. And before another father had to go through the pain, I was happy to pay the price, take the fall to save the world from that evil scoundrel because if I spared him and then later came to know about his other exploits, I'd never have been able to forgive myself. And to my surprise, the police never came for me. They charged poor Gayatri, and I realized they'd never be able to prove that because I knew she hadn't exterminated Maheep.'

'I knew from the start that the ludicrous charge would never stick.'

Silence again.

'What would you have done if someone had threatened your daughter?'

'Exactly what you did, Vansh, and I wouldn't have felt bad about it even for a second, I swear. No father should have to live in fear of anyone, no girl should ever feel threatened. Don't beat yourself up, Vansh. Destiny is a big force, it's an unstoppable juggernaut that destroys anything in its path, and sometimes it's the bad who get eliminated too. You were merely a vehicle in this case, not the doer. It might not have been lawful for this world, but it was justice … '

'What if they, the police, ever figure it out?'

'If they could, they would have by now. However, what surprises me is how come Priti or Gayatri or Vamini never realized that a hammer was missing from your house?'

'You've never been married, Akash. You really think the women in the household know or care what tools you have in the garage? There was no possibility of them missing a tool, no way.'

'Hmm … so there is no chance of them ever realizing that they lost a hammer?

'Nope.'

'Then I can comfortably assure you that we have only one job left.'

'What is that?

Akash stood up, walked to his desk, unlocked the lowest drawer, removed a brown cloth bag and held it up. 'The hammer—we have to dispose of it where no one can ever find it.'

All from God, thank you, God; Amen. Coltrane concluded *Love Supreme.*

Author's Note

Unlawful Justice is my sixth book to get published. Some of you might think it would have become easier to write by now. It has and it hasn't. I firmly believe that most of us know how to string words together, to put them in a sequence that builds an uninterrupted narrative, and to tell a story. The reason why most people don't write is not because they can't, but because it requires discipline. Days and months of sitting with a laptop, clacking at the keys. But that's the easy part. You write a story, it sells, readers like it and it sells some more. You want to write another story and the same cycle repeats itself yet again. Then you write the third, the fourth and the fifth story. Does anything change? Yes. Everything changes between the first and the sixth book. Like anything else, you've set an expectation for the readers. They start comparing your sixth book to the first five; they draw parallels with the works of other authors. The biggest change is they do not just evaluate your sixth book; they evaluate *you* now.

Unlawful Justice brings forth the point that all crimes aren't sins and vice versa, and what we humans think is justice isn't necessarily the final judgement in God's eyes.

As always, I thank my wife Nidhi for giving me time and space to write. After all these years she can tell when I'm thinking of some plot or scene in my mind by the involuntary movement of my hands.

My sincerest thanks to my literary agent, Mita Kapur, and the entire Siyahi team for endlessly working with me to give shape to the story.

I'd also like to thank the HarperCollins India team for believing in the story and for taking it through to publication.

And, lastly, I thank all my readers for reading my books. I hope you enjoy reading this book as much as you've enjoyed all the previous ones, if not more.

A word of caution: At any given point in time, there are more than three crore (30 million) cases pending in Indian Courts; if I stayed true to the timelines of a real trial, this book would go on forever and ergo I've taken the liberty of fast-tracking the case to bring it to a swift conclusion, and for that I apologize in advance.

Love, lots of it,
Vish Dhamija

Find me on:
Facebook: www.facebook.com/VishDhamija
Twitter: @vishdhamija
Email: vishdhamija@gmail.com
Web: www.vishdhamija.com